SHERLOCK HOLMES

The Patchwork Devil

Also Available from Titan Books

Sherlock Holmes: The Thinking Engine
James Lovegrove

Sherlock Holmes: Gods of War
James Lovegrove

Sherlock Holmes: The Stuff of Nightmares
James Lovegrove

Sherlock Holmes: The Spirit Box
George Mann

Sherlock Holmes: The Will of the Dead
George Mann

Sherlock Holmes: The Breath of God
Guy Adams

Sherlock Homes: The Army of Dr Moreau
Guy Adams

Coming Soon from Titan Books

Sherlock Holmes: A Betrayal in Blood (March 2017)
Mark Latham

Sherlock Holmes: Cry of the Innocents (July 2017)
Cavan Scott

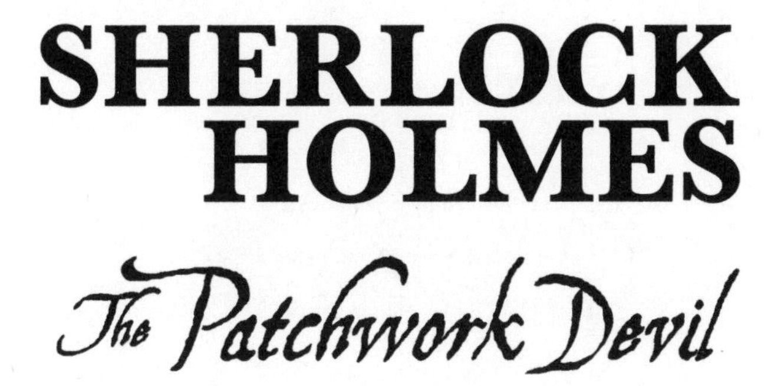

CAVAN SCOTT

TITAN BOOKS

Sherlock Holmes: The Patchwork Devil
Print edition ISBN: 9781783297146
Electronic edition ISBN: 9781783297153

Published by Titan Books
A division of Titan Publishing Group Ltd
144 Southwark Street, London SE1 0UP

First Titan Books edition: April 2016
2 4 6 8 10 9 7 5 3 1

A CIP catalogue record for this title is available from the British Library.

Printed and bound in the United States

For Clare

CHAPTER ONE

TO THE BEAT OF A DIFFERENT DRUM

From the papers of John H. Watson, MD

It wasn't every day that I witnessed Sherlock Holmes assaulting a police officer. I have to admit, however, that, in this case, the bounder had it coming.

It was the summer of 1919. The signing of the Treaty of Versailles had finally drawn a line beneath the dark days of war that had blighted Europe. The spectre of that dreadful conflict still hung over us, and would for generations to come, but for now the streets of the capital were a hive of industry. Preparations were under way for a citywide celebration, culminating in what the newspapers were already calling the Victory Parade. Companies of the French, Belgian and United States armed forces would join our own troops as they marched to be greeted by the King at Buckingham Palace. The route was being marked out by a series of temporary monuments, and I could already imagine the flags waving and the crowds cheering. After so much misery and uncertainty, the people of Britain were in dire need of some good old-fashioned pomp and circumstance, and by God, they were going to get it!

I myself was in exceptionally high spirits, warmed by the sun and buoyed by a visit from my long-time friend, Sherlock Holmes.

As I have stated in previous accounts, my friend had by this time retired from London, swapping the bustle of Baker Street for the tranquillity and solitude of a smallholding upon the South Downs. Usually, when he returned to London, Holmes would take rooms at the Goring, but on this occasion I insisted that he stay with Mrs Watson and me. My wife accepted his imminent arrival with her usual good grace, although after Holmes had descended on our Chelsea townhouse, I made every effort to ensure that we spent as little time as possible within its walls, for the sake of her continued sanity.

So began a whirlwind tour of museums and theatres; visits to old friends and even older haunts. It was thrilling to be in his company again, and, at times, more than a little infuriating, which of course was always part of the charm of our friendship.

The charm was, however, wearing a little thin when, in early July, towards the end of his visit, I found a note pinned to the mantelpiece by my regimental letter-opener. Pulling the offending item free, I opened the paper and read:

Watson,
Meet me at the Mallard Club, Duck Lane, 8.30pm sharp.
S.H.

"You're not going to go?" asked my wife as I swiftly moved a photo of her dear departed mother to cover the wanton act of vandalism. "You'll catch your death."

Gloomily, I glanced out of the window. The weather had taken a turn for the worse the previous day, gloriously blue skies banished by leaden clouds and driving rain.

I tried to counter her concern as I pulled on my greatcoat. "It must be important, dear. I haven't seen Holmes all day. He went out before dawn."

"And hasn't it been marvellous," I heard her mutter beneath her breath, as I hurried out into the downpour.

The drive into town was a quick one, the roads quiet due to the inclement weather. I parked my Swift on Broadwick Street and, considering that I should have listened to my wife, turned up my collar to traipse in the direction of our rendezvous.

Duck Lane itself was empty, although music was spilling out of an open door at the far end. I passed boarded-up warehouses and shops, the clamour of trumpet and drum increasing with every step. By the time I had crossed the threshold of the Mallard Club, I could barely hear myself thank the doorman who graciously took my hat and coat.

With more than a little trepidation, I entered the inner sanctum of the nightclub. Despite the exertions of the band, I was pleasantly surprised as I stepped through the door and found myself in what had obviously once been some kind of restaurant. The place was tastefully decorated, with a bar to the left of the room and a stage for the musicians at the front. Circular tables dominated the floor, save for an area near the band that had been cleared for dancing. The atmosphere was smoky, but no more so than the venerable clubs of St James's. It had to be said that the clientele certainly seemed to be enjoying themselves more than the dour-faced gentlemen who gathered in the Carlton or Boodles.

Indeed, while the music was not to my taste, the sheer joy exhibited on the dance floor was infectious. I found myself tapping my cane on the floor in time to the beat as I surveyed the room in search of my friend.

Any amusement I felt soon turned to annoyance as I realised

that there was no sign of Holmes at any of the tables. The man was my oldest friend and confidant, but he could try the patience of even the most tolerant of saints. I consulted my watch to find that it was now a quarter to nine, a mere forty-five minutes to last orders. Eight thirty sharp, indeed! I snapped my watch shut and considered walking out of the door to return home there and then. It had been good to see Holmes these last few weeks, but I was unwilling to allow him to fall back into his old ways, assuming that I would jump like a faithful hound whenever he called.

My mind made up, I started back for the entrance.

"Dr Watson?"

I turned to see a man sitting at a nearby table. He was almost completely bald, save for a strip of clipped grey hair above a pair of prominent ears, and the lines on his well-worn face put him at maybe ten years my senior, some seventy-five years old or so. He motioned me over, the glow of electric light bulbs reflecting in his large brown eyes.

"You have me at a disadvantage, sir," I said as he stood, his chair scraping across the black and white tiles. The stranger thrust out a hand.

"Albert Norwood, at your service," said he as I grasped his hand. It was warm and strong. "We have a mutual friend."

"One who wouldn't know the meaning of punctual if Big Ben struck him around the head?"

"The very same," said another, more familiar voice to my left. I turned to see a pair of intelligent grey eyes sparkling back at me. The thick eyebrows were now flecked with silver, as was the crop of once raven-black hair on the high domed head, but the angular chin was as well-defined as ever, the thin lips twitching with an amused smile.

"Mr Holmes," Norwood exclaimed before I could conjure up a suitably withering response, "thank you for coming. I am in your debt."

"No," Holmes replied, indicating for Norwood to retake his seat. "It is I who am in arrears, as well you know."

Holmes pulled up a chair, leaving me standing awkwardly. I waited for a second before, with a sigh, joining the two men.

"What is all this about, Holmes? Why did you call me here?"

"You found my note then?"

"Obviously."

"I had hoped to speak to you in person, but returned to the house to find you indulging in your afternoon nap."

The accusatory tone he placed on the last two words betrayed a distaste that only fuelled my frustration.

"A man is allowed to rest in his own home."

"Quite so," Holmes said, turning back to Norwood. "And you are looking well, Norwood. How is the garden?"

Norwood looked taken aback. "My pride and joy, Mr Holmes, although how—"

I had no time for Holmes's games in my current mood. "You have soil beneath your fingernails, Mr Norwood," I interrupted, "and your tan indicates that you have recently spent time in the sun."

Holmes regarded me with amusement. "Very good, Watson. I'm glad that some of my methods have rubbed off on you… eventually. But tell me, what do you think of the Mallard Club?"

"The music leaves much to be desired," I admitted, "but it seems pleasant enough, considering."

Holmes's eyes narrowed. "Considering what?"

"What one reads in the papers."

"Of course," said Holmes, "'the corruption of our once great city'. If you believe the gutter press, establishments such as these are the modern day Sodom and Gomorrah."

"Not just the gutter press," I pointed out. "The broadsheets also—"

"—insist that these dens of iniquity make the opium pits of

Limehouse look like genteel tea rooms. But now you've seen them with your own eyes. Does the excess and debauchery shock you to your very core?"

I glanced around, taking in the dance floor once again. "I see only young people enjoying themselves."

"A sight many of us thought we would never see again," Norwood added.

Holmes agreed enthusiastically. "I for one applaud their spirit, and find the choice of music intriguing. 'Jazz', I believe it is called?"

Norwood nodded.

"The sound of survival," Holmes continued. "A breath of fresh air rushing across the Atlantic, unequivocally modern and yet somehow primitive. No wonder it is upsetting the status quo."

"This is all very fascinating, Holmes," I cut in, "but I don't believe for a moment that you asked me here to discuss current trends in popular music."

"As astute as ever, Watson," Holmes said. "To business, then. Late last night, I received a telegram from Albert here."

I frowned. "I do not remember it arriving."

"It was after you and the redoubtable Mrs Watson had retired to bed." Holmes turned back to Norwood, regarding the man with obvious affection. "I have known Albert for many years, indeed, longer than you and I have been acquainted, Doctor."

"Is that so?" I bristled. "I can't remember you mentioning Mr Norwood's name."

"Please, Dr Watson, call me Albert," Norwood insisted. "I met Mr Holmes when he first started his practice in Montague Street."

"Albert Norwood was already a legend, Watson. A master of his craft."

"And what craft is that?"

"Theatrical make-up," Norwood said. "I worked at Drury

Lane all my life, my home away from home."

Realisation dawned. "Of course! Your disguises, Holmes."

Throughout his long career, Holmes had often applied the most astonishing make-up in order to pass unnoticed beneath the noses of both saint and sinner. From clergyman even to the fairer sex, his transformations were flawless, aided by my friend's natural talent for theatrics.

"We met while I was investigating Drury Lane's resident ghost."

"A ghost?" I exclaimed. "You?"

Holmes chuckled. "I trapped the spirit with his phantasmagorical fingers in the till, as it were."

"The theatre manager," Albert interjected. "Edmund Talbot. Knew he was a wrong 'un from the moment he arrived."

"I became fascinated by Albert's art," Holmes explained, "recognising immediately how it could aid me in my chosen profession. He, in turn, was generous enough to teach me everything he knew."

"You should have seen his early efforts," Norwood chuckled. "Plastering it on with a trowel, he was."

Even Holmes had the humility to laugh at his youthful shortcomings. "Albert pointed out that stage make-up is always heavy—"

"Due to the distance from the audience, and the lighting and what-have-you," I interrupted, having been the recipient of many a lecture from Holmes on the subject. Unfortunately, Norwood failed to pick up on my irritation.

"To fool someone close at hand demands a lightness of touch, you see, Doctor. Good make-up looks as if it's not there at all."

"Yes, yes," I said, rather more brusquely than necessary, "but what I don't understand is why we're discussing its merits in this place."

Norwood physically stiffened, his jaw setting. I knew that my tone had crossed the line, but not how far until Holmes explained.

"We are here, my dear Watson, because Albert's nephew *owns* this infernal place, and appears to be in quite considerable trouble."

CHAPTER TWO

ELSIE KADWELL

Suitably shamefaced, I apologised to Holmes's theatrical mentor. Thankfully, Norwood's demeanour immediately softened, a smile playing on his lips.

"Don't mention it, Doctor. Tempers have a habit of fraying around *some* people."

Holmes inclined his head in acknowledgement, taking the friendly ribbing in the manner that it was intended. "Before my character is completely assassinated, perhaps you would be so kind as to tell Watson what you told me."

Norwood leant forward, placing both arms on the table. "Marcus – that's my nephew – inherited this place from my late brother, Ted. Of course, it wasn't a nightclub back then. It was a restaurant, and a good one too. Not too expensive, not too shabby; perfect for theatre folk looking for something a little fancy on a budget. But then the war came. My brother's lads went off to the front and only one returned."

"Marcus?"

Norwood nodded. "My brother didn't have the heart for it

when the lads were away, especially when the telegrams started coming home." His eyes misted over for a moment, lost in grief. "Three, Ted lost in all. Broke his heart. Mine too, if I'm honest. He closed the place up, saying that it would be here for Marcus when he returned. Although he never saw that day."

"But you said—" I started, confused.

"Marcus Norwood returned from the war safe and sound," Holmes cut in. "At least, as sound as anyone who has experienced such horror."

"He won't talk about it," Norwood said. "None of the boys who came back will. Fair enough, I guess. But, my brother, you see; he had a stroke, just days before Marcus was shipped home. My sister-in-law found him upstairs. She's living with me and my Ada now. Needed to get away."

"Understandable in the circumstances," I sympathised.

"Marcus came back a changed man. Determined to make something of his life, grateful to have battled through. He came to talk to me about the restaurant, told me that he wanted to reopen the old place. I was pleased as Punch, but he had big plans. The West End was different now, he said. New clubs for a new generation. Did I think his old man would mind? Of course, I didn't. Ted was never one for looking back, but I told him, you've got to do it right. No funny business. I may not work round here any more, but I know what goes on in these places. That's why they brought in the Act, didn't they, first the midnight curfew and then the new closing times."

Norwood was correct, of course. Concerned that the situation in the West End was out of control, with clubs open all day and night, the government passed new laws. Restaurants, pubs and clubs had to call time by half past nine in the evening. A glance at the clock above the bar showed that we were nearly at that point already.

"But Marcus is a good boy, Dr Watson, with a good head for business too. 'I'm going to play it straight, Uncle,' he said, and I believed him. He saw an opportunity and took it. Bringing in the band. Meeting young Elsie. My Ada wasn't sure, but I said, he knows what he's doing."

"Elsie?" I asked.

"Elsie Kadwell. She was a singer, started off in Variety, before discovering the club scene. She came in here one evening and turned young Marcus's head. Reckon it went both ways, him looking so dapper in that dinner jacket of his. He invited her to sing with the band, if they had no objections. If they did, they soon changed their minds when they heard her. Voice of an angel, even singing *this* stuff."

"Was?" I commented, picking up on Norwood's choice of words. "You said, she *was* a singer."

A shadow passed over Norwood's face. "*Is* a singer," he corrected himself. "It's just that…" He paused, searching my face, as if he was unsure he could trust me.

"Please, Albert, go on," prompted Holmes.

"She's gone missing, Dr Watson. Just yesterday it was. I don't like it. Marcus won't tell me what happened, and he won't go to the police neither."

"The police?" I repeated. "So her disappearance is suspicious?"

"That's why I called on Mr Holmes, you see. One of my mates saw the two of you at the Palace the other night. Recognised you both and mentioned it to me. I thought, if anyone could help it's him. What did you use to say in your stories, Dr Watson – *The world's greatest consulting detective*?" Norwood turned to my friend. "I haven't got much, Mr Holmes, you know that, but what I have is yours if you can get to the bottom of this. Marcus is mixed up in something. I just know he is."

Holmes raised a hand at the mention of payment. "Albert,

know two things. First of all, I am retired and so no money need change hands; and even if I were still in practice, the service you have done for me over the years more than covers the cost of any investigation. More importantly, will your nephew see us?" Holmes looked around the still busy club. "The doorman told me that there has been little sign of him all evening."

"He's holed up in his office," Norwood said. "Hasn't come out all day. I wouldn't have even known any of this had happened if Annabel hadn't come to see me."

"Annabel?"

Norwood looked over to a pretty girl serving drinks behind the bar wearing a close-fitting cocktail dress and feathers in her hair. She glanced up, catching his eye, and gave the old man a sad smile.

"She's a good girl. Ada hoped that her and Marcus might get together, before Elsie arrived on the scene, that is. She's worried about him; has been for a while. Thinks he's getting in over his head."

"Getting into what?" I asked.

"A question I suggest we ask the young man in question," said Holmes, rising to his feet. "Which way is young Mr Norwood's office?"

"Marcus?"

Annabel had let us past the bar with a nod, Norwood leading us down a short gloomy corridor to a heavy wooden door.

He rapped on the wood for a second time.

"It's your uncle. Open up, lad."

"I'm busy," came a muffled reply.

"Annabel is about to close up out here," Norwood said. "By herself. You should be helping her."

There was no answer. Holmes and I exchanged a look, before

Norwood took matters into his own hands and turned the handle of the door. It wasn't locked, and swung open to reveal a young man sitting behind a desk. He jumped at the intrusion and leapt to his feet, knocking from the desk a bottle that smashed on the floor.

"What are you doing?" he objected. "I told you I was busy!"

"Busy losing yourself in a bottle!" Norwood said, striding forward. Holmes and I stepped into the office, keeping a respectful distance. The windowless room was small and airless, a solitary filing cabinet sitting beside the desk. There was no mistaking the stink of gin.

"You have no right, barging in here," the young man blustered, before focusing on his other unwanted guests. "And who are you?"

Holmes took that opportunity to step forward. "I am an old friend of your uncle," he began, before the young man cut him off.

"Then I hope you enjoyed your evening in the Mallard. Drinks are on the house."

His tone was anything but cordial. Holmes continued, unperturbed.

"My name is Sherlock Holmes and this is my associate, Dr Watson."

The flush in Marcus Norwood's cheeks disappeared in an instant.

"The detective fellow, from the stories," he mumbled, his eyes wide.

"One and the same," Holmes confirmed. "Your uncle was concerned about recent… events and asked for my advice."

"My uncle should keep his beak out," Marcus Norwood snapped, swaying slightly on his feet, both from inebriation and fury. "No offence to you, gentlemen."

"None taken," my friend responded. "And I understand that you are under a great deal of pressure today."

"I suppose your famous powers of deduction tell you that,"

Norwood slurred, only to receive an admonishment from his uncle. Holmes raised a hand to show that, once again, he had taken no insult.

"Albert has told us what has happened, or at least as much as he knows."

"And Mr Holmes and Dr Watson have come to help, Marcus," Norwood added. "If you'd let them."

Holmes took a step closer. "I realise this is hard for you. You are a proud man, and I would suggest that your anger is in fact directed towards yourself, rather than your uncle. You wanted today to be just like any other, so that the world would not know what has happened. Business as usual at the Mallard."

"You don't know what you're talking about."

"Do I not? You have been unable to concentrate from the moment you woke today, and you enjoyed very little of the eggs Benedict you ate for luncheon."

"How did you—"

"I count no less than four shaving nicks on your chin, alongside a patch of stubble you missed beneath your right ear. As for luncheon, there is a stain on your shirtfront where you spilt hollandaise sauce."

Marcus Norwood collapsed into his chair and clasped his face in his hands.

"I don't know what to do. If they hurt her..."

Norwood was beside his nephew in a shot, crouching beside him. "Hurt Elsie, you mean? Annabel said that she'd gone, but—"

Marcus Norwood looked up at his uncle. "But she didn't tell you how."

Now it was my turn to step forward. "Mr Norwood, you said 'if they hurt her'. Has someone taken Miss Kadwell? Is that what has happened?"

The young man merely stared at me, as if pleading for someone to make the decision for him. Albert Norwood did exactly that.

"Enough games, lad. We need to know the truth."

Resigned to having matters taken out of his hands, the young club owner led us to Elsie's dressing room on the first floor, opening the door with a key he kept in his waistcoat pocket.

Holmes wasted no time before sweeping into the room. The place was a mess. A deep purple chaise longue was on its side, and clothes rails were toppled over, spilling costumes across the polished floorboards. The dressing table was bare, its contents strewn over an oval red rug, the chair on its back, a long silk scarf draped over its seat where it had fallen.

"It appears there was a struggle," I said, following him in, although Holmes ignored my comment.

"And this is exactly how you found it?" the detective asked.

Marcus Norwood nodded. "I couldn't bring myself to tidy up. Not yet."

Holmes crouched down beside the girl's scattered possessions. There was a wooden wig stand, its black hairpiece tossed halfway across the room, alongside all manner of make-up palettes and lipsticks. Careful not to cut himself, Holmes picked up a framed photograph, the broken glass falling to the floor. "Is this Miss Kadwell?"

Norwood shook his head. "That's her sister, Beatrice."

"I didn't think Elsie had any family," Albert Norwood admitted. "Have you told her what's happened?"

"Bea's no longer with us," his nephew explained. "She passed away a year ago."

I shook my head at the news. Such tragic siblings. One dead and the other abducted.

Holmes had spotted something else, picking up a circular

yellow box, just one of several similarly shaped containers that were dotted among the dressing table detritus.

"More make-up?" I asked as Holmes rose to his feet again.

"I'm afraid not," he replied, removing the cardboard lid.

"Empty," I said, peering inside.

"Not entirely," Holmes said. "Perhaps you should consider reading glasses, Watson. Observe."

Holmes ran his index finger around the inside of the box, scooping up traces of unmistakable white powder.

I sighed, meeting his knowing gaze. "Cocaine."

"It can't be," Marcus Norwood insisted. "Elsie's no snow-sniffer. She won't touch the stuff, not since..." He caught himself, glancing nervously between Holmes and myself before changing tack. "I won't have it in my club. I know what the other places round here are like, full of that rubbish, but not here. Not in the Mallard."

I looked at Holmes, but my friend's eyes were set on the young man. He knew my thoughts on the drug. I had long been a campaigner for the criminalisation of the substance, and had even managed to wean Holmes off its use some two decades before, thank God.

However, it had taken the war for my views to become widespread. Moved by the suffering of our troops in France, well-meaning relatives had sent gelatine sheets laced with morphine and cocaine to the front, anything to make life in the trenches more bearable. The only result had been that thousands of men returned home with deep addictions. Soho had become a hotbed for the habit, supplying the drug of choice for London's bright young things, both male and female.

When the possession of both cocaine and opium became a criminal offence in 1916, I had been the first to cheer.

It was clear that the younger Norwood shared my repulsion, no doubt having seen the ravages of the drug at home and abroad.

To discover in such a way that his missing sweetheart was a user must have been a terrible shock.

"There's no hairbrush," Holmes said, abruptly changing the subject.

Marcus Norwood's dismay gave way to puzzlement. "I beg your pardon?"

"We have foundation, rouge and lipstick, not to mention numerous false eyelashes and bottles of perfume," Holmes explained, surreptitiously pocketing the yellow box, an action that made me nervous. There may have been only a few traces of the drug still in the container, but I was not keen for Holmes to have even the smallest amount of cocaine in his possession, even after all this time.

"And yet," continued the detective, "nothing for a young lady to comb her hair with. Is that not curious?"

"Not really," said Norwood, stepping over the chair to reach the dressing table. "Elsie keeps her hairbrush in her drawer. It's one of her most treasured possessions, a present from Bea before, you know..."

The club owner opened the drawer and stared in disbelief. "It's gone. It's usually right here." He started to rummage through the contents, but could find no sign of the brush.

"Could it have been stolen," I suggested, "by whoever kidnapped Miss Kadwell?"

"Kidnapped?" Marcus Norwood repeated mournfully, abandoning his search.

"That is what we're looking at, isn't it, Holmes?"

Holmes surveyed the scene. "There are certainly signs of a struggle."

"But who would do such a thing?" Albert asked. "Marcus, who on earth would want to hurt Elsie?"

"A good question," came a gruff voice from the door.

CHAPTER THREE

PRITCHARD

Standing in the doorway was a large man, nearly as broad as he was tall, with dark hair slicked to the side and narrow eyes that would scarcely have looked out of place on a ferret. The newcomer positively radiated arrogance, from his hands thrust into sharply creased trousers to his furiously masticating chin. Of all the habits brought back from the front, chewing gum was, in my mind, almost as unwelcome as reliance on cocaine. I understood why it had become popular in the trenches, helping Tommies focus during long hours of inactivity, but there could be no reason for the undignified custom to continue on the streets of London.

"Mr P-Pritchard," Marcus stammered, springing forward to greet the man. "I'm afraid we're closed."

Pritchard positively sneered. "Not to me, I hope."

Marcus attempted a weak smile. "The law is the law, sir."

"So, you *have* been listening to me, then," Pritchard commented, strolling into the room uninvited. His hooded eyes surveyed the devastation. "Quite a mess you've got here, Mr Norwood. Whatever has been happening?"

"A good question, Mr Pritchard," Holmes interjected, moving forward to stand beside Marcus Norwood. "And perhaps one you would be able to help answer, in your professional capacity, of course."

"Professional capacity?" repeated Pritchard, his brow furrowing.

"You are a police detective, are you not?" Holmes asked.

"And how would you know that, sir?"

"The slight bulge in your waistcoat pocket," Holmes informed him, prompting Pritchard to subconsciously pat his side. "A Metropolitan Police whistle, if I am not very much mistaken."

Bemused, Pritchard pulled out a cylindrical whistle attached to a silver chain, absently turning the article over in his hand.

"It is indeed, Mr…?"

"Holmes," my friend replied. "Sherlock Holmes, and I congratulate you on its upkeep. The 1905 De Courcy if I am correct, complete with an integrated penknife. Most ingenious. No wonder you still wear it, as do many of your colleagues in the plain-clothes division; a reminder of their days in uniform."

Throughout Holmes's explanation, Pritchard's eyes had been fixed on the detective. "I see your reputation is well deserved, Mr Holmes, although I'm surprised that Norwood chose to employ your services rather than come straight to me."

"You know each other then?" asked Holmes, looking between the two men.

"We're old friends," Pritchard confirmed.

"Did you serve together in the war?"

Pritchard shook his head. "No, we didn't have that honour. We met when the Mallard opened its doors, isn't that right, Marcus?"

Holmes gave the club owner no time to reply.

"Still, you were at the front, were you not, Mr Pritchard? I can tell from the way you hold yourself that you were a military man, ramrod straight like my colleague Dr Watson here. I must say, Doctor, it's agreeable to see our brave servicemen prosper, is it not?"

I nodded, confused as to where the line of questioning was heading. Pritchard was obviously wondering the same thing.

"Perhaps you can let me know what has been happening here, Mr Holmes," the policeman prompted, bringing Holmes back to the matter in hand.

"It would be my pleasure," Holmes said, stepping back to grant Pritchard full access to the sorry scene. "Mr Norwood returned to the Mallard yesterday to find Miss Kadwell missing and, as you can see, her dressing room in disarray."

"There's been a struggle," Pritchard commented.

"Evidently. But here is the curious thing. Miss Kadwell's hairbrush has also vanished, the only thing that appears to have been taken, other than the young lady herself."

"That is curious."

"I knew you would think so. A gift from her sister, Bronwyn."

"Beatrice," I interjected, surprised that Holmes would slip up on such a detail. It was quite unlike him.

My friend turned and positively glowered at me. I was hardly to blame that his extraordinary memory was finally betraying him. It comes to all of us, even the great Sherlock Holmes.

"Thank you, Watson. You are quite correct." He turned back to Pritchard. "What do you make of the hairbrush's disappearance?"

Pritchard continued to chew his gum. "Was it valuable?"

"I am not sure," Holmes admitted. "Mr Norwood?"

Marcus Norwood seemed lost in a dream. "Oh, I don't think so," he finally answered when prompted again by Holmes. "It was silver-plated, I think, and engraved with Elsie's initials, but had no real value."

"Except that of sentiment," Holmes suggested.

"As it came from her late sister?" Pritchard asked.

"Quite so. I don't suppose Miss Kadwell ever showed you the brush in question?"

Pritchard's frown returned. "Me? No. I barely knew the young lady, other than seeing her in the club downstairs."

"So, you've never visited her dressing room before?"

Pritchard's lips narrowed. "Why would I?"

Holmes raised a placating hand. "I merely assumed that, as you came looking for us—"

"I was sent up by the girl behind the bar," Pritchard said, obviously unhappy at having to explain himself. "She said I could find Mr Norwood up here."

"Because you were concerned about him."

"I'd heard that something was wrong—"

"And came to investigate." Holmes turned to young Norwood. "You are fortunate to have such a diligent friend in Mr Pritchard. Why you omitted to go to him in the first place is a mystery to me."

"I – I didn't want to bother him," Marcus muttered in response.

"Well, perhaps you can both help Marcus?" chipped in his uncle, speaking up for the first time since Pritchard's arrival. "Two heads are better than one, after all."

"I doubt Mr Pritchard requires assistance from a relic such as myself," Holmes said, showing rare and surprising humility. "I trust that Dr Watson and I can leave the case in his capable hands."

"Thank you, Mr Holmes," Pritchard said, nodding sagely. "I've tried to warn Marcus how dangerous this game can be. Opening a club in Soho can put folk's noses out of joint, if they think you're muscling in on their patch. Dangerous folk."

"You think this could be the work of another club owner?" I asked.

"The Mallard's been something of a success, thanks to Mr

Norwood. It's attracted attention, not to mention customers. I've seen this kind of thing before. Intimidation. Violent attacks."

"You don't think they would hurt Elsie?" Marcus Norwood said, his voice laced with concern.

"I doubt it. This is probably a warning. You're an honest man in a dishonest world, Marcus. That doesn't always go down well."

"Surely we can do *something* to help?" said I, addressing my friend.

"I would gladly offer any assistance, if our friend from Scotland Yard believes I could be of service," Holmes replied.

"No," Norwood cut in. "There's no need." The force of the interjection surprised us all. Realising his manners, he added, "I mean, Mr Pritchard will be able to help me, I'm sure he will. You needn't trouble yourself, Mr Holmes. My uncle was right; I should have gone to the police in the first place."

Pritchard smiled. It was hardly a pleasant sight. "I appreciate the offer, Mr Holmes, but, as Norwood says, this is police business. I'll ask around, see if anyone saw anything yesterday and take it from there."

Holmes nodded his agreement. "A capital idea. You know the area, after all. We shall leave you to your investigations." Holmes turned to Marcus Norwood, and held out a hand. "I hope that you and Miss Kadwell are soon reunited, Mr Norwood."

Minutes later, we were trudging back up Duck Lane, Holmes sheltering beneath a wide umbrella while I braved the elements in my hat and coat.

"And that's it?" I asked, struggling to match Holmes's stride. "We walk away?"

"I had hoped you would be able to help," Albert Norwood added, bitterness evident in his voice.

"And what makes you think that I am not able to do so?" Holmes asked, leading the way to the end of the lane.

"But you said—"

"I know exactly what I said, Watson. Now where is that car of yours?"

"Just down here," I replied, pointing down Broadwick Street. "Would you like a lift home, Mr Norwood?"

"Oh, we're not going home, Watson," Holmes announced.

"We're not?"

"Quickly now," he called over his shoulder as he rushed towards the Swift. "Time is against us."

And so we found ourselves, having been bustled into the car by Holmes, parked further up the street, watching Duck Lane like a band of thieves planning a robbery.

"It won't be long now," Holmes observed.

"What won't be?" I asked, not happy to be left in the dark.

"It's Pritchard," Norwood said, pointing over my shoulder. Sure enough, the policeman had stridden out of the lane wearing a heavy double-breasted coat and felt homburg. As we watched, the man turned to the right and walked towards Wardour Street.

"Wait," Holmes hissed.

"For what?"

On the street corner, the policeman paused to flag down a passing taxi.

"Excellent," Holmes said, instructing me to start the engine. "But whatever you do, keep your headlights extinguished."

"Why on earth would I want to do that?"

"Do you wish Pritchard to know we are following him?"

"And that is what we are doing?"

"Evidently. Hurry now, Watson, before the cab gets away."

Grumbling beneath my breath, I turned onto Wardour Street, the cab by now two cars in front of us.

"Albert, has your nephew ever mentioned Pritchard before?" Holmes asked as we continued along the road.

"Not that I can recall."

"And yet Pritchard claims they are friends."

"Marcus certainly didn't act as if they were close," I commented.

"Indeed," Holmes said, peering through the windscreen into the gloom. "The boy could barely bring himself to look in Pritchard's direction."

"I can't say I took to the man, myself."

"Nor I, Watson. Nor I."

"I could tell. What was all that nonsense about being successful?"

"Guff?" Holmes repeated. "Really, for a man who claims to be an author your vocabulary leaves much to be desired, as do your powers of observation. Did you not notice the man's suit?"

"I can't say that I did."

"A most fashionable cut, favoured by Wilkinson of Cork Street I believe."

"Wilkinson of Cork Street? How the devil—"

"Living in the countryside doesn't mean one loses the ability to read the papers, Watson. Leslie Garnham Wilkinson trained in Boston and, after a period operating out of Antwerp, opened premises on Cork Street earlier this year, or so a fascinating piece in *The Times* recently informed me. His designs are quite distinctive, and far beyond the purse of most Metropolitan Police detectives. The curious thing, however, was that the suit could not have been more than two months old, and yet is already straining at the seams. It appeared the detective is enjoying a fine diet – as well as more dubious pleasures."

"Such as?" I asked, wishing that Holmes would at least let me turn on the lights. As if driving in these conditions wasn't dangerous enough.

"His gum. A disgusting habit, and yet one often employed to disguise the clenching of the jaw so indicative of those who have recently taken cocaine."

"He's an addict?"

"An occasional user would have no need for such deception. And again, if he is funding an addiction…"

"You think he's on the take?" asked Albert from the back seat.

"He certainly seems to have a secondary income, and for a man so intent on helping investigate a girl's disappearance, he seems in rather a hurry to return home."

The cab had halted in front of a three-storey house in Marylebone. I pulled over to the side of the road and turned off the engine.

"Pritchard lives here?"

"We shall see," Holmes commented, as the policeman exited the cab, paid the driver and climbed the steps to the front door. Seconds later, he was inside, the door closing behind him.

"Well, we know he has a key, at least," I said.

"Again, how many detectives do you know who could afford to live in a neighbourhood such as this? Come on."

Without another word, Holmes opened the passenger door and was on the pavement.

"Now where are you going?" I asked, clambering out after him.

"To make a house call," my friend replied. "Albert, find a policeman immediately."

"A policeman?" I repeated, "Pritchard *is* a policeman." Holmes was already marching towards the steps to Pritchard's house, swinging his furled umbrella as he walked. "And besides, the man might be a rum sort, but surely—"

"We should be chasing down whoever has spirited away poor Miss Kadwell?" he interrupted, knocking sharply on the door.

"Well, yes," I concurred.

Holmes was about to respond when the door was yanked open and we found ourselves staring at Pritchard's startled face.

"Mr Holmes? What are you—"

Holmes gave the detective no opportunity to finish. "We are here to see Miss Kadwell."

"We are?" I asked, as bewildered as the owner of the house.

"I don't understand," exclaimed Pritchard. "Why on earth would you think she's here?"

"Because she was no more abducted than I am the Queen of Sumatra," Holmes insisted. "Now, I suggest you let us enter."

"And I suggest you clear off," came the angry retort, as Pritchard began to swing the door closed in our faces.

Holmes thrust his foot forward, stopping the door from closing. He pushed it back against Pritchard, determined to gain entry to the house.

"Oi! What do you think you're doing?"

"I believe I have made my intention abundantly clear."

"As have I," Pritchard responded, his hand flashing towards Holmes's face. There it hovered, his police whistle between his fingers, the penknife's vicious little blade now extended. "Leave now, old man."

Holmes glanced at the penknife and actually smiled, before feinting to the side and attempting to barge past the policeman. Pritchard lunged with the knife, but Holmes was already pivoting to the side. He pushed Pritchard's knife-wielding hand aside using the edge of his umbrella, before cracking the policeman on the nose with the curved handle. The younger man staggered back, but not before Holmes had hooked the end of the umbrella around Pritchard's neck. With a practised move, Holmes pulled Pritchard off balance, the policeman landing at Holmes's feet.

A cry went up from inside the house, a woman's voice, shrill and alarmed. "Charlie, are you all right?"

"Stay in there," Pritchard spluttered from the floor, but Holmes had stepped over the flailing policeman and was darting into the hallway. I followed him through an internal door to find a pretty young woman wearing little more than a silk slip and a surprised expression.

"Miss Kadwell, I presume," Holmes said, bowing slightly.

Behind me, Pritchard crashed, still dazed, into the doorframe.

"Don't say anything, Elsie," he commanded, drawing a chuckle from my friend.

"What exactly do you expect her to tell me, Mr Pritchard? Nothing that I don't already know, I'll be bound."

"Is that right?"

"It was clear that you lied back in Miss Kadwell's dressing room. You claimed never to have visited her room before, but the moment I mentioned the missing hairbrush your eyes flicked towards the dressing-table drawer. How would you know the lady kept it there if you had never been in the room before?

"Then, there was my intentional misnaming of Miss Kadwell's dear departed sister, Beatrice. Despite my colleague's over-zealous correction, I noticed a twitch in your lips, detective. You knew that I had made an error, perhaps because you first met Elsie when investigating Beatrice Kadwell's unfortunate cocaine overdose. Even if I hadn't recalled your name from the newspaper report at the time, you certainly knew that Beatrice was dead, even though no one in the room had mentioned the regrettable fact. 'Her late sister', those were your exact words."

"But why kidnap Miss Kadwell at all?" I asked.

"I didn't," Pritchard insisted, nursing his swollen nose.

"Of course not," Holmes concurred. "The abduction was well staged, but not a bottle smashed on the floor? No, they were placed there carefully by Miss Kadwell herself, who also ensured that she took her beloved hairbrush before fleeing the scene. As for why, Watson, Mr Pritchard told us himself."

"He did?"

"Marcus Norwood is an honest man in a dishonest profession. As Mr Pritchard noted, he did attract attention. Not, however, from his rivals—" Holmes turned to face the scowling policeman, "—but from an unscrupulous officer of the law. I would suggest that Pritchard here approached young Mr Norwood, offering protection for the right price. When Norwood turned down this generous, and no doubt expensive, offer, Mr Pritchard decided to show him exactly why he needed protection in the first place. What better argument than the apparent abduction of the Mallard's star turn, aided and abetted by the lady herself? I wonder how many other clubs in Soho have been forced to employ Mr Pritchard's dubious services. Someone has to pay for this house and those fine suits, after all."

"I'll kill you," Pritchard started, and instinctively I placed myself between the disgrace of a police officer and my friend. However, there was no need for any further heroics.

"I think not, sir," came a voice from the hall. Pritchard whirled around to see a stern-looking police officer in a rain-soaked cape, standing beside Albert Norwood.

CHAPTER FOUR

LIVING IN THE PAST

"A bittersweet success, Holmes," I observed as I drove us back to Chelsea. It was well past midnight, now that we had furnished the police with our statements. "Young Marcus Norwood is in for a shock when he discovers that his lady friend plotted against him."

Even in the gloom of the witching hour, I could see the grin that tugged at my companion's lips. "I swear that you adhere to the sensibilities of the last century as firmly as a limpet clings to crumbling rock."

"And what's that supposed to mean?" I snapped, my temper shortened by the lateness of the hour and the distance to my bed.

"I can hear it in your voice, Watson; your disdain for our client's romantic entanglement. His *lady friend*, indeed."

Now it was my turn to pick up on Holmes's words. "Our client, eh? Now who's living in the past? I thought you were retired."

Holmes waved away my admittedly feeble taunt. "Force of habit, nothing more, although I would wager that your puritanical tendencies are more deeply rooted. When will you learn that times change, and so must we? Are you even aware of the year?"

I took the corner to Cheyne Walk faster than I ought, clipping the kerb in the process.

"Have a care, Watson. You nearly had us over."

"If you don't like the way I drive, next time I suggest you take a cab."

"Come now. There's no need—"

"No need?" I cut him off, screeching the Swift to a halt in front of the house, no doubt attracting the notice of several of my more inquisitive neighbours. Since Holmes's arrival the curtains of Cheyne Walk had twitched so much you could be forgiven for thinking that they had developed a life of their own. "You drag me out in the middle of the night—"

"I would hardly call eight o'clock the middle of the night," Holmes interjected, clambering out of the passenger seat.

"What you call it is neither here nor there. You summon me to a sordid little nightclub—"

"If you think the Mallard is sordid, I dread to think what you would make of the rest of Soho."

"*A sordid little nightclub*, without a word of explanation, and have me charging around the streets of London on a personal crusade that has little if anything to do with me."

"Watson, you do yourself a disservice."

"Do I? Exactly what purpose did I serve this evening, other than that of chauffeur? Or perhaps I was just there so that, once again, I could be dazzled by your brilliance as you remind me how dull-witted, ignorant and laughably out-of-touch I am."

I punctuated my last sentence with a slam of the driver's door, not caring a jot if it attracted the attention of our regiment of nosy neighbours.

"Watson, you are tired."

"Outstanding, Holmes," I said, barging past the detective and marching up to my front door. "However did you know?"

I turned the key and pushed the door open, stepping inside. Holmes followed me, a look of smug amusement written across his face. I knew I shouldn't rise to the bait, but could scarcely help myself.

"And for your information," I continued, hanging my still damp hat and coat on their customary pegs, "I am all too aware of the age that we live in, and what the last few years have done to our country. You say I cling to the last century? Well, maybe I do. Maybe I yearn for a time when the police could be trusted, when a woman stood by her man rather than stab him in the back, and when an honest chap who had defended his country was rewarded, not broken by the very powers that have pledged to protect him."

Holmes merely laughed, shrugging off his own coat and stowing his umbrella in the stand. "And when exactly did this fairy-tale age exist, Watson, outside your rose-tinted imagination? Have you learnt nothing from our various misadventures over the years? The purity of the human spirit is a dangerous myth, as are the restraints of polite society. Time and time again, the gullible fall prey to those who truly understand human nature with all its complexity and foibles."

"Folk like you, I suppose."

"Folk like criminals, con-artists and swindlers," Holmes replied, his voice as infuriatingly calm as my own was agitated. "Not to mention the patrons of clubs such as the Mallard. Those young men, dancing the night away, they have stared horror in the face, Watson; they have seen beyond the lie of a happily-ever-after, seen what man will do to man. No wonder that they lose themselves to the primitive beat of a drum or a line of white powder."

"No wonder you find yourself so at home," I threw back, pushing past him to take the stairs.

If Holmes was stung by my words, he had no chance to show it.

"John Watson, what in heaven's name do you think you are doing, shouting the odds at this hour?"

I looked up to see my wife at the top of the stairs, hands on hips.

"I am sorry, Mrs Watson," Holmes replied in my place. "The blame is mine, not your husband's. Watson was merely pointing out that I have overstayed my welcome somewhat."

My tirade interrupted, I found myself becoming flustered at Holmes's words. I turned back to face him. "Now, I never said—"

"He is, of course, correct," Holmes continued, expertly avoiding my gaze. "It appears that I am living in the past: expecting our partnership, and indeed our friendship, to resume where we left off, and for that I also apologise. I shall leave first thing in the morning."

With that, Holmes climbed the stairs, leaving me fuming in the hallway. My wife stood aside on the landing to let him pass, which he did with a loaded expression of thanks.

It was typical of the man. Picking a fight and then, when the argument was lost, taking the high ground. Maybe it was the throb of my rheumatism, the chill of night, or the sudden realisation that some things never change, no matter what Holmes said, but if my former companion wanted to cut short his visit, then so be it. He would be the one returning to a cold, empty cottage, not I.

After a fitful night's sleep, I awoke early to hear movement downstairs. I glanced at my bedside clock to see that it was but seven o'clock. My wife was still sleeping peacefully, so unless we were being burgled it could only mean that Holmes was up and about. The memory of our quarrel hanging heavily over me, I struggled out of bed, ignoring the creaks of my knees to throw on my gown.

Closing the bedroom door as softly as possible behind me, I stole downstairs to spy a suitcase packed and beside the door, Holmes's coat draped over it. Of the man himself, there was no sign, until I walked through to the kitchen and found the detective writing a note at the wooden table.

I cleared my throat to announce my presence.

"Ah, excellent," said Holmes, glancing up and rewarding me with the tightest of smiles. "I was composing a letter of thanks to your dear lady wife, but now you are awake, you can relay my gratitude in person. Capital."

He stood, taking care not to scrape his chair against the tiles.

"Holmes, I—"

"It has been more than agreeable to see you again, Watson. I do hope I can repay your hospitality in future. You and your wife are of course welcome to visit—"

I stepped forward into the kitchen, cutting him off.

"Please, Holmes. There's no need for you to leave like this. What I said last night—"

"Was completely understandable, and, I would admit, somewhat justified. You were correct; there was no need for me to – how did you put it so eloquently? – *summon* you to the Mallard. I could, and indeed did, bring the matter to a satisfactory conclusion without your assistance, on this occasion at least."

He replaced the chair beneath the table and flashed me yet another smile that singularly failed to reach his eyes.

"And now I must make haste if I am to catch the eight o'clock from Waterloo." He marched straight past me and into the corridor. "I can hail a cab on the way, so there is no need to worry about providing transport. You should get back to bed. After all, you had a late night."

"I won't hear of it," I said, following him towards the front door. "If you must go today, I'm sure that you can catch a later train. Let me get dressed, and we can have some breakfast before I drive you to the station."

Stubbornly, Holmes slipped on his coat and picked up his luggage.

"No need, Watson. No need. I have put you and your good lady out for too long. Besides, by the sound of the footsteps approaching your front door, you have a new visitor."

"Footsteps? What do you—"

Before I could complete my question, Holmes swung open the front door to reveal a portly individual reaching for the knocker.

The fellow started to find himself caught in the act, before a wide gap-toothed grin spread across his bearded face. He clapped his hands together with glee and laughed heartily.

"Ha-ha. Just the man I wanted to see. Sherlock Holmes, back where he belongs in old London town – and not a moment too soon!"

CHAPTER FIVE

INSPECTOR TOVEY

"Bless my soul," I exclaimed, staring in amazement at the hirsute gentleman on my doorstep. "Inspector Tovey, is that really you?"

"Indeed it is, Dr Watson," the newcomer replied. "Larger than life and twice as ugly. May I come in?"

"Of course, of course," I agreed, ushering Tovey into the hallway, before tugging self-consciously at the belt of my dressing gown. "You will have to forgive my appearance."

Tovey dismissed my apology with the wave of a broad hand. "Please. I'm the one banging on your door at this god-forsaken hour – or I would be if Mr Holmes hadn't opened it first!" He waggled a thick finger at my friend. "What was it, Mr Holmes? The scrape of my boot on the pavement, or the fact that I had kippers for my breakfast?"

Now it was Holmes's turn to smile. "You know my methods too well, Inspector, although I dread to think how long it has been since we last saw each other."

"Nearly ten years, sir."

Holmes's thick eyebrows shot up. "Really? So long?"

"You think I'd forget the Blackheath werewolf?" Tovey chuckled, patting the left side of his belly. "The scars still itch whenever it rains."

I looked at the two men in wonderment. "The Blackheath what?" I asked. "You never told me about that!"

"A man is allowed his secrets, Watson," Holmes said. "Even from his official biographer. Now, do you expect the good inspector to stand on ceremony, or should we make him more comfortable?"

Remembering my manners, I led our visitor through to the drawing room, and begged him to take a seat on the settee. He did so gratefully, the frame creaking slightly as it took the not inconsiderable strain. While the inspector had never been a slim man, he had unquestionably piled on the pounds since I last saw him.

We had first met Inspector Tovey in his native Bristol, during the unfortunate business with the League of Merchants in '91. Back then, Abraham Tovey had been an up-and-coming police detective in his early twenties, determined to tackle the crimes that his colleagues worked hard to ignore: cases that confounded logic and, in many cases it seemed, natural law. It was little wonder that he had crossed paths with Holmes and me, although Tovey had barely survived his first encounter with the pair of us. Nearly thirty years later, and now at Scotland Yard, the inspector bore the marks of that terrible investigation: a glass eye that stared permanently ahead. The fake orb was the work of a true artist, but could never hope to match the vitality of the original. Tovey's frame had blossomed, while his dark beard was now flecked with grey, but the intelligence and good humour that shone like a beacon from his surviving eye had diminished not one iota.

"There, that is better," Holmes said, marching across to the curtains. "Now, if we could shed a little light on the matter…" He pulled back the drapes to be greeted by a sky still beset with heavy clouds. Holmes let out a sigh. "Less illumination than I had hoped. I would suggest turning on the lights, but I would not want the flicker of the bulbs to trigger one of your migraines, Inspector."

I regarded our friend with sympathy. "I could prescribe something if that would help, Inspector. My wife suffers from the same affliction." I stole a glance at Holmes. "Especially during times of stress."

"Thank you, Doctor, but I've learned to live with them," Tovey replied, "although I'm waiting with bated breath to discover how Mr Holmes made his diagnosis."

Holmes took a chair by the fireplace and steepled his fingers. "There is no great mystery, Inspector. As you passed me in the hallway, I noticed a patch of yellow residue on the right side of your neck."

Tovey laughed, rubbing the offending stain.

"Of course, I remembered your fondness for homemade remedies." Holmes turned to me. "Any ideas, Doctor?"

"A mustard bath?" I guessed.

"The very same," the inspector said, "with just a touch of baking powder."

"A panacea that dates back to Roman times," Holmes said, slipping easily into a lecture. "Also said to aid congestion and stiff joints. As the inspector's sinuses are obviously clear, and he is having little trouble walking, a propensity for migraines seemed the obvious, if regrettable, choice. While I usually leave medical matters to Watson, may I also recommend two tablespoons of honey before bed."

"Fascinating though this consultation is," I cut in, eager to steer the conversation away from homespun nonsense, "I'm sure the inspector didn't come all this way to discuss his health."

"Indeed, I didn't," said Tovey, tapping his forehead, "although I will make a note about the honey. A good tip, Mr Holmes, and one I shall try tonight."

I couldn't help but roll my eyes.

"But as the doctor said, we should get down to business," Tovey continued, "especially if I am to persuade Mr Holmes to abandon his journey to Waterloo Station."

Holmes raised an eyebrow, amused that Tovey was trying to beat him at his own game. "You spied my suitcase in the hallway, of course," he acknowledged.

"And had a word with the cabbie waiting out in the street," Tovey said. "I'll gladly pay him for his trouble if you hear me out."

"You have my full attention, Inspector."

"And I am glad of it. You won't believe how relieved I was to hear your name mentioned at Scotland Yard this morning." The inspector shook his head. "Always knew that Pritchard was a bad 'un. Glad someone finally exposed him."

"It was nothing," Holmes insisted, modestly.

"Nothing or not, I was about to take a trip of my own, seeking you out on the South Downs – but here you are, solving crimes, on the streets of London town, thank the Lord. If I need any man's help at the moment, it's that of Sherlock Holmes."

"Help in what way?"

Tovey shifted forward on the settee, lowering his voice, as if worried that he would be overheard. "Two days ago, a hand was found on the banks of the Thames, not far from Tower Bridge."

"A human hand?" I replied, feeling a shiver of anticipation at the inspector's macabre revelation.

Now it was Holmes's turn to roll his eyes. "I doubt the inspector is talking about a monkey's paw, Watson!"

"I only wish I were, Mr Holmes," Tovey replied. "It was human all right, and as fresh as a daisy, as if it had been severed that very day."

"Intriguing," I admitted. "And you hope that Holmes can identify its original owner?"

Tovey shook his large head. "No need, Doctor. We know exactly whom it belonged to. I had the damned thing fingerprinted, you see?"

"And found a match?" Holmes asked.

"Samuel Pike," came the reply. "Small-time crook, arrested for burglary back in 1911. Sentenced for two years, he was, but got himself released after just eleven months for good behaviour. By all accounts, a likable enough fellow, despite having light fingers."

"Then it sounds as if you have your man," said Holmes.

"That's just it," Tovey replied. "I thought I did, until I did some digging. You see, Pike volunteered for service in 1914."

"Making amends by serving his country," I commented. "Admirable."

"And tragic," Tovey said. "I decided to pay a visit to his last known address."

"Was Pike there?" Holmes enquired.

"Nursing a bloody stump?" Tovey asked. "That would have been nice and easy, wouldn't it? But no, I questioned his wife, who just sat there shocked as you like, the colour draining from her face."

"Fearing for her husband's safety," I suggested.

"That's what I thought, Doctor, until she insisted that the hand couldn't belong to Pike at all. 'It can't be Sammy's,' she said. 'It just can't.' But there was no doubt about it, the fingerprints were conclusive. The hand was Pike's.

"And then she gets up, Mrs Pike, and walks across to the dresser on the other side of the room, like she's in a trance. I continue with my questioning, assuming that she's in shock. When did she last see her husband, does he work down by the river? That kind of thing."

"And whether he had fallen back into his old ways, I should imagine," said I.

"She didn't answer," Tovey continued. "She just stood there, her back to me, hands on top of the dresser. I tried again: 'Mrs Pike,' I said, 'if you think your husband is in trouble...' She just made a noise, either a sob or a laugh, I couldn't tell which. 'Sammy's long past trouble,' she said, and opened a drawer. When she turned round, she had an envelope in her hand, which she passed to me without another word."

Tovey turned to face Holmes. "I don't mind admitting that my blood ran cold when I recognised what it was."

The inspector reached into his jacket pocket and retrieved a small rectangular notebook.

"Too many of those letters have been delivered, Mr Holmes."

I knew what was coming even before he read the words he had copied from the dreadful missive:

Dear Madam,

The King and Queen deeply regret the death of your husband in the service of his country, and I am commanded to convey to you the expression of Their Majesties' true sympathy with you in your sorrow.

Yours very faithfully,
Keeper of the Privy Purse

"So he died during the war," I said.

"The letter was dated the seventeenth of May 1917," Tovey revealed. "'Now do you see why that hand can't be Sammy's?' Mrs Pike asked as she took back the envelope. If I didn't believe a letter from the Palace, I could ask a fellow called Mallory who drank in the local pub. He served with Pike in France, and had seen him killed."

"And did Mr Mallory corroborate the widow Pike's story?" Holmes asked.

Tovey slipped the notebook back into his jacket pocket. "He did, and said there was no doubt about the matter. Samuel Pike took a bullet to the head and was dead before he hit the ground. Mallory said he'd never forgot it, Pike staring up him, with half his head blown off."

"But you said that Pike's hand was fresh when you found it," I said, struggling to make sense of Tovey's sorry tale.

"I did, Doctor," the inspector confirmed. "No sign of decay whatsoever."

"Which leads us to ask," cut in Holmes, as calm as a man commenting on the morning's weather, "how a freshly severed hand could find itself in London, two years after its owner was killed some two hundred miles away."

CHAPTER SIX

THE HAND OF MYSTERY

Not an hour later, I was washed, dressed and standing in a Scotland Yard laboratory. Tovey's gamble had paid off – as soon as Holmes heard the inspector's strange story, my friend had taken his suitcase back to the guest room, changed from country tweeds to city attire and was waiting back in the hallway, hurrying me along.

My wife, now awake, had watched Inspector Tovey bustle us out of the front door and stated through thin lips her delight that Holmes had decided to extend his visit after all.

I knew she would have more words to say on the matter when we returned, but for now my attention was focused on the waxy appendage laid out on a tray on the pathologist's slab.

"What do you make of it, Watson?" Holmes asked.

I bent to examine the hand, gently testing its joints, lifting each finger slightly in turn.

"There's no sign of rigor mortis," I reported, "which means, judging by the state of the skin, that the hand was removed more than forty-eight hours ago." I looked up at Tovey. "When did you say it was found?"

This time, the inspector had no need to consult his notebook. "Ten past ten on Monday morning."

"Which means that it was amputated no more than twelve hours before its discovery."

I glanced up from the grisly artefact. "Remember how hot it was on Saturday, Holmes, before the weather broke in the evening?"

Holmes nodded. "If, then, the hand had been exposed to the warm air before that point—"

"I would expect the rate of decay to be significantly accelerated," I confirmed, standing again.

"You mentioned amputation," Holmes prompted, "suggesting surgical removal, rather than loss of the appendage in a fight?"

I turned the tray so that Holmes could see the sheared bone. The hand still possessed a length of forearm, three inches or so from the wrist.

"I assume that you have brought a magnifying glass?"

"As if I would leave the house without one," Holmes declared, producing a large glass, which he delivered into my hand.

"Force of habit once again?" I countered, turning the lens on the two rings of exposed bone. I checked the cuts myself, before moving aside so that Holmes could make his own study.

"Ah yes," he said, peering through the glass. "I see them."

"See what?" asked the inspector.

"Grooves cut into the bone by a surgical saw," I explained. "On both the ulna and the radius."

"Does it have to be surgical?" Tovey enquired. "Butchers have been known to cut through bone."

"They have," replied Holmes, "but in this case, the doctor is absolutely correct." He angled the glass so that Tovey could observe the markings.

"As you can see here and here, whatever implement sliced through these bones possessed fine teeth, capable of precision work. Butchery saws are positively barbaric in comparison with modern medical equipment."

Pleased though I was that Holmes had jumped to my defence, my analysis of the bones was as yet incomplete.

"That may be true," I said, taking back the glass, "although I would suggest that whoever performed the amputation, while obviously skilled, was in something of a hurry. Examining the cut itself, I would suggest that he got halfway through, before either the saw caught or he was disturbed. See? The angle of the cut changes slightly—"

"Meaning that our mystery surgeon shifted position to resume the operation," Holmes said. "Excellent work, Watson. Now, what of these?"

Holmes was pointing to a thin line of puckered scars that ran an inch or so from the wrist.

"I thought you would never ask," I said, eagerly. Carefully, I turned the hand over onto its back so that the bloodless palm faced upwards. "The scarring continues all the way around the wrist."

"A perfect ring of stitches," Holmes said, gently attempting to prise the scar apart with his middle and index fingers.

"Stitches?" Tovey repeated. "You mean that Pike – or whoever this is – attempted to slash his wrist and was stitched back together?"

"Suicides tend to stop at the wrist," I pointed out, "not slice all around the arm."

"What would produce such an injury, then?" the inspector asked.

"Replantation," Holmes replied without hesitation.

Tovey was still none the wiser. "Which is?"

"Impossible," I said. "Replantation is the theorised surgical reattachment of a body part."

Holmes took up the explanation. "Say a farm worker loses an

arm in a threshing accident. There are those who believe that one day it will be possible to reattach the limb."

"What? To sew it back on?"

Holmes nodded. "Reconnecting the vascular system and reattaching both muscle and bone. After a period of recuperation, the patient would be able to use his arm as if it had never been severed from the body. A medical miracle."

"*If* the process were ever perfected," I countered. "Even if muscles and blood vessels could be successfully stitched back together, infection would be inevitable. I have no doubt that one day such an operation may be possible, but not for decades, maybe even centuries."

"And yet we have Mr Pike's wrist," Holmes said, once again examining the scars. "One enigma after another, eh? Whatever your doubts, Watson, even you must recognise the skill demonstrated in such needlework?"

Holmes was right. Whoever had produced such regimented sutures was no mere skilled surgeon; he was an artist. I had never seen work so delicate and yet secure, each stitch perfectly placed along the long white scar that circumnavigated the wrist.

"So, you're saying that our hand had been severed before and reattached, only to be severed again?"

"Of course not," Holmes said, bluntly. "That would be, as Watson explained, impossible – although I would think that the good doctor is itching to open up the wrist and see if there are any other signs of replantation beneath the skin."

Undeniably the thought had crossed my mind. "Perhaps that would be an examination best left to the police pathologist," I said, however, with a certain regret in my voice.

"Luckily, there is much we can learn from Pike's hand without resorting to the scalpel," Holmes said. "You say that it was discovered near Tower Bridge?"

Tovey nodded. "St Katharine Docks, to be precise."

"The western or eastern basin?" Holmes asked, running his glass over the palm of the hand.

The inspector reached for his notebook, flicking through pages of neat handwriting. "Western," he eventually reported. "Near the dockmaster's house. He noticed it while checking the lock, discarded in a clump of weeds according to the first officer on the scene."

"So that's where it happened?" I asked. "Whatever *it* was?"

"I don't think so, Watson," Holmes said, passing me the lens once again. "What do you make of these lacerations? Here, across the distal palmar, and also on the thenar eminence."

I examined the areas Holmes had indicated, first the bridge of skin beneath the fingers and then the cluster of muscle beside the thumb.

"They're punctures rather than cuts," I exclaimed, looking back up at my friend. "Bite marks, maybe. Some kind of dog?"

"A Jack Russell, I would suggest," came the reply, "according to the distance between the wounds. Possibly a Border Terrier at a push."

I continued my examination. "There's no sign of inflammation around the marks—"

"Meaning that they were incurred after the hand had been removed from Pike's body."

A gruesome thought occurred to me. "Good Lord. Could the hound have been attempting to eat it?"

Holmes dismissed the notion with a shake of his head. "There are no signs of gnawing, although if we turn the hand over we can see similar wounds on the reverse."

The detective did so, revealing a series of punctures in corresponding areas on the back of the hand.

"Carried then?" I suggested, the image of a small dog, trotting along the Thames with a human hand in its mouth, no less disturbing than the thought of the appendage being chewed.

"That would be my hypothesis," Holmes agreed.

"So the hand was found by a dog," said Tovey, his police-trained mind filing the evidence into a plausible course of events, "and transported to the docks."

"Where it was dropped, ready to be discovered the following morning," Holmes concluded.

"Then we're no nearer to understanding where the dratted thing originated," I sighed, instantly castigating myself. It was all too easy in cases such as this to reduce body parts to objects; mere evidence to be studied and then discarded when their usefulness had passed, a habit I always fought hard to resist. Whether I was in a pathology lab, or examining the mummies of the British Museum, I tried to remember that these *things* had once been parts of living, breathing people. They were neither artefacts nor evidence; they were human remains, and it was necessary to treat them with respect.

Of course, Holmes would have scoffed at such sentimentality. My friend had elevated professional detachment to an art form. Leaning closer, he held out his palm to me as if I were a nurse assisting at an operation. "Tweezers, Watson."

Used to his brusqueness, I did as I was asked and watched as Holmes, keeping the tweezers closed, scraped beneath the fingernails.

"A dish if you please, Doctor," he instructed, and I started to rummage through the pathology cupboards for a petri dish, Holmes hurrying me along.

"Give a man a chance," I scolded him as I found a stock of glass containers and passed one over. Carefully, he tipped a scrap of dark sludge into the dish.

"Mud?" I enquired.

"Clay. In particular, London Clay of the stratigraphic range associated with the Ypresian age. Naturally it possesses a bluish-grey appearance, which turns brown when weathered."

"Yes, yes. If you could spare us the geological seminar..."

Holmes sighed. "It's found throughout the London Basin, from Wiltshire to Essex, but in the capital itself is most likely to be found near the Thames."

"So our man was working on the river," Tovey said, "before the hand was removed."

"A logical conclusion, Inspector."

"But if the hand *was* found by a dog..." I pointed out.

"We still have no idea where," Tovey concluded.

I nodded. "The Thames covers a lot of ground."

"Which is why I require hydrofluoric and perchloric acids, plus a hearty breakfast," Holmes announced. "I assume that the pathology department has stores of the former, if not the latter?"

Soon, Holmes, Tovey and I had repaired to a local café for sustenance, while the clay sample settled in a solution mixed by my friend from the two acids. It may appear remarkable that we could even think of food after such a grisly examination, but the exertions of the previous evening and the strange thrill of being back on a case had left me ravenous. As Napoleon himself said, an army marches on its stomach, as do detectives of the law, especially in the case of Inspector Tovey. The amount of food the man could put away was almost as astonishing as the crimes he investigated, although the conversation was light and the friendship we had kindled all those years ago burned as brightly as ever.

Our appetites sated, we returned to the laboratory where Holmes boiled away the liquid, ready for the soil to be dried and filtered.

Then the waiting began anew, as Holmes tested and analysed the sample, while I whiled away the rest of the morning with *The Times* in Tovey's office, which I was pleased to report was as neat and tidy as his vast beard was wild and unruly.

It was mid-afternoon before Holmes burst into the office, a large book in one hand and his results in the other.

"I thought as much," he enthused. "If I am correct, and I know I am, I can pinpoint the last known location of our mystery hand before it was liberated from its arm."

"We stand ready to be amazed," Tovey said, flipping open his notebook in readiness.

Holmes deposited his papers on the desk. "It's all there for you, Inspector. As I hypothesised, the sample was riverbank clay, and I have found significant traces of both copper and arsenic."

"Arsenic?" I repeated, concerned by the mention of the deadly poison.

"Do not worry yourself, Doctor," Holmes said, raising a calming hand. "In this case the chemical comes from an innocent source, if not an eminently wise one. Both copper and arsenic are used in the manufacture of the emerald green dye so beloved of wallpaper manufacturers and even confectioners these days."

"Arsenic in confectionery?" Tovey exclaimed. "Next you'll be telling us it's used in toys."

"Indeed it is," Holmes confirmed, "which is why the practice has largely been discontinued. In fact, according to the gazetteer in New Scotland Yard's surprisingly comprehensive library, only a handful of factories still practise the method."

"Including one on the Thames?" I suggested.

"Not half a mile from St Katharine Docks," Holmes revealed triumphantly.

"Then that is where we shall go," I said, folding my newspaper and slipping it under my arm.

Holmes regarded me with amusement. "Watson, surely you are not telling me you are ready to charge around London on another crusade with me?"

"Someone has to look after you," I replied. "Especially if you don't have an umbrella to hand."

Tovey looked between us in bewilderment. "I'm not going to pretend I know what you're talking about," said he, "but I can get a car outside for us in five minutes flat, if you don't mind an old bloodhound of the law tagging along."

"Of course not," Holmes replied. "It *is* your case after all – and besides, I can hardly see you staying behind when you hear what else I discovered."

"And that is?" I prompted.

Holmes's eyes sparkled. "There was something else beneath Pike's fingernails. A minute trace of a mud from a foreign shore."

I could guess what was coming as Holmes slammed the book he had been carrying down on the desk, revealing it to be an atlas, full of colourful maps.

He found the page he was looking for and jabbed a finger at the map in question.

"Northern France," I said, peering over.

"The Douai Plains," Holmes confirmed. "Now, as we know from personal experience, Watson, the trenches were muddy places indeed."

"More like hell on earth," I murmured, trying not to dredge up memories that I had hoped to bury for ever.

"So, it *is* Pike's hand?" Tovey asked, dragging me back to the here and now.

"The fingerprints alone tell us that, Inspector," Holmes replied. "Of the fact that the hand belongs to Samuel Pike there is no doubt. What I want to know is where he has been for the last two years, and how he survived a German bullet to the brain."

CHAPTER SEVEN

OF MUD AND MURK

Thankfully the rain of the previous day had yet to reappear as Inspector Tovey drove us towards Wapping, although ominous storm clouds were already brewing on the horizon.

I sat up front in the passenger seat, while Holmes watched the streets of the capital speed by from the back. We drove in silence, until Tovey picked up on one of Holmes's earlier comments.

"So, what did you mean about personal experience of the trenches, Mr Holmes?"

My friend ignored the question.

"I mean," Tovey continued, pressing the point, "forgive me for saying, but neither of you are of the age to serve on the front line. Unless, Doctor, you were there in your medical capacity?"

Before I could respond, Holmes's sharp voice rang out from the back seat. "As I am sure you are aware, Inspector, much of what happened during the war remains shrouded in secrecy, for the sake of national security. I would ask you to put my momentary lapse of discretion down to the excitement of the case and never mention it again."

Tovey mumbled an apology and the car fell into an awkward silence, as far removed from our jovial breakfast earlier that day as London is from the fields of northern France.

Of course, Holmes was correct. Both he and I had been employed by the state on numerous occasions during the war years, serving our country here and abroad. While I was obviously glad to do it, the distressing events I witnessed will haunt me for the rest of my days, far worse even than my experiences in Afghanistan. Fortunately, my involvement was limited to half a dozen cases or so. As for Holmes, even I had no idea of the extent of his wartime service.

The subject had arisen not a few days earlier, when I suggested that Holmes had played a significant role in the defence of our realm.

"I merely played my part, Watson," he said, "as any Englishman would. The true glory, if one can use such a word, belongs to those brave men who sacrificed their future for ours."

I had let the subject drop then, as Tovey did now. Thankfully, when we pulled up on Wapping High Street, the atmosphere between the two men lifted as we lost ourselves in the mystery once again.

"This way," said Holmes, leading us down a narrow alleyway between the Hoop and Grapes public house and the walls of a rag and bone yard. We emerged on the banks of the Thames to find that the tide was thankfully out, silt sloping down to the water's edge.

"Here we are," said Tovey, making his way along an uneven pathway to our right. He pointed to a faded sign that hung from a redbrick building on the river's edge.

ROUD AND COMPANY,

DYE AND PIGMENT MANUFACTURERS

Marching up to the large green doors, the inspector tried a handle only to find the place locked. Cupping one of his hands, he tried to peer through the grimy windows, but it was obvious the factory was empty.

He stepped back onto the walkway of uneven planks and looked up at the dilapidated sign. "You would think they might at least give it a new coat of paint. Not the finest advertisement for their wares, is it?"

Holmes, meanwhile, was examining the clay beneath his feet. It was undoubtedly the same shade as the muck he had found beneath the fingernail of the hand.

"The pigment industry in this country has floundered of late," Holmes said, wiping his hand on a handkerchief. "Meanwhile, it has positively flourished on the continent, specifically in Germany." He returned the now mud-smeared cloth to his pocket. "Where do you think the military had to go to buy the khaki pigment needed for British Army uniforms at the beginning of hostilities?"

"Nothing surprises me any more," Tovey commented. "Where now? The place is shut up."

I surveyed the stretch of riverbank before us. Most of the buildings were in the same sorry state, many seemingly abandoned if the broken windows and boarded-up doorways were anything to go by. Peace might have been restored, but the country was still suffering, many industries unable to man their workshops and factories, while injured and disenfranchised servicemen huddled unemployed beneath railway bridges. My mind wandered back to those young people dancing with such abandon back at the Mallard Club. Maybe Holmes was right. Maybe you couldn't blame them for seeking escapism when the real world was so resolutely bleak.

Holmes was also looking up and down the river. I followed his gaze, my eyes resting on another crumbling pile along the bank, its windows without glass and signage long gone. All except for one architectural feature that caught my attention.

"Holmes," said I. "That building there…" I was already marching down the pathway, the boards shifting beneath my weight.

"What of it?" Tovey asked, following me along the bank. Holmes was matching me step for step and had clearly noticed the same thing.

Above the doorway, chiselled into a large stone, was a long serpent wound around a staff.

"The Rod of Asclepius," I said, stopping in front of the building.

"A place of medicine," agreed Holmes, stooping down to retrieve what at first looked like a length of driftwood, but on closer examination was revealed to be part of an old noticeboard. Holmes's handkerchief was out again in a flash, this time rubbing a thin layer of grime from the wood to reveal long-obscured words.

"Abberton Hospital," I read over his shoulder. "Have you ever heard of it?"

"Not before now," Holmes admitted, "although by its current state, that is hardly surprising. It looks as if it has lain derelict for decades, although bearing in mind the marks on Pike's wrist bones…"

"A surgical saw," Tovey chimed in. "But surely no one would be operating in a place like this?"

Holmes regarded the squat building, which in days gone by would have tended those who worked in the surrounding factories. "You would think not. However…"

He thrust the filthy piece of wood into my hands and bent to examine what little could be seen of the step beneath the hospital's heavy double doors.

"There's a footprint," he declared, "or at least half of one, poking out from beneath the doors. Do you see, Watson?"

I replied in the positive, and marvelled that it had not been washed away by yesterday's rain. Holmes pointed at the stone ledge that extended above our heads.

"The porch would have offered at least some shelter. But details, Watson. Details."

At first I was puzzled by his remarks, wondering what else I was expected to notice, when my eyes widened. "It's covered by the door!"

"Meaning that the door must have been opened recently to allow whoever passed this way to leave a mark," confirmed Holmes. He stood, trying the doors themselves. Like those of the factory, they were locked shut.

"Do you still carry a set of skeleton keys to go with your magnifying glass?" I asked, not relishing the idea of scrambling through any of the windows.

With a snort of frustration, Holmes slapped his palm against the all-too-sturdy wood of the door. "Watson, you appal me. I am an apiarist, not a housebreaker. Besides, I foolishly left them in my suitcase."

"Then perhaps I can be of assistance?" cut in Tovey, producing a small leather pouch from his breast pocket. "If you gentlemen would give me a little room."

"Gladly," smiled Holmes, gently pulling me aside.

Tovey knelt, and, opening the wallet, extracted a small penknife and a single lever pick. His tools in hand, the inspector went to work, inserting the blade into the keyhole. Listening to rather than looking at the lock, he manipulated the knife, easing it up within the casing. I knew enough of such practices from my time with Holmes to imagine that he was trying to raise the bolt within the mechanism. Satisfied that the knife was in position, it was in with the lever pick. Stepping to the side to get a better look, I was amused to see the pink tip of the inspector's tongue poking out of the side of his mouth, in the same manner as a child concentrating on a drawing. There was nothing infantile about the man's dexterity, however, those thick fingers gently easing the pick into the workings, searching for the correct groove, before with a satisfying *click* the bolt gave way.

"Bravo," remarked Holmes, rewarding the inspector with a sotto round of applause. "Expertly done, Inspector. I couldn't have managed better myself."

"And you a bloodhound of the law," I remarked, offering the large man a hand as he hauled himself back up to his feet.

"I wasn't always a policeman," Tovey replied enigmatically, pocketing his tools before trying the door once again. It swung open with remarkable ease, emitting barely a squeak of rusty metal. Inspector Tovey ran his index finger across the hinges.

"Oiled," he reported, rubbing the tip of his now slick and blackened finger against his thumb. "And recently too."

"And here is the rest of our footprint," said Holmes, once again squatting in the doorway. There was no need for a glass to make it out, clear against the grime of the step.

"Small," I pointed out. "A woman?"

"Possibly," Holmes said, rising again, "although the edges regrettably lack the definition required for conclusive analysis."

"Then what about these?" Tovey said, stepping into the lobby of the abandoned hospital. Sure enough, by the light spilling into the room from the now opened door, many more footprints were clearly visible in years' worth of dust. The inspector pulled a torch from his pocket and flicked it on, tracing the footsteps back to the bottom of a flight of distinctly rickety-looking stairs.

"Definitely a woman," Holmes said, following the inspector inside, "and more besides. Inspector, if you would swing your light this way."

Tovey did so, revealing the imprint of a larger boot. "Looks like a man this time," he said, "according to the size and tread."

"Inspector, if I may borrow your torch?" Holmes asked, holding out his hand in anticipation. Tovey handed it over, and Holmes illuminated another set of prints. "That *is* odd," he said, crouching on his haunches.

"What is?" I asked, walking over to him.

"The man stood still here," Holmes explained, showing me the marks in the dust. "See? His feet are at shoulder width."

"And how is that peculiar?" I enquired. "Other than why anyone would want to linger in such a place like this?"

I am not embarrassed to admit that there was something in this relic of a hospital that unnerved me. It wasn't the dust motes spinning in the beams of light, or even the distant scrabbling of tiny claws behind the wainscoting. The air simply seemed wrong, as if it held a tang of the unnatural. Ridiculous, of course, and I am certain that Holmes would have dismissed my unease as the overactive imagination of a second-rate novelist, but I felt it all the same.

Attempting to stop myself from shivering, more from apprehension than the damp cold that seemed to pervade the building, I studied more closely the prints that Holmes was examining so diligently. "They look perfectly normal to me, if a little on the large side."

"But that's just it, Watson," he replied. "The size. The right foot is at least three sizes larger than the other."

I looked more carefully still and could now see the truth for myself.

"So it is, although that is less unusual than one might expect. Why, my wife—"

"Has a larger left foot than her right," Holmes interrupted. "Of course she does. In eighty per cent of cases the left is larger than the right, but the difference is usually minimal, as in Mrs Watson's case; a size four on her left and three on the right."

"If you say so," I sniffed.

"I do indeed, but the difference between the left and right in these prints is far too pronounced."

"A false leg, maybe?" Tovey suggested.

"Possibly, yes," Holmes conceded, standing again.

"Do we know what size shoes Pike took?" I asked.

"I doubt the letter from the privy purse bothered with such detail," Holmes deadpanned, before pointing up the stairs. "Whoever the prints belonged to, it appears that our mismatched male and his female companion spent most of their time here traversing up and down these steps."

Holmes swept the torch around the remainder of the lobby. The dust to the side of the stairway was undisturbed, a thick blanket covering the space between us and a number of internal doors, most of which remained shut.

However, as Holmes angled the light to sweep up the staircase, we could clearly see a host of footprints on the steps. Whoever had been here regularly walked up and down the stairs, ignoring the rest of the ground floor.

Gripping hard the handle of my walking stick, I swallowed my nerves, taking the first step.

"Then we had better see what's up there, had we not?"

CHAPTER EIGHT

THE DYNAMO

I cried out as my foot went straight through a step.

"Tread carefully, Watson," Holmes said, springing forward to catch me as I tumbled onto my knees.

"Yes, thank you, Holmes," I snapped, pulling my foot free from the jagged hole in the wood. "The thought had crossed my mind. Of course, it might help if you pointed the torch in the direction we're walking, rather than darting it here, there and everywhere."

Inspector Tovey rushed up beside me, testing with his foot the rest of the step that had given way.

"This one's rotted through, but the next looks solid enough."

He dragged himself up over the broken wood using the handrail. The next step creaked, but remained firm beneath his sturdy boots. "I reckon we'll be fine heading further up," he speculated with little in the way of evidence, "besides, if they can take my weight, you should have no bother at all, Doctor."

"I'll judge that when we reach the top," I murmured, holding onto the banister and rubbing my throbbing ankle. A shard of wood had left a nasty scratch, but thankfully the skin was unbroken, although I could feel that an angry welt had already risen along the length of the injury.

"You could wait here," Holmes suggested, "or return to the lobby. I am sure the inspector would be happy to accompany me from this point on."

"No problem at all," Tovey confirmed.

"We could even give you the torch."

"Don't be ridiculous," I said, resuming my ascent. "I've come this far, haven't I?"

I was reluctant to admit that I would rather take my chances falling through another rotten stair than waiting alone in that disconcerting place below.

We were climbing towards the second storey of the hospital now, the light failing with every passing minute. The first floor had been much like the lobby, the thick layer of dust on the floor undisturbed save for marks left by tiny scurrying paws. Instead the human footprints continued upstairs.

All around us the building groaned, wind whistling through the empty corridors. Doors caught in the breeze, banging open and shut to shred what little was left of my nerves. We continued up, loose strands of cobwebs brushing across our faces, and our nostrils full with the cloying stench of a building submitting to ruin.

And all the time, my knees threatened to rival the creak of the wood beneath our feet.

Inspector Tovey paused at the top of the flight, calling us to join him. "This is it," he said, pointing towards a set of double doors. "The footprints head that way."

"And that is not all," I added. "Look, Holmes, something was pulled across the landing. Something heavy."

A path had been cleared through the dust, a channel with straight edges at either side, some two feet apart.

"A trunk maybe," Holmes commented absently, following the

path to the doors. He opened them, peering around the corner, his surprise evident as he saw what lay beyond.

"Watson. Inspector. Come and see."

I hobbled forward, my ankle still aching, and made my way through the doors.

A series of wires hung from the walls, laden with electric light bulbs that dangled like forgotten Christmas tree decorations. It was clear that the cables were not part of the hospital's original fittings and fixtures. The wires were thrown between the inert gas lamps that dotted the walls, the supply long disconnected.

"Wait here," Holmes ordered, darting ahead. I called for him to wait, but instead he turned left into a room, the torchlight vanishing, shadows immediately rushing in to claim the corridor.

"Holmes," I cried out. "Holmes, what have you found?"

"Let us see," he called back, and I heard what sounded like a lever being thrown.

With the buzz of a hundred angry wasps, the hanging bulbs blazed with yellow light. I raised my hand to protect my eyes, blinded by the sudden glare. When I lowered it again, blinking against the artificial incandescence, the shadows of the corridor had been banished. We could now see both the paint peeling from the walls and the detritus that littered the floor: papers, files, even an upended chair, the remnants of a working hospital, scattered around. The bulbs fizzed and flickered, making the scene yet more unsettling, and beneath it all came the throaty growl of machinery.

Holmes's head appeared from around the door. "Watson, you have to see this."

The inspector and I entered what looked once to have been some kind of administrator's office. A wooden desk was pushed to the far corner and shelves stretched around all four walls. Once these would have been lined with notes and ledgers. Now they held only dust.

Holmes was standing, facing the door, his face full of anticipation, waiting to see how we would react to what we saw. Behind him, wheezing like a grampus, was an incredible device. A bicycle wheel, stripped of its tyre, had been bolted upright to a wooden plinth, the spokes replaced by six thick metal rods. At its centre was a core that spun like a Catherine wheel, producing a worrying number of sparks with each revolution.

"An electrical generator?" I asked, keeping a safe distance between myself and the device.

"The very same, and an ingenious one at that." Holmes took a step closer to the machine, and it was all I could do to stop myself pulling him back for his own safety. The damned thing looked as if it might go up in flames at a moment's notice.

"These static rods are magnets," he said, pointing out each component as he talked, "the rotating armature at the centre generating the current. I cannot see for sure, but I would think, from the positioning of the cables, that there is a communicator at the dynamo's heart, converting any generated current to workable power."

"For all these lights," said I, glancing up at the strings of bulbs.

"And possibly more," commented Holmes.

The inspector did not share my friend's enthusiasm. "I've seen more sophisticated rigs," he sniffed. "This looks practically homemade."

"Not to mention decidedly unsafe," I added.

"And that's precisely why it is so impressive," insisted Holmes.

"That it might combust at any second?"

"No. Just think of it, Watson. If whoever created this machine can generate power with such crude materials, just imagine what they might do with the right components. Inspector, you are correct; it is primitive, laughable even compared to industrial dynamos, but surely you can see that there is a craftsman at work here? Look at the welding. Such precision. Elegance, even."

Holmes's passion was rubbing off on me. "But how is it powered?" I asked, intrigued. "There are no oil or petrol canisters."

The detective waggled an amused finger at me. "A good question, Watson. Here."

Holmes pointed towards a thin rubber tube, the kind found on Bunsen burners in every laboratory across the land, tracing its path from the back of the device to a small slit of a window near the ceiling. Then he crossed the room and tried the gas lamp that was fixed to the wall above the desk.

"The gas supply to the building is cut off," he said, "so our clever engineer has found a way to siphon the required fuel for his dynamo from the mains. I would imagine that the tube finds its way down the back of the building, thin enough to remain unnoticed, unless one knows what one is looking for."

"A great deal of effort to go to," Tovey said, scratching the back of his neck.

"Indubitably," came Holmes's reply, "so let us see what is so important."

Holmes darted back out into the corridor, following the long line of bulbs. We followed, splitting into two teams; I explored the rooms to the right with Holmes, while Tovey took those to the left.

The chambers were small, the first empty save for rusty bed frames and mouldering mattresses. No bulbs had been strung around the gas-fittings and we found nothing of apparent interest, except a pile of yellowing medical notes beside a broken table leg. Holmes snatched up the notes, only to return them to the floor a few seconds later.

The fourth room, however, was illuminated by a single light above the doorway. Inside there was a bed, like the others, but again the dust on the floor was disturbed. Furthermore, Holmes spotted something beneath the bed. He dropped to his knees and fished it out.

"A book," he announced as he returned to his feet. He turned the paperback volume over in his fingers and gave its cover a cursory glance, before flicking through the pages. "A novel, no less."

"I'm not going to ask if it is important," I said, "knowing full well what your answer will be."

"Everything is important, Watson," Holmes said, thrusting the book towards me. I took it and turned it over, noticing immediately that the title was in French.

"*Le Triangle d'or*," I read. "One of Leblanc's Lupin stories?"

"Not among the best," Holmes commented, as he cast his eye around the rest of the room. "Lupin is all but absent for the first half, and I guessed the culprit's identity within three pages of his appearance."

"You've read it?" I asked in amazement. This was a man whom I had once categorised as possessing a complete absence of interest in literature other than that of the ghoulishly sensational kind. I suppose the exploits of Maurice Leblanc's outrageous gentleman thief certainly matched the latter.

"A fellow must occupy himself one way or another, Watson," Holmes replied. "In days gone by you berated me for escaping the mind-calcifying boredom of inertia by means of the needle. I thought you would be pleased that these days I prefer to lose myself in the pages of a good book."

"Or even a bad one? And to think you have the temerity to criticise *my* stories."

Holmes laughed. "I have made the acquaintance of a young curate in the village who imports such dubious delights from the continent. He allows me access to his growing library in return for a few jars of royal jelly."

As he spoke, my ever-surprising friend had finished his

examination of the room and, finding nothing else of note, turned to face me.

"However," he continued, "your astonishment about my new-found passion for the written word has distracted you from the most obvious of conclusions."

"Which is?" I asked, still bemused.

"Look at the publication date, Watson," Holmes instructed.

Doing as I was told, I flipped the book open, finding the front matter. Running my finger down the text, I found the date in question.

"1918," I reported.

"Indeed it was; November, if I remember correctly. Now, does this institution look as if it was open for patients eight months ago?"

"I sincerely doubt it," said I.

"And you would be correct. Every scrap of paperwork I have found dates from before the war."

"So the book wasn't left here by a patient," I concluded.

"And instead was read by a recent occupant, unequivocally male, possibly French, with a low level of literacy, poor personal hygiene and the habit of sleeping in his working clothes."

With that, Holmes marched out of the room, leaving me to hurry after him as fast as my aching legs would allow.

"Now, Holmes. The French origin I can see from the book itself, and the gender of the reader from the large unequal footprints in the dust," I said, finding Tovey and the detective in an adjacent room, "but as for the rest?"

Holmes sighed, turning to me. "It is as clear as day. Turn to any page, and you will see smudges caused by someone running their fingers beneath the lines as they read. The size of the fingers can only be that of a male, and the grime consistent with someone who has little acquaintance with water."

"And the fact that the person concerned sleeps in his clothes?"

"There are numerous sturdy threads – such as those used to make hardy working attire, not a man's nightclothes – snagged around the buttons of that poor excuse for a mattress. Now, unless you need me to explain further, I should very much like to know what the inspector has discovered in the room opposite."

It was moments like this that had caused me to paint Holmes in a more flattering light than he often deserved. There was always a fear that the readers of the *Strand* would struggle to identify with the more irritating aspects of his personality. He could be the most charming of companions, and yet, at times, I had to fight the urge to bludgeon him over the head with my stick.

Indeed, at this precise moment, when he turned to face the inspector and presented me with the back of his head, the urge was all too great. Thankfully, the impulse brought a smile to my lips rather than a swing to my arm. Intolerable or not, this was exactly why I had spent so many years in Holmes's company. The thrill of the hunt.

"I'm afraid I'm going to disappoint you," Tovey told Holmes, "other than that I think you're right about a woman having been here."

Before Holmes could respond, I stepped forward, having made a quick assessment of the room myself. It was as dirty as the previous chamber, save for one small detail.

"There are sheets on the bed," said I, "although that in itself is not enough to suggest that the occupant was a woman, Inspector."

"No," Holmes agreed, flaring his substantial nostrils, "but the odour from the sheet makes such a conclusion more likely."

He bent over, leaning on the bed, and inhaled deeply. "Notes of orange blossom and sandalwood, with just a hint of jasmine."

"I don't know about all that," Tovey said. "But it certainly smells like a woman to me. Bought something similar for Mrs

Tovey a few years back. Narcisse Black, or some such. Wedding anniversary. Gave me a right rollicking when she found out how much it cost, she did."

"So our lady has no problem living in such squalor," Holmes said, turning around to take in the rest of the room, "but still strives to maintain standards. The sheets, while not exactly fresh, are cleaner than the mattress they cover."

"And she still wears scent," I added.

"Which may or may not cost a pretty penny."

"But if she can afford expensive perfume, why live in a place like this?"

Holmes's eyes locked onto a small detail on the floor. Recognising the look, I stepped aside, allowing him to pounce on whatever had attracted his attention.

"What is it?" Tovey asked, but I too had noticed the tell-tale marks splattered across the floor, minute but still visible.

"It's blood, isn't it, Holmes?" I asked.

CHAPTER NINE

A CHARNEL HOUSE

"Unfortunately, yes," came Holmes's reply. "And recently spilled too. See? It fell *on* the dust, rather than being covered by it. But where, or whom, did it come from?"

"Our perfumed lady?" asked Tovey.

"Perhaps," Holmes said, prowling across the floor on his hands and knees like a cat. How I envied his suppleness, even if he was crawling around in the dirt.

"There," he said, springing back to his feet and charging out of the room.

"There's more?" I asked, following him into the corridor. Holmes had his magnifying glass out now, sweeping it across the floor.

"Only a few drops," he responded, "but yes. The beginnings of a trail."

He hurried further down the corridor, finding more traces, which he announced with some excitement were increasing in size. Only Sherlock Holmes could become so enthused about drops of blood, and yet my own heart was racing as he swung open a set of double doors at the end of the corridor.

The scene that greeted him made even Holmes stop in his tracks.

"Good Lord," said I as I joined him, pausing to stop the door from slamming into Inspector Tovey's face as he hurried in behind us.

There was blood everywhere. Splattered on the floor, sprayed across the once-white tiles of the wall, dried where it had pooled beneath the rusted metal base of a table at the centre of the room.

And then there was the offal. My gorge rose in my throat as I walked towards the table. To its left, lay an overturned metal bin. I could tell from the reek what I would find inside.

"An operating theatre?" said Inspector Tovey from the door, his voice but a whisper, not out of respect, but disgust.

"More like a charnel house," I replied, slipping the end of my cane into the overturned bin and lifting it back onto its base.

The meat inside was lousy with maggots, wriggling white against the slimy black of the decaying flesh.

"The contents, Doctor," Holmes asked, as he stalked slowly around the room, his thin head turning to take in every depraved detail.

"Viscera, most probably human," I said, my voice thick. "Intestines, liver, kidneys—"

I had to break off, for fear of gagging. Understand that I am not a squeamish man. I have seen plenty of operating theatres in my time. Sterile. Clean. Stinking of disinfectant and bleach. Not this place. The inspector had mentioned butchery in the pathologist's lab, but even the most slovenly of butchers would have struggled to stomach the conditions of the room. The dirt, the mould. The stench of offal and stale bodily fluids.

My horror was only intensified by the floodlights that cast the abominable contents of the room into stark relief, as if it were a tableau in one of the sensationalist waxwork emporiums that had sprung up following the exploits of Bloody Jack thirty years earlier.

"What kind of man could operate in such a room as this?" Tovey asked.

"If it was a man at all," said Holmes, who had ceased circling the room and was now crouched down beside the operating table. "More footprints in the blood, and this time there is no doubt. A woman."

Steeling myself, I walked over to join him and could not help but gasp. The footprints were dainty and thin, but not those of a shoe.

"She walked through all this barefoot?"

"This is a woman who sprays herself with perfume and covers filthy mattresses with cotton sheets to effect a semblance of normality. We know that she owns shoes. Perhaps she prefers not to soil them. Whatever happened to Samuel Pike, I would suggest that you have discovered more of him in that bin."

"A severed hand discovered near this bloodbath?" I said. "It would be naive to pray that this is all a coincidence."

"Coincidence is rare, Watson. Unfortunately, depravity is not. And that is exactly what we have here. Something sinful."

"Says the only atheist in the room."

"Says the man who may not believe in God, but has no doubt that devils walk the earth, be they demons of flesh and blood, rather than fire and brimstone."

"I've seen enough flesh and blood for today, thank you very much," said Tovey from behind us. The policeman was crouched in the corner of the room. "And bone, for that matter."

"Bone?" Holmes enquired, as we crossed over to the inspector, taking special care not to step in the dried blood around the operating table.

"Never seen anything like this," Tovey said, standing so we could see what he had found, "and I've seen a lot of strange things in my time."

The corners of the room were in shadow, the floodlights having been angled to illuminate the operating table. Holmes pulled out Tovey's torch and directed the beam downwards. A length of white bone shone back at us, reflecting the glare. Like everything else in this place, it could only be described as wrong.

I reached into my coat pocket to retrieve my leather gloves and, putting them on, picked up the bone, turning it over and over in my protected hands.

"Intriguing," I said, walking back into the gleam of the floodlights. "It's a fragment of clavicle."

"A shoulder blade?" asked Tovey.

"No, the collarbone," I replied, indicating the position of the bone on my own shoulder. "It belonged to a child, eight or nine years of age judging from the size, but..."

My voice trailed off as I continued to turn the bone over and over.

"Watson?" Holmes prompted.

I looked more closely. "It's covered in some kind of growth, almost like a fungus. No, that's not right. It's a solid plate, running its entire length, growing out of the bone itself."

"But made out of what?" Holmes asked. He had returned the torch to his pocket and was holding out his hand expectantly.

I passed the puzzling object to him. "I would say more bone, if I didn't know better."

Before Holmes could respond there was a thud from outside, the unmistakable sound of the stairwell's double doors slamming shut. Someone else was in the building.

Holmes and I glanced at each other, before the detective thrust the curious bone back into my hand and started for the door.

"Holmes," I hissed. "Wait!"

My friend raised a silencing hand and, stopping at the doorway, listened.

There was a crank of a lever and every light in the building went out, plunging us into darkness.

"The generator," cried Holmes, and before I could stop him, he had clicked on the torch and was halfway up the corridor. Tovey rushed past me and, slipping the bone into my pocket, I followed suit, both of us trying to catch up with Holmes.

He had paused, just before the generator room, with his back to the wall and the torch angled down. He silently indicated that he would go first, but Tovey was having none of it, his Webley revolver held tight in his right hand. Nodding, Holmes handed over the torch and prepared for the inspector to strike.

With surprising grace for one so large, Tovey swung around into the room, his gun raised in one hand and the torch in the other.

I expected him to shout a warning, or at least to continue into the room, and therefore was unprepared when he didn't move at all.

"Empty," he reported a second later, relaxing his firing arm.

"Then who turned off the generator?" Holmes asked, as we entered.

"Could it have broken down?" I enquired.

Holmes examined the device. "After we heard the doors, Doctor? What was that you were saying about coinc—"

The door slammed behind us, causing us all to spin around. In the light of Tovey's torch, I rushed forward to grab the doorknob, but it wouldn't budge.

"We're locked in," I gasped.

"There was no key in the door," Holmes insisted, pushing me aside to try the knob himself. He pulled, but produced the same result, although his reaction was more rational than my emotional outburst. "The wood has warped," he concluded. "It's jammed in the frame, that's all."

"Let me," Tovey said, pocketing his gun and handing me the torch. He braced his left hand against the wall and grasped the doorknob in his right. He yanked once, twice, and with a squeak of twisted wood, the door opened on the third attempt. He was out in the corridor in an instant, his gun back in his hand. I moved to turn on the generator, but Holmes stopped me.

"Keep the lights off," he hissed.

"But we won't be able to see!"

"Then neither will our assailant, Watson."

There were crashes from down the corridor, in the direction of the operating theatre.

"The torch, Watson," Holmes ordered.

"I thought you wanted it dark!" I said, offering the torch to him.

"Just hand it to me," he said, snatching the torch to shine its light down the corridor. The doors to the operating theatre were closed, although it was clear from the racket that someone was tearing the place apart.

"What should we do?" I whispered.

"Change our mind," came Holmes's response.

"Head back outside, you mean?" asked Tovey, his gun pointing directly towards the door.

"You would never forgive me, were I to do such a thing," said Holmes, disappearing into the next room. He returned a moment later carrying the table leg I had spotted earlier. "No, I mean, about the lights. Watson, when I indicate, throw the lever."

"Of course, but—"

A hand was raised in the air, another call for silence. Holmes crept forward, the table leg held in front of him like a rapier. What was he planning to do? Throw open the doors and attack whoever was on the other side with a scrap of broken furniture? Still, I had seen what damage he could inflict with an umbrella. The table leg appeared considerably more solid.

As Holmes inched towards the doors, whoever was on the other side continued their act of vandalism, and I winced as I heard the metal bin kicked across the floor, imagining its grim contents slopping across the tiles.

Holmes reached the double doors, but did not open them. Instead, he slipped the table leg between the door handles to lock them in place, and called over his shoulder. "Now, Watson!"

I rushed back to the generator and threw the lever, the dynamo spinning back into life. The lights flared on, both in the corridor and, I could imagine, in the operating theatre itself.

The noises from the room ceased immediately.

I returned to the corridor as Holmes addressed the invader through the door. "Now, listen to me, whoever you are. We are armed and will not hesitate to fire."

As he spoke, he nodded towards Tovey who, Webley outstretched, was inching towards Holmes's position. I followed, wishing that it were my service revolver I clutched in my hand rather than my cane. Still, I would do some damage with it, if required.

"You are surrounded with no way out," Holmes continued, "so tell us who you are, and what you are doing here."

There was no response. No noise at all.

Then an attempt was made to force open the doors, which caught immediately on the table leg. My cane came up further, Tovey freezing where he stood. Our prisoner, as that is exactly what he had become, tried again, rattling the doors before falling silent once again.

We stood there waiting, minutes seeming to stretch into hours. My ears strained for any indication of activity behind the doors, and I became acutely aware of every sound: the growl of the generator in the room behind us, punctuated by sparks of electricity; the cry of a distant gull in the skies outside; the wind whistling past splintered window frames. Even the sound of my own watch seemed impossibly loud, as if we were inside a clock tower, the march of the second hand reverberating through the air.

Tick.

Tock.

Tick.

Tock.

And still nothing. Holmes stood as still as a statue, waiting for a response.

Tick.

Tock.

Tick.

The response came. A great weight threw itself against the doors, snapping the table leg in two. In an instant there was confusion and panic. Holmes cried out in pain as he was pinned between the opened door and the wall, his head cracking on the exposed brickwork.

The figure that had burst from the operating theatre didn't stop as Holmes slid to the wall, momentarily dazed.

"Stop, or I'll fire," Tovey yelled, but the juggernaut ignored the warning. In the glare of the electric light, I caught a glance of pallid skin, long lank hair and a snarling mouth, but what truly shocked me was the size of the brute.

He must have been eight feet tall.

This wasn't a man. It was a monster.

CHAPTER TEN

DEVIL IN THE DARK

Inspector Tovey gave no further warning. His Webley spoke twice, its harsh report like cannon fire in the oppressive space.

The giant didn't go down. He flinched at least, the bullets thudding into his broad shoulder, but only growled in response; a deep, guttural noise, not of pain but of anger. With one stride he was upon Tovey, bringing back a club-like arm. I cried out an impotent warning, for the monster had already backhanded Tovey across the face. The inspector's head snapped around with such severity that I feared that his neck had been broken like a dry twig. He was lifted from his feet and sent, despite his great bulk, sailing through the air like a paper doll caught in a gale. His weight became obvious again only when he crashed bodily into the wall, a plume of shattered plaster and dust billowing out from the impact.

Now it was down to me, the only one of our band still standing. Screaming a primal battle cry, I rushed forward, cane raised. The monster was coming right at me, but I cared nothing for the danger. I brought my stick down hard, its length smacking against his barrel chest. The regimental head of the cane, polished to within an inch of its life, was ornamental no more. It struck hard against his prominent cheekbone like a cudgel, and I fancied that I heard a painful crack. The man may have stood a good head and shoulders above me, but I was determined to bring him down, for Holmes and Tovey. Yesterday Holmes had proved that age need not equate with frailty. Now was my chance to show my mettle.

Or so I hoped.

The reality of the situation was somewhat less heroic.

Striking the brute was like trying to demolish a brick wall using a length of reed. To my dismay, the force of the blow snapped the shaft of my stick against the man's chest, the wood splintering. I had little chance to mourn my faithful cane. Before I could react, an enormous hand was around my neck and I was being lifted from the floor. I clawed at my assailant's thick forearm, my fingernails catching on the thick weave of his jacket. It was useless, the muscles beneath the fabric like stone.

My feet waved in the air as if I were a toddler plucked from the ground by an adoring father, and yet there was nothing paternal about this embrace. I gasped for breath, staring into the snarling face of my assailant. My vision was already blurring, but I could make out the deep-rucked scars that scored his sallow features. His heavy brow was furrowed beneath a thick curtain of greasy hair, so black that it was almost obsidian. And then there was the eye, glaring out from beneath the unruly fringe. Never had I seen an eye like it; bloodshot to such an extent that the sclera was a whirlpool of broken veins swirling around a watery yellow iris. At its centre lay the fiend's pupil, a mere pinprick, devoid of light or reason. Inhuman. Abhorrent.

It was almost a relief when dots clustered in front of my own vision, blotting out the world. As my breath rattled in my crushed throat, I could only curse the fact that this abominable face would be the last thing I ever saw.

Then, with a shout and a dull thud of fist against flesh, I was saved, snatched back from oblivion for a short while at least. My release was not peaceful, the gruesome goliath losing interest in my murder and tossing me aside like a discarded plaything. I landed heavily on my shoulder, the pain immediately dulled as my head met the floorboards, and the world flared white all around me.

I could hear shouts, voices that seemed both near and far at the same time. There was the shuffling of feet, disturbingly close to my throbbing head although I had neither the inclination nor the ability to roll out of their way. A boot in the face was almost something to be welcomed, anything to knock me senseless and release me from the confusion of pain and disorientation my life had suddenly become.

The sounds of a desperate struggle played out above my head: crashes and grunts, curses and bellows. And then it was over, with a cry cut off too abruptly to be healthy, and the thud of something hitting the ground heavily nearby.

"Holmes?" I wheezed, as thundering footsteps receded into the distance, giving way to an awful silence.

I couldn't move. I could barely think. It felt as though I had been lying there in the dirt my entire life, before there came the scrape of a boot, and a gentle touch on my shoulder.

Someone was speaking, repeating a name, over and over. It took me a moment to realise that the name was my own.

"Dr Watson. Dr Watson, can you hear me?"

"Inspector?" I slurred weakly.

"Thank God. Just lie there. I'll get help. It's going to be all right."

All right? Why wouldn't it be? The man was obviously a fool. I might have giggled, but I had no idea why. There was nothing to laugh about. I couldn't even open my eyes, but Tovey had already gone, leaving me where I lay.

For a moment, I found it impossible to remember how I had got there, or where indeed *there* was. I think I must have drifted off, because it seemed only seconds before the inspector was calling my name again, more urgently this time.

"Dr Watson. Wake up. We need to get you out of here."

"Wha—?"

"Can you stand? Here, I'll help you."

"No. I… I just need to rest."

"Not here you don't. Dr Watson, please."

I wanted to tell the man to shut up, that I would get up when I was good and ready, but the words refused to form.

There were more footsteps now, all around me. I had no idea how many. I tried to open my eyes, and after what seemed an eternity they finally obeyed my command, flickering like broken blinds. Not that it helped. The world was a mess of unrecognisable shapes and blurs. There was something in front of me, but I was unable to tell what it was.

A face? Yes, that could be it, inches from my own. Familiar too, but somehow not quite right. What was wrong with it? What could it be?

I felt like laughing again, a hysterical cackle welling up from deep within my chest.

It was too ridiculous to comprehend, you see, the dreadful realisation that dawned second by second.

I was staring into the face of Sherlock Holmes, my oldest and dearest friend, and yet he had undergone a ridiculous transformation. His skin was blanched, and covered in blood that ran in rivulets from a ragged gash in his forehead. His lips were slack, his teeth stained crimson – but it was the eyes that were wrong. They should have been piercing and effervescent, windows into a vibrant soul, bursting with an intelligence that defied categorisation. Yet now they were staring straight at me, with no indication that my friend recognised me at all, that he even knew I was here.

"No," I groaned, struggling to push myself up, only to be thwarted by a tidal wave of pain that radiated out from my shoulder. I didn't care. This couldn't be happening.

My friend. My friend who had cheated death so many times, was lying prone in front of me, a lifeless husk. Surely it was not to end here, on the cold hard floor of a forgotten ruin.

This could not be the place where Sherlock Holmes died.

CHAPTER ELEVEN

THE COLD ROOM

For a man who has spent the best part of his life in medical facilities, one might think that I would have been comfortable in the hallowed halls of Charing Cross's famous hospital. The doctors insisted that I was suffering from concussion, and they were probably correct, but I knew the real reason for my distress as I paced up and down the long echoing corridor.

On the other side of the thin brick wall, in a private room secured by Tovey, lay Sherlock Holmes. He flitted in and out of consciousness, and on the rare occasions when he was awake, his ramblings and moans were those of a madman.

They had wanted to admit me as well, of course, but I would not hear of it. How could I lie in bed, knowing that my friend was in a critical condition? Yes, my head hurt abominably, and my shoulder ached from where it had become dislocated, but the throb behind my eyes would ease and the sling the nurses had insisted I wear would rest my arm. The sickness in my stomach? That would pass only when I knew Holmes had recovered.

The door to Holmes's private room opened, and Tovey walked

out, followed by the doctor who had been ministering to my friend, a handsome young fellow with the already careworn face so common on medical men.

I took a step forward, feeling a sudden wave of dizziness, and leant heavily on the wooden cane the hospital had provided. Tovey sprung forward, ready to catch me as if I were a lady falling into a swoon.

"Dr Watson?"

"I am fine, thank you, Inspector," I said, a little too brusquely, "please do not fuss."

He took a respectful step back as I regained my balance and turned to face the young doctor.

"Dr Gibbs, how is my friend?"

Gibbs gave me the same sympathetic smile I had offered hundreds of patients during my career.

"There has been no change, I'm afraid, Dr Watson. Mr Holmes has suffered a serious head injury resulting in oedema, and he is having some trouble breathing due to at least three broken ribs. For a man of his age—"

"Holmes is as strong as an ox," I interjected, incensed at the very suggestion.

That smile returned, mirrored by professional sympathy in the doctor's eyes. "I'm sure he is, but you know what can happen when anyone suffers a trauma such as this."

"You yourself should be recuperating, Doctor," added Tovey. I chose to ignore the comment.

"May I see him?"

Gibbs glanced at the nurse in the stiffly starched uniform who had followed them from the room, before returning his gaze to me.

"Of course, but please, try not to excite Mr Holmes. He needs his rest."

"He is awake then?" I asked.

"Barely," the nurse replied. "Dr Watson, Mr Holmes is very ill indeed."

"Then he needs his friends around him," I insisted, shifting uncomfortably on my cane. I wasn't used to being on this side of such a conversation, and was all too aware that I was being difficult. I took a deep breath, forcing my expression to soften. "Dr Gibbs, you can trust me. Holmes is your patient and I respect that. I realise that he is in the best possible hands, but as I am sure *you* can understand, this is difficult for me. That man in there has been under my care for over thirty-five years, not only as a patient, but more importantly—"

"As a friend," the young doctor interrupted. "I do understand. My father adored your stories, Dr Watson, and following his death, I have become quite a devotee myself. It's an honour to meet you both, albeit under difficult circumstances. Be assured I will do everything I can for Mr Holmes."

He reached out and gave my good shoulder what was obviously supposed to be a comforting squeeze. I am sorry to say that I stiffened, fighting the urge to pull away.

Noticing my discomfort, Inspector Tovey rode to my rescue. "I'll stay with Dr Watson," said he. "We realise that you have other patients to attend to."

Gibbs nodded and stepped aside to let us enter Holmes's room, Tovey noticeably limping from his own altercation with that brute in the deserted hospital.

"Five minutes, please," said the nurse, pulling the door closed behind her. "And no more."

"Of course, nurse," said Tovey. "Thank you."

I uttered not a word. Instead I simply stood and stared at the gaunt figure lying in the bed. His face was as pale as the crisp white sheets beneath him, the sharp angles of his cheeks never more pronounced. Nearly three decades ago, Holmes had used self-starvation and the liberal application of Vaseline, belladonna, rouge and beeswax to convince all that he was at death's door. His charade had fooled even me, and all to expose a terrible blackguard for the rogue he was. How I wished that Holmes would throw back the covers now and laugh, mercilessly teasing me for falling for another of his japes, but this was no trickery. The man before me was a shadow of his former self. I had never seen my friend look so old, so fragile.

All at once, a moan escaped from Holmes's mouth, barely audible, but there all the same. I sprang towards the bed, a wave of vertigo threatening to overwhelm me, but I steadied myself on the bedside cabinet.

"Holmes?"

Beneath thin lids, my friend's eyes rolled in their sockets. Was he about to wake once again?

Another moan, louder this time. My name? Was he trying to say "Watson"?

"Yes, Holmes. I'm here. I'm right beside you."

Nothing. No response at all. His eyes ceased their movement and the only sound was his rasping breath. I felt my whole body sag. Had I really believed that my mere presence would be enough to rouse him from his stupor? What a foolish old man I had become.

"Maybe he's dreaming," Tovey offered, and I realised that the inspector had moved to stand behind me, perhaps concerned that I was about to end up sprawled across the floor. "Pleasant ones, I hope."

I doubted it, although I remained silent. I myself dreaded falling asleep. The hour was late, and heaven knows my body was in desperate need of slumber, but I knew that, as soon as I shut my eyes, I would see the hideous face of that monster looming out from the shadows.

The inspector spoke again, returning my thoughts to the cold, sterile room. "So, that young doctor's diagnosis..."

I studied Holmes's face as I replied. "They will keep him under observation. The cerebral oedema is a concern, although it may decrease in time."

"The swelling of the brain, you mean?"

I nodded. "If not, they may resort to more drastic methods."

Tovey's next word turned my stomach. "Trepanning?"

The thought of anyone drilling a hole in Holmes's skull was too much to bear, even if it might release some of the pressure on his remarkable brain. It seemed so barbaric, especially in our so-called modern age. I had read of cave paintings showing our savage ancestors wilfully cracking each other's skulls to release bad spirits or whatever mumbo-jumbo those primitives believed in. Could we really be performing the same operations millennia later?

"I hope it won't come to that," I said.

We fell silent, and I stood fighting the tears that threatened to well up in my eyes. Holmes would have been appalled, but perhaps now, more than ever, I was aware of what a void would be left in my life when the two of us were eventually parted. It seemed ridiculous. We lived miles away from each other, in different counties, living different lives, seeing each other but a few times a year, but nevertheless I knew Holmes was there, tending his bees and writing his monographs. All I needed to do was pick up the telephone or start up the Swift, and I would see my old friend. If that ever changed, where would I be? While Holmes drew breath I was still somehow the same person who had found him bent over a Bunsen lamp in St Bart's nearly four decades previously. If that connection was broken, then I feared that the anchor to my very existence would also be lost, I would be adrift, a man left only with stories scrawled in fading ink.

"Doctor?" It was Tovey, trying to summon me out of my self-imposed trance. I started, looking at the inspector.

"Yes. Yes, of course. Holmes must rest."

"And so must you."

I nodded, letting my gaze wander back to the bed. "I'll call a cab."

"No you won't," Tovey insisted. "I'll have a car take you home. Mrs Watson will never forgive me otherwise."

My wife all but ordered me to bed when Tovey's policeman delivered me to my doorstep. She fussed around me, telling me that she knew something like this would happen – and yet as she clucked like a mother hen, I noticed the look of concern on her face when she asked after Holmes. After all, she had herself known him for many years now, no matter how infuriating she found him. He infuriated us all; that was simply his way, and none of us would have it otherwise.

Of course, all sympathy was lost when, taking my coat, she shrieked and dropped something to the floor as if it were a hot coal. The object of her disgust bounced across the hall carpet, coming to rest by the umbrella stand.

"What in the name of all that is holy is that?"

I bent to investigate, nearly pitching over with the effort.

"No, no, I'll pick it up, if I have to," said my wife.

Opening a drawer and pulling out a pair of gloves, Mrs Watson slipped her hand into one of them and tentatively plucked the item from the floor between thumb and forefinger.

"The bone," I said, as she handed it to me, "from the operating theatre."

"From Charing Cross Hospital?"

"No, from our investigation, before we were set upon by that animal."

"Why in heaven's name would you be carrying it around in your pocket?"

For the life of me I couldn't remember. I had obviously thought it important when we had been disturbed by the arrival of the giant. "A lucky chance," said I.

"Lucky? Carrying around old bits of bone doesn't sound lucky to me, unless it's a rabbit's foot." She looked uncomfortably at the relic. "Is it… human?"

"Undoubtedly," I replied. "And it's not as if you haven't seen human bones before." A full medical skeleton hung in my study, although my wife tried hard not to look at it whenever she entered my inner sanctum. "But don't you see, if I can find out what happened to this, what these growths on the bone are, then we might be one step further in understanding this damnable business. When Holmes recovers…"

My voice faltered, and suddenly I felt every inch my age, the late hour and the events of the day weighing heavily on me.

My wife gave me a kind smile. "When he recovers, he can listen to your findings and tell you exactly what you've got wrong before leading you off on another merry dance. But before that, you are going to sleep, John Watson. And no arguments, or, so help me, I'll have that Inspector Tovey throw you in a cell. Do you understand?"

"Yes, doctor," I replied, allowing her to take the bone from my hand.

"Good. Now, upstairs with you, while I lock this delightful object in your study."

Thanking her, I started the long climb up to my chamber, trying not to think of Holmes lying alone in his hospital bed.

CHAPTER TWELVE

UNWANTED VISITORS

My fears of night terrors proved to be unfounded, and I slept like a proverbial babe, until the first rays of sunlight glimmered through the curtain. Mrs Watson was still fast asleep, but from the moment my eyes opened, my mind was buzzing with the thought of the strange bone in my study downstairs. So as not to wake my wife, I crept from our bedroom and dressed in the guest room. The sight of Holmes's case standing still packed beside the wardrobe dampened my enthusiasm a little, but I was determined not to squander the day in morose contemplation. Holmes was relying on me to keep the investigation alive, so that once he had recuperated – and I was determined to focus on the *when* rather than the more worrying *if* – he would have the full facts at hand.

Leaving my sling neatly folded upstairs, I stepped out of the house, carefully closing the door behind me. The morning was thankfully free of rain, although the air was as heavy as the clouds that hung waiting to burst in the sky above. I considered taking the car, but, having enough sense to realise that driving after a blow to the head was never wise, hailed a cab.

With the bells of All Saints yet to strike seven o'clock, the streets of London were clear as we drove to my practice on Queen Anne Street. Sitting in the back seat, I stared out at the empty pavements and turned over the events of the last few days in my head. From nightclub to nightmare in the space of forty-eight hours, yet, grey as it was, this was a new day. I vowed there and then that I would find the monster that had hospitalised Sherlock Holmes and hold him to account. Whoever the brute was, he had a connection to that bloodbath in the deserted hospital. Solve the riddle of what had happened in that sorry place and we would find the man. He had been looking for something or someone; maybe the mysterious couple who had set up home in those dismal rooms by the light of a makeshift generator. Indeed, a thought struck me as we turned the corner into Queen Anne Street. Maybe our devil in the dark had been the Arsène Lupin fan whose discarded book we had found beneath the bed?

I paid the cabbie, and hurried up the stairs to my practice. I had spent many happy years living here before my second marriage, at the heart of London's medical community and a short walk from Baker Street. It had been a wrench, when my wife insisted we move out of town to Chelsea, but I had kept the practice going, renting out my old chambers to a surgeon from the nearby Welbeck Hospital. Recently, Mrs Watson had started a fresh campaign, attempting to persuade me to sell up once and for all and retire, but I was determined to put off that inevitability for as long as possible. I prized these book-lined walls as highly as my study back on Cheyne Walk. There, surrounded by the memorabilia of my second career, I was John Watson, biographer and author. Here, surrounded by medical texts and behind the same wooden table that had sat in both my Paddington and Kensington practices, I was John Watson, MD.

Leaving my coat on the hat stand, I turned on the brass

desk lamp and placed the puzzling clavicle on my blotter. To the relentless beat of the clock on the mantel, I turned it over, examining the macabre item in detail. It was utterly unlike anything I had seen before. As I had first suggested in the derelict hospital, the unnatural growths seemed to be made of bone. It was thick, like muscle that had turned to stone, solid to the touch and smooth, free of any discernible impurities.

Intrigued, I stood, crossing to the bookcase that housed my medical encyclopaedias. The mutation must have been some kind of medical disorder, a blight that would bring considerable distress to the sufferer, especially if it spread beyond the collarbone. Indeed, there was evidence of further growths along the medial end of the bone. If they continued on to the sternoclavicular joint, they might have restricted the movement of the arm itself. Of course, I could scarcely help but wonder why such a patient would be operated upon in the filth and grime of an abandoned hospital, but banished such thoughts as I searched for the correct book. This was a time for facts, not speculation.

My fingers fell upon the volume concerning skeletal abnormalities, but as I started to ease the book from between its neighbours, I heard the front door to the building open. I paused, the book half removed from the shelf, and turned to face the door to my consulting room, which I had left slightly ajar.

"Mr Stillwell?" I called out, thinking that it might have been my surgical lodger leaving for the day. "Is that you?"

There came no reply, save for the sound of the door shutting once again, more softly this time, not the carefree slam of a fellow heading off to work at all.

I listened intently, but there was no other sound, until the sudden creak of the loose floorboard in the hall.

"Hello? Who's there?" I asked, fetching the cane I had left leaning against my desk and stepping into my waiting room. "I'm afraid that the surgery is closed until further—"

I broke off, as the door opened and two men entered. They both wore rounded collars beneath tweed jackets and waistcoats, dark stains on their cloth caps telling me that it had started to rain outside. The fellow to the right was short, with a thick moustache and piercing blue eyes. The other was clean-shaven with a noticeable scar on his top lip and eyes the colour of tar pits. A gold watch hung from his herringbone waistcoat, and, unlike his stockier companion, he wore a smart bow tie, expertly tied, and matched with a dandyish red carnation.

"I'm sorry, gentlemen," I began, all too aware of the menace exuded by the newcomers, "but as I said, the practice is currently closed. If you need medical assistance then I can recommend a number of my colleagues."

The stocky man sneered, his moustache bristling. "Oh, no one is in need of medical assistance yet, Doctor."

"Then I must ask you to leave."

"And that's funny," said his clean-shaven colleague, hooded eyes sparkling with amusement. "Because we've got something to ask you too, haven't we, Mr Hartley?"

"That's right, Mr Burns."

Their voices were thickly accented, the unmistakable flatness of the Black Country. Holmes would have no doubt been able to tell me exactly what part of the Midlands they hailed from, but all I knew was that I wanted them out of my practice as soon as possible.

"I'm sure I'm not interested in anything you have to ask me," I said, walking forward to show them to the door, trying to disguise the slight hobble in my step. It was never wise to show any sign of weakness with men such as these. "Now, if you do not leave, then I'm afraid I shall have no option other than to call for the police."

"And that's your problem right there, Dr Watson," Hartley said, stepping forward to block my path. "Always running to the police, stopping them from getting on with their business."

The ruffian had moved so close that I was forced to take a step back, if only to escape the reek of stale whisky on the man's breath.

"You have something we want," said Burns. "Something that should never have been found."

The bone. He must be talking about the bone.

Burns's wolfish smile widened. "Something which I reckon I'll find in that room through there." He pointed with tobacco-stained fingers to my consulting room.

"I don't know what you are talking about."

"I think you do, Doctor. You see, I've read some of your stories. Oh, there's no need to look so surprised. I can read, you know."

"I wouldn't presume to suggest otherwise—" I blustered.

"Picked up a few tricks, I have, from your pal Mr Holmes. Like how you went to look over your shoulder when I mentioned the bone. Because it is a bone, isn't it, Doctor?"

I cursed myself, angry to have fallen for the same ruse that Holmes had used to ensnare Pritchard in the Mallard Club. It occurred to me once again what an old fool I had become.

"Now, this is what's going to happen. I'm going to go in there, collect what we came for, and you're not going to stop me. Is that clear?"

"You have no right—"

"No, but I'm going to do it anyway."

Burns took a step forward, but I would be damned if I was going to let him simply stroll past me to steal valuable evidence. I went to step around Hartley, my cane already raised, when the thug of a man slapped a tattooed hand onto my bruised left shoulder. Waves of agony swept through my body and I sank to my knees, my cane clattering across the floor. The brute maintained his vice-like grip, rendering me near immobile with pain as his partner sauntered into my consulting room to reappear mere moments later, patting his jacket, the bone no doubt secreted in an inside pocket.

"You have what you came for," I hissed through gritted teeth, fighting back nausea, "so I suggest you leave. Unless you're also planning to finish the job on me."

Burns paused, trying to look offended. "Finish the job? You must think us barbarians."

"You have no qualms about torturing a helpless old man," I gasped. "What am I supposed to think?"

The man laughed. "Old, yes, there's no doubt about that. But harmless?" He gave another snort of derision. "I don't think so. As I said, I've read your stories, unless they really are fiction."

He nodded at his companion, who released his hold on my shoulder. I slumped forward, gasping for breath. Burns's polished brogues stepped towards me and he crouched down.

"The thing is, Doctor, this is a story you should abandon, a case that does not concern you."

I reached for my stick, aiming to stand and regain what little was left of my dignity. Instead, Burns denied me even that.

"Here, let us," he said, standing and looping a hand beneath my arm. Before I could resist, he and his compatriot had hauled me painfully to my feet. I cried out again, and staggered back, Hartley manoeuvring me to land awkwardly in one of the waiting room chairs, breathing heavily. I glared at the two men, even as Burns bent to pick up my cane.

"Forget about what you saw, Doctor. Forget about what you found."

"And if I don't?" I panted in reply, straightening myself in the chair.

"Then a dodgy shoulder will be the least of your worries, and as for Mr Holmes…"

He left the words hanging in the air.

"What of him?" I asked, the insinuation of the pause too much to bear.

"He should return to his bees, that's all I'm saying," came the reply. "Keep eating that honey of his. Stay healthy, if you know what I mean."

All the time, the lout was turning my cane over and over in his hands. He stopped, grinning again, showing a row of uneven yellowing teeth. "Do we understand each other?"

"Absolutely," I spat.

"Good," said he, throwing my cane towards me. Instinctively I snatched it out of the air, drawing another agonised gasp as my aggrieved shoulder burned in response.

"Then we'll be off," Burns said, touching the brim of his cap. "It was a pleasure meeting you, Doctor. Shame that I didn't bring one of your books. You could have signed it for me."

And then he strutted out, his hands thrust deep in his trouser pockets, his bulky companion falling in behind. I had neither the energy nor the inclination to try to stop them, not even when I heard the latch to the front door click open and that damned voice call out again.

"Of course, I could drop round and leave one with your wife. Sixty-seven Cheyne Walk, isn't it?"

Growling with anger, I pushed myself from the seat, but they were already gone, slamming the door behind them. I struggled out into the hall, pulling the front door open and stepping out into the rain. I looked from right to left, but of the two invaders there was no sign. My shoulders sagging, I stepped back inside, shutting out the bad weather. My two visitors had left, but their threat remained. They knew where I worked and where I lived. That they had wanted to frighten me, there was no doubt. That they had succeeded was obvious, but if they thought that John Watson could be intimidated, they had made a grave error.

My heart still hammering in my chest, I limped into my consulting room to fetch my coat, pausing only to note that, as expected, the bone was gone.

It mattered not. I had overcome worse obstacles in my life, and had been threatened before, but with the Almighty as my witness, had never capitulated. Damned if I was going to start now.

CHAPTER THIRTEEN

CLOSED SHUTTERS

"That is not possible. I saw him only last evening."

The desk sergeant at New Scotland Yard could only shrug.

"I don't know what else to say, Dr Watson. I asked after Inspector Tovey, but apparently he left early this morning."

"For Cornwall? Why there?"

"An important case, by all accounts, and one that requires his…" The sergeant chose his words carefully, "…own particular methods."

I gripped my new cane hard, trying not to take out my frustrations on the poor man before me. He was merely the messenger.

I had travelled straight from Queen Anne Street to the Yard, intending to inform Inspector Tovey about my disagreeable callers, sure that he would help get to the bottom of their warning, and yet now found that Tovey was already hundreds of miles away, rushing towards a new investigation. It made no sense. Tovey was a tenacious sort, the kind of man who was incapable of resting until a task was completed. For him to abandon London after the events at Abberton Hospital was unthinkable, and yet it had happened nonetheless.

"What of Inspector Gregson?" I asked, clutching at what few names I still knew at the Yard. In days gone by, I would have asked for Lestrade, God rest his soul, but I was sure that Tobias Gregson was still active, although he too would be reaching retirement.

"I'm afraid that Inspector Gregson is also unavailable, sir," the sergeant said, matter-of-factly.

I frowned. "You know that without checking?"

"He is currently investigating a crime in the East End, and we won't be expecting him back until sundown. I wish there was something I could do for you."

"Well, you could tell me who else I can see, unless every detective in the Metropolitan Police Service is currently occupied."

"Crime does not rest," the sergeant replied, without a hint of irony. "And neither must we. Now, if you leave me your details, I can enquire about the possibility of an appointment—"

"An appointment?"

"Do you have a telephone, sir?"

"Of course I do, however—"

"Then if you leave me your number, I'll make sure that someone contacts you as soon as they're able."

I was flabbergasted. To think of all the times I had assisted Scotland Yard in their investigations, and here I was being dismissed like a stranger; no, worse than that, I was being treated like an irrelevance.

"Sergeant, I don't think you understand. Not one hour ago, I was assaulted by a pair of ne'er-do-wells in my own medical practice. I have reason to believe that this intrusion has everything to do with an investigation being carried out by Inspector Tovey, an investigation that he invited us to be a part of."

"Us, sir?"

"Sherlock Holmes and myself."

"Ah, but Inspector Tovey is not here..."

"So you have said—"

"So, if you leave your telephone number, I will make sure that he gets back to you as soon as he returns."

"From Cornwall."

"From Cornwall, yes."

I could feel my blood pressure preparing to erupt. "Oh, this is intolerable. They threatened me, Sergeant. Worse than that, they threatened my wife. Do you see? They said that they would hurt us."

"Did these ne'er-do-wells of yours specifically use those words, Doctor?"

"Not exactly, but their meaning was clear."

"I see. Then, until we get in touch, I suggest you go home and make sure Mrs Watson is safe. I'll send someone presently to take a statement."

It was clear that I could protest as much as I wanted, but the sergeant would remain unmoved. Reluctantly, I left my details as instructed and traipsed back out into the drizzle, fuming that I had been dismissed out of hand. If this was how people were treated when they turned to the police, no wonder that crime flourished on every street corner.

I consulted my watch. It was just turning ten. I would heed the sergeant's advice, exasperating though it had been, and check on my wife. But first, as I was in town, I decided to visit Holmes and see if there had been any improvement in my friend's condition. Not fancying the four-mile walk in the rain, I hailed a cab and sat brooding in the back, more injured by my treatment than by any trauma suffered at the hands of Burns and Hartley earlier that morning. At least the day could only get better, I considered. If Holmes was awake, we could discuss what had happened and make sense of it together.

It was a vain hope. On arrival at the hospital, I made my way to Holmes's room, but was astounded and not a little dismayed to find the bed without an occupant, the sheets neatly made.

"Oh no," I gasped, fearing the worst, and looked around for assistance. "Nurse? Nurse!"

A blonde nurse immediately ran up. "Can I help you, sir?" she enquired, her accent cheerfully cockney. "Are you all right?"

"No, no I am not. My friend, Mr Sherlock Holmes. What has happened to him?"

A look of confusion passed over the girl's pretty young face. "I don't know what you mean, sir."

"The patient who was in this room, where is he?"

She shook her head. "I'm afraid I don't know. I've just come on duty, and there's been no one in there all morning."

"But that's impossible. Dr Gibbs, is he here?"

"Dr Gibbs?"

"Yes, he was treating my friend. He'll know what's happened."

"I'm afraid Dr Gibbs is on holiday, sir."

"On holiday?"

"So I believe. Taken his family to the coast I've heard, lucky souls. I hope the weather's treating them better than us."

She smiled, but my head was spinning. "He didn't mention he was going away," I said. "I was talking to him here, last night. There was another nurse with him, older than you perhaps, with dark hair."

"Nurse Eddison?"

"Maybe, I don't know."

She smiled again. "Let me check for you. I'll be right back. Why don't you sit down for a moment? You look as though you could do with taking the weight off your feet."

I had to admit that she was right. My mind was racing, imagining all kinds of horrors: that Holmes had deteriorated in the night, his injuries proving too great, the swelling in the brain, internal bleeding. It was too much to bear.

I was roused from my fears by the light footsteps of the returning nurse. "I'm sorry, Dr Watson, but there's no sign of Nurse Eddison, and no one seems to know anything about a patient in that room. Are you sure you're not mistaken? Was it definitely this room?"

"Yes," I cried, rising from the seat, frustrated beyond belief. "I sat right here, waiting for Dr Gibbs to examine Holmes."

"But Dr Gibbs is on holiday, sir."

"Well, he wasn't last night," I bellowed, the concern on the nurse's face disappearing with my outburst.

"Doctor, please. This is a hospital."

"It is," I replied, incensed. "And one, it seems, that loses its patients!"

The nurse crossed her arms, and it was clear that I had exhausted her goodwill. Not that I cared one jot.

"Sir, I am going to have to ask you to leave. There's obviously been some mistake, and I'm afraid I can't help you. We have no record of your friend, and even if we did, your tone is not helping."

"Very well," I said, incensed beyond measure. "But don't think for one moment that this is at an end. I shall be writing to your council of governors. Sherlock Holmes has served this country all his life, and for him to be treated in such a manner in his hour of need is an outrage."

The nurse indicated the exit at the end of the corridor. "Good morning, Doctor."

I took my leave without another word, storming from the corridor and, minutes later, from the hospital itself. First Scotland Yard and now here? Doors were slamming in my face, and, worst of all, I now had no idea where to find Holmes. For that damned nurse to suggest that he had never been in the room in the first place, why, it was preposterous. I had seen him there with my own eyes, lying in that bed. If Tovey hadn't fled for the West Country, he could have attested as much. I had half a mind to go back to the ward and read the riot act to the girl. She obviously had no idea who she was dealing with.

Then it struck me. She *did* know who I was. "Dr Watson", that was what she had called me, using both my name and my title, and yet I had never introduced myself properly, I was sure of it. She knew who I was, and yet still she claimed to have no knowledge of Holmes.

I staggered, dizziness washing over me. A passer-by stopped, ready to be a good Samaritan, grabbing my arm, asking if I needed to sit down. That was the last thing I needed. I thanked him, sending his fine intentions on his way. He couldn't help. Perhaps no one could. Everything had suddenly become clear. The louts in my surgery, Inspector Tovey's sudden absence, and now Holmes's disappearance; these events had to be connected to the case, to the amputated hand, the attack in the hospital, the mutated bone, that blood-stained operating theatre. Whatever we had stumbled upon had led to my being threatened and turned away by the authorities. And if that had happened to me, what of Holmes, in his weakened condition?

With no one else to turn to, I knew there was at least one man I could rely on, one man who would never turn me away. Stepping into the road, I hailed a cab.

"Where to, guv?" the cabbie asked, scratching absently at well-established ginger whiskers.

There was only one destination left open to me. "The Diogenes Club," I instructed. "And hurry."

CHAPTER FOURTEEN

THE STRANGER'S ROOM

It was almost noon when the car pulled onto Pall Mall. The drive across town had been erratic to say the least, my driver seeming to have very little understanding of road safety, or indeed the width of his car. Nevertheless, he had conveyed me to my destination and I felt a flutter of excitement to be back among familiar streets.

"There," I said, leaning forward in my seat. "That door, near the Carlton."

"Right you are, guv," said the cabbie, pulling over. "Do you need me to wait?"

I exited the vehicle, pushing a handful of coins into the driver's open hand. "That won't be necessary. Here, keep the change."

"Much obliged," the cabbie said, driving off to leave me outside an anonymous building with a navy-blue door. Finding the door locked, I rang the bell, waiting for what seemed an eternity before it was opened.

The doorman was a gentleman of African descent, with three lines of ritualistic scars carved across his dark cheeks. If I had never visited this place before I might have been taken aback by the fellow's aspect, but, while not a regular visitor, I had made enough jaunts to this particular establishment to find nothing out of the ordinary in his appearance.

"Dr Watson," the doorman intoned, as if he had seen me only yesterday rather than the ten years it had actually been. The gatekeeper to the Diogenes prided himself on a photographic memory for names and faces.

"Sapani, thank heavens," I exclaimed. "I have never been more pleased to see anyone in my life. Is he here?"

Sapani nodded and bade me enter. Without a word, he closed the door behind me, and gestured to take my hat and coat. I allowed him to do so, remaining absolutely silent myself, and was led along a long hallway lined with glass panels. Through the windows I could see men sitting in booths, their collective heads stuck in the pages of books and newspapers. No one spoke. No one even showed any inkling that others were present. Such was the way of this remarkable institution. Within its hallowed walls, members were required to remain completely and utterly silent. To speak but one word would bring a stinging rebuke from the committee. To speak again was unthinkable. To commit a third offence was to risk immediate and permanent expulsion. It was the perfect place for the antisocial and awkward, a sanctuary where human contact was discouraged and interaction illegal. If a chap had secrets, it was the perfect place to keep his lips tight, which was probably why the man I sought spent so much time within its chambers.

Sapani led me into a small room and, nodding once, exited, shutting the door behind him. I let out a sigh, relieved to find myself within the Stranger's Room, the only chamber in the building where noise was permitted. While Holmes had told me time and time again that he considered the atmosphere of the Diogenes Club to be relaxing, I found the place positively stifling.

I found it hard even to breathe while walking its corridors, and fought the urge to shout nonsense at the top of my voice simply to break the oppressive silence.

Whatever I thought of the club, at that moment, it had become my own personal haven. For the first time that day I had not been turned away, treated like an irritation or threatened with my life. What's more, as I heard footsteps so heavy that not even the Diogenes' thick carpets could soften them, I knew that help was, finally, at hand.

The door opened, and a corpulent figure strode in, wearing both an ill-fitting black suit and a look of great concern. "John, my dear fellow," he said, crossing over to me and extending a vast hand. "I am so glad you have come. Please take a seat."

He showed me to one of two severe chairs that rested beside an empty fireplace and lowered himself onto the nearest seat. This was a man who was designed for sitting down, although usually his chairs of choice were considerably more robust.

"Now tell me," said Mycroft Holmes, ignoring the creak beneath his considerable bulk, "where the Dickens is my brother?"

"That is exactly what I hoped you could tell me," I admitted, and proceeded to recount the entire sorry tale. Mycroft listened, his jowls quaking as he nodded at every twist and turn. Finally, after my account had reached my arrival in the Stranger's Room, I fell silent, waiting for Mycroft to comment.

Instead, my friend's older sibling merely sat and stared at me for longer than was strictly comfortable before reaching into his jacket pocket and drawing out a cigarette case. "Will you join me?" he asked, flipping open the case with large fingers.

I resisted the temptation, having turned my back on the habit a few years previously following a bout of bronchitis, and watched the elder Holmes go through the ritual of lighting a cigarette and drawing a thick plume of smoke into his lungs.

"I had rather hoped," he eventually said, "that conversations such as these would have come to an end when Sherlock retired."

I took the comment with more than a pinch of salt, knowing how much Mycroft had relied on his brother – especially during the war – since Holmes's so-called retirement. Even after all this time, I was unsure exactly what position Mycroft held at Whitehall, but I knew enough not to ask. I was also aware that the two brothers corresponded regularly, Mycroft often employing his younger sibling's unique talents in matters of national security.

"Something has happened to him, Mycroft. I know it has."

Mycroft sighed. "Very well. Leave it with me."

"Thank you, Mycroft. They were hiding something, the people at Charing Cross Hospital, that much was obvious."

"Don't you worry about that. Don't you worry about anything."

"It's just so damned frustrating that those ruffians took the bone. If I could only make a proper study—"

"John, let the matter rest."

Mycroft's tone gave me pause. There had been a change, almost imperceptible. The kindness that had been evident was gone, replaced by steel. He was no longer advising me, he was delivering a command.

"I can't," I insisted. "Inspector Tovey asked us to help him."

"But as you say, Inspector Tovey is away on another investigation—"

"A damned convenient investigation. I can't help but think—"

"And that is your problem, Doctor." So, it was "doctor" now, not John. "You over-think matters. It's an unfortunate by-product of spending so much time with my brother."

I could hardly believe what I was hearing. "Mycroft, you're talking as if I don't know you, that I haven't worked with you on numerous occasions."

"Your services to King and Country are beyond reproach,

Doctor. In fact, only the other day your name was mentioned at the highest level."

"It was?"

"I shouldn't say this, of course, but you're to be offered a knighthood. Sir John Watson. How does that sound?"

It sounded like one thing, and one thing alone. I know what people say of me. Dr Watson is an idiot. A bumbling fool eclipsed by the genius that is Sherlock Holmes. Granted, it is a reputation that I have no doubt reinforced in my stories, reducing my own part in proceedings to that of a stooge for my friend's great powers – but I knew what was happening here. So far today I had been warned off by devils and ignored by those who I had hoped were working on the side of the angels. Now, sitting in this small room on Pall Mall alongside a man whom I would have trusted with my life, I was being bribed. There was no warmth in Mycroft's revelation, no joy. It was a statement of fact. Run along like a good boy and you'll get a treat. Arise Sir John, neutered lapdog to the authorities. I had served my purpose, and for reasons that I could not begin to fathom, I was being dismissed.

I felt sick to my stomach, but all the time Mycroft kept talking.

"Just because my brother continues to refuse the honour, there is no reason why His Majesty's government should not recognise your part in the defence of the realm. Of course, officially the honour will be given for services to literature and medicine—"

"But we know the truth, eh, Mycroft," I interrupted. "Secrets and scandals."

For the first time in our interview, for that was what it had become, Mycroft looked uncomfortable, and it was not the chair that brought about his lack of ease.

"Quite so. Now, I am sure you will want to go home and tell Mrs Watson the good news. She will no doubt be after a new dress for the investiture. I hear good things about that Selfridges place, although I have never been there myself."

"Yes, we shall want to look our best, won't we? When I accept my thirty pieces of silver."

"John?"

"And I'm John again. All friends together. No doubt you will be inviting me to join this august institution next. 'Come in, come in. Now, pull up a chair, sit down and keep your mouth shut.'"

"Doctor, I would ask you to lower your voice."

"You're asking me to do more than that. No, not asking – instructing!" I stood, my chair scraping across the floor. "Go away, John. Keep quiet, John. Mind your own business, John."

Now it was Mycroft's turn to stand. His mouth was a thin line and, strangely, I realised that he looked more like his brother when he was angry than in repose.

"Doctor, that is enough!"

"Is it? I don't think so. I came to you for help. I came to you because your brother – my friend – is missing. Yesterday, I thought he was dying. Today, for all I know, he is lying in a mortuary, and the worst thing of all is not that he may have died, although by God it breaks my heart even to say those words, but that I think you know where he is."

"I assure you, I have no—"

"Liar."

"I beg your pardon?"

"I think you know what has happened to Holmes. You knew before you came into this room. Everyone I've talked to, Inspector Tovey, Dr Gibbs, even that nurse, they've all mysteriously disappeared. New cases in Cornwall, holidays to the coast. And now you want me to disappear too? To run home, so grateful that you have deigned to bestow an honour on me that I forget what I have seen and heard; that I forget who I am!"

The door opened and Sapani stepped in. I must have been

shouting by the end of my diatribe, my voice carrying beyond the Stranger's Room, but I cared not one iota. Let them all hear.

"Is everything as it should be, Mr Holmes?" the doorman asked.

"Unfortunately not," I replied on Mycroft's behalf.

The elder Holmes fixed me with another icy stare.

"You are tired, Doctor. Exhausted even. It is not surprising. You suffered a blow to the head—"

"Oh, so *you* are a doctor now, are you? And what do you prescribe?"

"That you go home and get some rest."

"Or what, Mycroft? What will happen if I don't? Do you know what the curious thing is? I should feel safe here with you. An old friend, an ally, and yet I would rather take my chances with those thugs who broke into my practice this morning. At least they were honest in their villainy. At least they didn't try to sugar-coat the poison."

"Dr Watson," Sapani said, softly. "I think you should leave."

"Don't worry, I'm going," I said, delivering one last glare in Mycroft's direction before I thundered out of the room, Sapani stepping aside. "And thank you for your kind and generous offer, Mycroft," I shouted over my shoulder, well aware that I would be attracting shocked glances from the members reading their newspapers on the other side of the glass. "But I would rather choke than accept any 'honour' from a man who obviously has none of his own."

"Dr Watson, please," Sapani implored, but I marched ahead, reckless of the club's rules and regulations. I stood seething as the doorman returned my hat and coat. I snatched them, making sure I bade a loud farewell to Mycroft who was standing at the other end of the corridor, his usually ashen face flushed with fury.

"Goodbye, Mycroft," I shouted, my chest puffed out with

indignation. "Enjoy your silence and communal solitude. I hope it will give you the opportunity to think about what you have done!"

Sapani opened the door of the Diogenes Club and I exited gladly, in desperate need of fresh air, no matter how inclement the weather. As the door closed gently behind me, a sound somehow as deafening as if it had been slammed, I stood on the pavement, leaning on my cane, my breast heaving with short, angry breaths.

So that was the way of it. I understood now. I was alone, but I knew what I must do.

I stepped forward, hailing a cab. One pulled over to the kerb immediately, the driver cheerfully asking my destination.

"Where to, guv?"

My blood ran cold. It was the same smiling face as before, the same thick ginger beard. It was the cabbie who had brought me from Charing Cross not an hour before. A coincidence? I would have said so yesterday, maybe even a few hours ago. Now, suspicions raged in my mind. Mycroft had known what was going on, I was sure of it. His eyes had told me that, even if his words had not. What if Sapani really had expected to greet me when he opened the door? What if Mycroft had known I was coming all along, what if he had been tipped off? Had I stumbled into a web of lies? Holmes and I had seen enough conspiracies in our time to recognise one as it closed around us. Around me.

"No thank you," I said to the driver with forced jocularity. "The rain is easing. I think I shall walk."

"All the way home, sir?"

Yes, because that was where they wanted me to go. Home. To share my good fortune with my wife.

I touched the brim of my hat.

"That will be all. Thank you."

"Please yourself," the driver sniffed. "You wouldn't catch me walking the streets today. It'll be the death of you."

I watched him drive off. Did his parting comment contain another threat? It was hard to tell – and if it did, where had it originated? From the thugs who invaded my rooms, or the government man behind the anonymous blue door? There was very little between them at present.

Glancing around myself, I pulled up the collar of my coat and set out.

CHAPTER FIFTEEN

THE SCENE OF THE CRIME

When I finally reached Wapping High Street, having trudged along the streets for nearly an hour and a half, I was cursing my stubbornness. I could have hailed another cab along the way, but there was no way of knowing whom I could trust, not today. Better that they thought I was walking home.

The thought of home brought with it a pang of guilt. Perhaps I should have tried to contact my wife, but what could I have done? Should I have stopped at a random door, hoping that the occupants would let me use their telephone? I could have sent a telegram, but what would it say? And she would have no way to reply, no means of letting me know that she was safe. No, I would continue on the path I had chosen and, I hoped, return to her before evening. No good would come of worrying her unduly.

"Come now, John," I muttered to myself as I took the alleyway beside the Hoop and Grapes. "You're just a man taking a stroll."

The ludicrousness of the statement made me chuckle as I carefully descended to the river's edge. All pretence of humour evaporated, however, as I set eyes on Abberton Hospital. I had hoped never to set foot in the building again, but I knew what I had to do.

Glancing at the boats that chugged by on the water, I walked purposely towards the accursed place, my right hand deep in my coat pocket, clutching the torch I had purchased en route as if it were a lucky charm.

This time there was no need to jemmy the lock. The front door to the hospital swung open easily and, clicking on the torch, I stepped into the lobby. Nothing had changed. I am unsure why I thought it might have. The same dust and litter on the floor greeted me, although there were more footprints now, most probably those of the police officers whom Tovey had called to whisk us to Charing Cross following our altercation with the monstrous man on the second floor. I sent the beam of light up the stairs. That was where I was heading, back to where the nightmare had taken place.

I was steeling myself to make the ascent when the front door slammed shut behind me. I spun around, illuminating the door with the torch's beam. I waited, expecting a creak on the step, or maybe for the handle to turn, but when neither came, I strode forward to fling the door open again.

No one was there.

"Nervous old fool," I murmured, heading back in. "Must have been the wind."

This time I didn't wait but marched up the stairs, swallowing any trepidation I felt. I had survived much in my life, both on the battlefield and in the streets of London. What had I to fear from a forgotten building?

Repeating this mantra, I climbed to the second floor and, not stopping to think, pushed through the swing doors, into the corridor where we had attempted to trap a monster and tasted its wrath. Yet things had changed.

I swept the torch around. The light bulbs and cables were

gone. I hurried to the room where the curious dynamo had been stored. It too was missing. I inspected the two bedrooms that had been occupied. The sheets were gone from the woman's bed, as was the novel from the chamber opposite. In fact, the floors were free of dust. I bent closer to see. Yes, they had been swept clean, the rusting bed-frames and the overturned chairs pushed neatly against the walls.

Had it been the police, gathering evidence? Since when had His Majesty's constabulary tidied up after themselves so meticulously?

A thought struck me and I rushed to the double doors at the far end of the corridor. They were open, and even as I approached I could see that the chamber beyond was as spotless as the rest. The operating table was gone, as were the metal tables at the sides. The buckets. The equipment. All missing. Even the floor was freshly mopped and the tiled walls scrubbed. If I had entertained any hope of finding fresh evidence, even by my meagre abilities, it was gone. The operating theatre was as sterile as it had ever been, even when the sound of patients and staff had echoed down these empty corridors.

I stood in the silence, numb with the realisation that I had hit another brick wall. Surely the investigation had come spluttering to an end. There was nowhere else to go, no one to turn to, and without Holmes I was lost, hopelessly out of my depth.

Admitting defeat, and hating myself for it, I turned and uttered a cry of alarm. There, in the open doorway, stood a man, staring at me with amused eyes. A tattered cloth cap perched on his head while a thick ginger beard almost covered his smirking mouth. It was the cabbie who had taken me to the Diogenes Club. So he *was* involved.

"What are you doing here?" I demanded, raising my cane. If the man had been sent to deal with me, then by God I would make it difficult for him.

The fellow raised his hands, still leering. "Now, we don't want to get excited. After all—" The hands dropped and with them the driver's north London accent. "—we have both suffered considerable injuries over the last couple of days, if the bruise on your forehead is any indication."

The end of my cane clattered on the floor.

"Holmes?"

The cabbie smiled, and his body underwent a remarkable transformation. He stretched, and I realised for the first time that the man had been hunched over. Now, standing erect, he pulled off both his cap and wig to reveal tousled grey hair, which he attempted to smooth with long fingers. Next came that damned beard, yanked free of the theatrical gum that had glued the fake whiskers to a very familiar face.

"It's good to see that the knowledge dear Albert imparted all those years ago can still pull the wool over your eyes, Watson. I feared that you would see through my disguise outside the Diogenes. Tell me, how is brother Mycroft?"

Stuffing the beard into the pocket of his jacket, my friend strolled around the room, his eyes sweeping the floor as thoroughly as the mops that had cleared away every last remnant of gore.

"B-but I saw you," I stammered, "in the hospital. You were barely conscious."

Holmes nodded. "Indeed I was. I have to tell you, I am still not feeling quite myself. The blow I received to my head has left me with a rather persistent case of tinnitus, and I admit I am finding it considerably harder than usual to concentrate."

A realisation hit me. "I let you drive me around London."

"Oh, you were quite safe," Holmes laughed. "I nearly blacked out only once. Maybe twice."

Now, when I looked at my friend, devoid of his disguise, I could see how tired he still looked, how grey. Perhaps his appearance had actually aided his subterfuge.

"We should get you back to hospital," I insisted.

"After I worked so hard to escape?" said the detective. "I think not."

"You discharged yourself?"

"Nothing so official, I'm afraid. I first became aware that something was wrong when I came to. I could hear voices, fading in and out, including yours I think, and that of friend Tovey."

"We didn't leave your side, at least until the inspector insisted we go home."

"And I'm glad you did, otherwise I may never have slipped away, and I mean that in terms of extrication, not passing into heaven's embrace."

"Extrication? You believed you were in danger then?"

"Not until a certain voice pierced my stupor. And a familiar voice at that. My brother's."

"Mycroft?"

"At first, his presence hardly seemed peculiar. I was at death's door, after all. But then, as I began to come around, I was unable to work it out. What was my brother doing there?"

"As you said, you were quite unwell, or so we thought."

"Come now, Watson. You know my brother. He is usually to be found in one of three places. His offices in Whitehall, his chambers in Pall Mall, and within the club he founded. If he can avoid travelling anywhere, he will, and he has a legion of lieutenants scampering all across London, probably the entire planet, gathering information and delivering messages on his behalf. And yet he was there, talking to young Doctor… what was his name?"

"Dr Gibbs," I supplied.

"Ah yes, Dr Gibbs. You'll have to forgive me. As I said, my faculties are unfortunately a touch impaired. So, I lie there, listening to my brother quiz Dr Gibbs. What is my condition? Does he expect me to make a full recovery? A man expressing concern for his sibling, or so you would assume if you were unacquainted with Mycroft."

"You think he had an ulterior motive for being there?"

"Think? I know it! The questions continued, but I could hear in his voice that something else was coming. Gibbs was outlining the treatment he had planned for me, the tests he would perform the following morning, and so on. It soon became apparent that Mycroft had no intention of leaving me in the good doctor's capable hands. 'Thank you, Doctor,' said my brother. 'My family is in your debt, but I shall be moving Sherlock to a private facility. I need to ensure that he receives the best possible care if there is hope of him recovering.'

"Gibbs argued, his professional pride affronted and rightly so. He assured my brother that Charing Cross Hospital had my best interests at heart, and would stop at nothing to nurse me back to good health, if such an aim were even possible. My brother remained resolute and I became aware that another man was present in the room.

"'I need you to go with my colleague,' Mycroft informed the doctor. 'He will take a statement, and then you can go about your duties.'"

"A statement?" I repeated. "To what end?"

"A pertinent question, Watson, and one I asked myself. If Mycroft was going to transfer me to this 'private facility' he would have full access to the doctor's notes. Why would there be need to interrogate the poor fellow?

"And yet, Dr Gibbs was removed and I was left alone with my brother. Thankfully I had enough of my wits about me to play dead, or at least to convince him that I was still unconscious."

"Did he try to hurt you?"

"No, of course not. He merely stood there, in silence. I could feel his eyes upon me, Watson, examining my face, looking for any sign that I was awake.

"'Oh, Sherlock,' he finally said. 'Why did you have to involve yourself in all this?' And with that he turned and left. I realised that I had only a few moments. Before he could return, I got myself out of bed – which was more difficult than I had anticipated – and struggled to the door. To be honest with you, I struggle to remember how I made my exit from the hospital."

"I'm not surprised."

"I have scraps of memory. Stealing into another room to help myself to a fellow patient's clothes, coming across a stairwell, missing a step to find myself sprawled on a half-landing."

"Holmes, you were in no fit state..."

"What choice did I have? I couldn't stay. Finding myself on the ground floor, I stumbled into the laundry, where to my good fortune the women boiling the sheets were engrossed in tittle-tattle. Thank the Lord for gossips and tattlers. I was sure they would notice me as I opened the back door, but I was out and away in seconds."

"Where did you go?"

"I still have boltholes across the city, Watson, and so I squirrelled myself away, making use of the pharmaceuticals I had stored for such an occasion. A wash and a change of clothes and I felt a new man, albeit one who could barely remember his own name."

"So, you rested..."

"Briefly, although I knew I had to see Tovey."

"As did I," I interrupted, "but he has gone away."

"So I understand. To Cornwall of all places, if you believe the story."

"Which I don't."

Holmes nodded. “I have no doubt that the inspector is on a case, but one that was hurriedly found for him, rather than one that he chose himself.”

“And the cab?”

“One of the Irregulars is now a cabbie. Young Geller, do you remember him? Not so young any more, but happy enough to lend me his taxi – for a good price, of course.”

“He was always a shrewd businessman,” I said, recalling the grubby lad I had once known, part of the ragtag bunch of urchins employed by Holmes to be his eyes and ears on the street.

“No one pays attentions to cabbies,” Holmes said. “Especially when they already have a fare in the back.”

“Geller again?”

“I had him jump out when I saw you outside the hospital.”

I shook my head. “I thought you were part of it, Holmes. The cabbie – you, I mean.”

“I must admit I was surprised when you opted to walk earlier this afternoon. I can only imagine that your appointment with Mycroft did not go the way you hoped.”

“He is involved in all of this,” I said, “whatever this is.”

“Reluctantly, I am inclined to agree,” Holmes said, genuine sorrow in his voice. “I am surprised they failed to clean the lobby as well as these rooms. His footprint was unmistakable.”

“Whose?”

“My brother has four pairs of shoes, all of which were crafted by Mr John Lobb of St James’s Street, on the recommendation of the Prince of Wales no less. The tread is quite familiar. Mycroft has travelled more of London in the last twenty-four hours than he has in the last twenty-four years. Something is afoot, Watson, and I shall get to the bottom of it, whether Mycroft wants me to or not. Now, I suggest we leave. My earlier self-medication is wearing thin, and my chest feels as if it is on fire. I assume that you have painkillers at home?"

"Of course, but—"

"To Chelsea it is then," Holmes cut in, placing the cap firmly back on his head. "This time there is no need to walk a marathon. I know of a cabbie who will be pleased to drive you home."

"I don't think you should get behind the wheel again," I said, following him towards the stairwell.

"Nonsense," came the reply. "I am more than capable of—" My friend stopped, his nostrils flaring. "Watson, can you smell that?"

"What? Holmes, I—"

I took a sniff, and realised what Holmes was talking about. "Something's burning."

"Your torch," instructed Holmes, grabbing my arm and pointing the beam of light at the swing doors. Smoke was billowing from beneath them. Dark. Deadly.

"Watson, the building's on fire!"

CHAPTER SIXTEEN

LIKE SOLDIERS OF OLD

Holmes yanked open the door, yelping as he gripped a handle that was already too hot. Smoke rolled in, stinging our eyes and forcing us back.

Covering his mouth with the cabbie's cap, Holmes strode into the thick cloud, almost disappearing from view. I followed, peering down the stairwell, the glow of the flames flickering from below.

"Come on," Holmes shouted, charging down the stairs straight into the inferno.

"Are you mad?" I shouted after him. "Those steps were treacherous enough before!"

"Somehow I can't see either of us throwing ourselves out of a window," he called back, coughing on the fumes. "Not in our current condition."

Grudgingly I was forced to agree, and began my own descent, barely able to see, so thick was the smoke. It needed only another rotten step and we would tumble down into the blaze.

My chest felt heavy and I struggled for breath as we passed the first floor landing to turn down to the lobby. Holmes stopped abruptly and I did not need to ask him why. Flames were dancing along the lobby floor, blistering already blackened paintwork on the walls and spreading up to meet us. Our escape route was well and truly blocked. We would never make it to the bottom step, let alone the front door.

"Back upstairs," Holmes commanded.

"But you said—"

"Save your breath."

I wanted to stop. I wanted to sink to the steps and wait for the inevitable. I knew such thoughts were tantamount to suicide, but it felt that my lungs were about to burst and I could barely see. The heat was unlike anything I had ever experienced, the smell unbearable; but the noise? That is what you never understand about fires until you are standing in the heart of one. The crackling. The roaring.

"Watson! Come on!"

I couldn't give up. We were at each other's side once more, as we had always been. Holmes and Watson. As close as any brothers.

Grabbing the banister, I took the first step, and then another. I felt the hairs on the back of my neck singe, imagined the skin blistering, sparks catching my coat, but I ran, not as Mycroft had hoped I would, but towards escape, one step at a time.

"That's it, Watson," Holmes said, as I wheezed onto the first floor landing. "Almost there."

"Almost where?"

"I'm a fool," was his only reply.

"What do you mean?"

He pushed open the doors.

"Give me your torch."

It was a miracle I hadn't dropped it in my flight. I passed it to him and he swept it across what little we could see of the floor.

"This way," he half-choked, pulling me to the right. I stumbled blindly after him, until we reached a door at the end of the corridor. He flung it open and we found ourselves standing in a small box-like room.

"No!" Holmes cursed, stepping back into the smoke-filled corridor. "It must be here somewhere."

"What are you looking for?" I spluttered, blinded by the smoke, although I could hear Holmes running his hands along the walls.

"This," came the triumphant cry, accompanied by the opening of a door. A hand emerged from the murk, grabbing my shoulder and pulling me forward. I cried out as pain lanced up my arm, but found myself in an enclosed stairwell that was thankfully free of smoke. The flight curved around a service elevator that would be useless without power, but the stairs themselves were still passable. Holmes was already racing down them, and I followed suit, holding onto the handrail as if my life depended on it, which it probably did. Smoke billowed up the shaft like a chimney, but there was no sign of flames save for an ominous glow from the gap beneath an already steaming internal door.

We reached the bottom, and spied another door. Holmes tried the handle, only to find it locked. He handed me the torch, but before I could ask him his intentions he surprised me by drawing a revolver from his belt and firing once, twice, three times into the lock. The noise was deafening, even above the clamour of the blaze, and I threw up a hand to protect my face from flying wooden shrapnel.

Holmes threw his weight against the door, tumbling forward as it flew open. I cried out, rushing forward to help him up, only to find the man flat on his back, laughing hysterically. I felt cool air on my face and saw the sky above us. We were out.

Struggling to my feet, I stood over my amused companion.

"What the devil is wrong with you, Holmes?"

He grabbed my forearm and, placing more strain on my already near-ruined shoulder, levered himself up. "Twice this building has tried to kill us, Watson, and twice we have escaped."

"We're not clear yet," I said, looking around. We were in a tiny loading yard, trolleys that would have once housed piles of linen overturned against a six-foot wall. "How do we get out?"

"Down here," Holmes said, pointing out a tiny alleyway that ran along the side of the burning building. I cast the light of the torch down the passage, noting with dismay a wooden door that blocked our exit. Holmes limped down to investigate and, rattling the barricade, realised that it was locked from the other side.

"What are you waiting for?" I asked, hobbling up behind him. "Use your gun again!"

"That is the unmistakable sound of a padlock," Holmes said, pushing past me, back into the yard. "Even if I were at the height of my powers, striking a lock through a solid door would be a trick shot worthy of Wild Bill Hickok."

"Then how will we get out? We can't go through the blaze again."

"Indeed we can't. Help me with this," Holmes said, trying to raise one of the trolleys back onto its castors.

"You can't be serious."

"Watson, please," my friend croaked. "My resources are wearing dangerously thin. I haven't the strength by myself."

Pocketing the torch, I joined Holmes and manhandled the trolley upright. We rattled it over to the passageway and, lining it up with the locked door, gave each other one last look. From somewhere in the building there came an almighty crash as a floor or ceiling gave way. Grinning despite myself, I looked into Holmes's soot-covered features.

"This is why my wife doesn't like me spending time with you," I said.

"Nonsense," came the reply. "It keeps you out from under her feet."

With a cry born chiefly of desperation, Holmes and I charged down the alley, pushing the trolley with all our might. It crashed into the door, the impact causing both of us to cry out in pain, although there was no time to nurse either shoulder or ribs. Instead, we pulled back and let fly again, like soldiers of old attempting to batter down the gates of a castle.

This time the door gave a little more, wood splintering. At last, on the third attempt, the latch sprang open. The trolley trundled through the open door and Holmes had to catch me before I fell flat on my face.

We staggered around the side of the building, like drunkards returning from a night in a gin palace. We stopped only when we reached the riverbank, turning to gaze at the flames that were claiming the ruined hospital from within.

Flames that had very nearly claimed us as well.

CHAPTER SEVENTEEN

AN ULTIMATUM

My wife was at the kitchen table, her head in her hands. I hovered at the door, not quite knowing what to do. I had heard her sobbing from the hallway, and knew all too well the reason for her despair. When Holmes and I had entered the house, she had appeared at the drawing-room door, her face ashen. What a sight we must have looked, blackened from the soot and as weary as the dead. I tried to explain what had happened, but she refused to meet my eye. Instead, she bustled around me, rushing upstairs to run our guest a bath, instructing us both to bundle together our smoke-infused clothes for washing. Holmes had insisted that I bathe first and retired to his room to smoke a pipe, as if his lungs had not yet sustained enough damage.

I washed and changed into my bedclothes and dressing gown to find that my apparel from the day had been dutifully whisked away, although the stink of the fire lingered in the bedroom. Then it was Holmes's turn to freshen himself, although by the look of the man it would take more than a long soak in the tub. I wished I could march him straight back to the hospital, but considering everything that had happened I could scarcely be assured of his safety, even within the previously trusted walls of Charing Cross.

My head was still spinning with what he had suggested: that Mycroft himself was somehow involved in a conspiracy to stop our investigation. Just what had we stumbled upon?

My body ached for my bed, but I knew my mind would gain no rest until we had discussed the recent occurrences. Who had started the fire, and, worst of all, had they been aware that we were inside the building?

Such questions faded when I found my wife in the kitchen. For a moment, I considered leaving her to her grief, but immediately I scolded myself. What kind of man and husband would I be then?

"My dear," I said, as softly as possible, stepping forward. She started, pushing back her chair to rise quickly, trying to hide her tears from me even as she dabbed at her eyes with a handkerchief.

"There you are," she sniffed. "Feeling more human, I hope? I shall fetch you a drink."

"You'll do nothing of the kind." I would hardly insult her intelligence by asking what was wrong. "We're quite all right, you know, a little singed around the edges, but other than that—"

"It's not funny, John." She pulled away, her back to me. "None of this is funny. You could have been killed tonight."

"But we weren't. We—"

"Escaped?" Now she turned towards me, but the sorrow was gone from her face, to be replaced by anger. "Yes, this time. But what about tomorrow, or the day after that?"

"You don't understand. After the day I've had—"

"After the day *you've* had? Do you have any idea about the day *I've* had, John? Yesterday, you were delivered to our door by a policeman, with your arm in a sling and suspected concussion. Today, I awake to find you've gone, sneaking out to heaven knows where before dawn."

"It was hardly before dawn, and I went to the surgery, that's all."

"How was I supposed to know? How am I supposed to know anything any more? I'm your wife, John, but how many more days will it be until I become your widow?"

"There's no need for that kind of talk."

"Isn't there? Yesterday, it was a knock on the head. Today it was near immolation. What will it be tomorrow? A knife in the back? I tell you, he won't rest until he sees me put you in the ground!"

"Who won't?"

"Who do you think?"

I had never witnessed such ire from my wife, and, while I knew that she had every right to be aggrieved, I was not about to be addressed in such a manner, not in my own home.

"Now, that's enough. None of this is Holmes's fault. I am your husband and—"

"Then start acting like one!" she cried, cutting me off. "None of this is Holmes's fault? Now I *know* that knock on the head did some damage. Did any of this happen before you invited him to stay? Did we have policemen at the door morning, noon and night? Don't you dare suggest otherwise, John Watson. That man up there will get you killed!"

"And what am I supposed to do, eh? Turn him out on the streets? Forget any of this happened?"

"He has a home to go to, doesn't he? A life of his own that's far enough away that it won't turn yours upside down. This isn't one of your silly little stories, John. This is real life. *Our* life, not some childish fantasy."

Now she had gone too far. "Childish fantasy? They were real. You know that; all of them. They happened to me. To us. They're part of who I am."

"Who you *were*, John. They're in the past now, or so they should be."

I snorted with derision. "I didn't see you complaining when my 'silly little stories' paid for this house!"

"A house for us to grow old in together," she replied, "not for me to live in alone, grieving for you for the rest of my days."

"Then perhaps you should leave!"

I don't know who was more stunned by my words, my wife or I. She stood there, staring at me in disbelief. If my aim had been to shock her into silence, there was no doubt it had worked, although the words had tumbled from my mouth with little in the way of thought.

No, that wasn't right. They hadn't tumbled. I had spat them, like bullets from a gun, and I had no way of putting them back in the chamber.

She straightened, trying to retain her dignity, her lip trembling with both fury and sorrow. "Perhaps that would be the best, until things settle down," she admitted. "I can go to my sister's."

I took an appeasing step forward. "I didn't—"

She backed away, brushing an imaginary crease from her dress. "Millie's been asking me to visit for months now," she continued. "But I've been too busy. I can leave in the morning. Maybe stay for a week or two."

She granted me no opportunity to argue. I had done enough of that already. Instead, she swept around me, head held high, and disappeared out of the kitchen.

"I'm going to bed," was all she said as she climbed the stairs.

I stood in the kitchen, uncertain what to do. Should I go after her, attempt to dissuade her? I doubted it would do any good. She was a strong-willed woman. It was one of the reasons I had been attracted to her in the first place. Once her mind was made up, she stuck to her guns, come what may. Besides, and this was what truly twisted the knife, part of me was glad she wouldn't be around. Oh, I told myself it was because she would be safe, miles away from whatever was happening here, but that was another lie, to myself this time. I knew I wanted to see this through to the bitter end, and had no need of the distraction of quarrels at home. I hated myself for admitting it, but it was true nonetheless.

How selfish had I become?

There was a sound from the drawing room. The creak of a chair. I walked down the hallway to find Holmes sitting in the armchair in his dressing gown, a book on his lap. He looked better, if still dreadfully pale, glancing up at me as I entered the room.

"You heard?" I asked.

"It was difficult not to, I am afraid."

I eased myself into the other armchair, my shoulder still throbbing. Holmes closed the book. "I shall leave in the morning."

"Holmes, we've already gone through this."

"I am sure the Goring can find a room for me."

"There is honestly no need."

"Watson, if it is a choice between me and your wife, there is nothing more to discuss. I am only sorry that my involving you in this case has led to such hostilities at home."

"You didn't involve me. Tovey did. Besides, the one thing no one seems to be taking into account here is that I may want to find out what's happening." Glancing at the door, I lowered my voice and leant towards Holmes. "The last couple of days have seen me attacked, threatened and nearly burnt alive. I need to see this through to the end, Holmes. Besides, those men from the surgery, Burns and Hartley; if we don't get to the bottom of this, how do I know they won't crawl out of the woodwork again? No, it's better my wife goes to see her sister. At least she'll be out of the firing line. It really is better this way."

Holmes regarded me in silence. I could see from his eyes that my resolution had pleased him, but he spoke not another word about it. Instead, he steepled his fingers in the way I had seen him do so many times during our long friendship. "Then let us review the evidence."

I shrugged. "What evidence do we have? I doubt Scotland Yard will let us get near that infernal hand again and everything in the hospital was scrubbed clean even before it went up in flames."

Holmes tapped the side of his head. "Everything I need to know about the hand is up here. No, we must turn our attention to our mystery collarbone."

"The clavicle? But even that was taken—"

"By Burns and Hartley, yes, but you examined it, did you not? And would recognise a similar specimen?"

"Of course, if we could find such a thing."

Holmes smiled thinly. "In that case, Watson, I believe we should look in your attic."

CHAPTER EIGHTEEN

THE ATTIC

My wife was not fond of going into the attic of our townhouse. It was no surprise. She was, after all, a woman who prided herself on the tidiness of our home.

"A place for everything and everything in its place," she would say. It's a principle that I myself have lived by my entire life, one of the many reasons that we were so well suited.

It is also why I found that the habits of my fellow lodger so rankled with me during my years at Baker Street. It wasn't to say that the man was slovenly. Indeed, when it came to his appearance, Holmes was fastidious to the point of obsession. However, any man who would amuse himself by shooting bullets into the wall of our drawing room was obviously someone whose ideas about tidiness were at the raffish end of the spectrum.

I still wonder why I agreed to store Holmes's archive when he finally moved out of 221B. Thankfully, my wife had been out on the day that wagon after wagon had trundled down Cheyne Walk, each fully laden. That evening, after everything had been crammed into its new home, she had paid a brief visit to the attic, but had quickly descended again, her face as pale as snow, vowing never to venture up into such "chaos" again.

Now, as I opened the attic door, I sympathised. The merest glance at the jumbled mess of crates and boxes was enough to send the sanest mind into panic. There had been no plan, no organisation. My friend had simply deposited his life's work into the empty space and shut the door behind him.

"I thank you, Watson," he had said that day fifteen years ago, as he opened the bottle of champagne that he had purchased to toast the end of an era. "I shall have little use for the archive in my new life, but I cannot bear the thought of it being discarded."

I had suggested that he could donate both his library and the vast index to Scotland Yard. Needless to say, the proposal was met with considerable disdain.

And so, in the subsequent years, his collection of books, clippings and periodicals had mouldered, gathering dust. Now, as the musky stench of paper welcomed us, Holmes all but danced up the stairs, the sight of his once precious volumes a positive elixir.

"Excellent, Watson. Simply excellent."

I tried to hush him, not wanting to upset my wife any more than I already had. Holmes seemed conveniently oblivious to my pleas.

"It is good to be among my things again, Watson, even after all this time. A man could lose himself up here."

"Or break his neck," I suggested, stepping over a pile of books only to narrowly avoid turning my ankle on a discarded phrenology bust.

"Watch that," Holmes said, already rummaging through a tea chest. "It was a gift from dear Hollander."

"If it means so much to you, then maybe you would like to keep it, or at least return the wretched thing to Bernard at the first opportunity."

Holmes made no reply, but instead abandoned the chest to continue rummaging through other boxes. "Watson, I sincerely hope you have not been moving things around up here?"

"Perish the thought. Besides, I would have no idea where to start."

"But they should be here, next to the obituary albums."

"I promise you, I haven't touched a thing. What are you looking for?"

Ignoring me, he went to work, pulling the tops off boxes and nine times out of ten not replacing them, having failed to find whatever he was looking for inside. All the time he muttered about my suspected interference in his filing "system". I half decided to leave him with his books and boxes, but, while bed was calling me, my curiosity had been piqued by this sudden activity. What was he hoping to uncover?

"Aha," he finally exclaimed, straddling a mahogany trunk to pluck a hefty-looking tome from a straining bookcase.

"What is it?"

"*Butterworth's Almanac of Medical Curiosities*," came the reply, as Holmes sat on the trunk and opened the book on his lap. "Have you not read it?"

"I can't say I have. When was it published?"

"Oh, 1867 or thereabouts."

"And you think it will help identify the bone?"

"Do you think I would go through all of this if it could not?"

"Stranger things have happened, Holmes."

Perching on the edge of an overturned crate, I waited patiently for him to flick through the yellowed pages, pausing to peer at faded illustrations.

"No... no... no... no... no..." he said, dismissing one page after another.

"No luck then?"

Holmes's face darkened, until he turned the last page and a sheet of paper fluttered down from where it had nestled between the endpaper and the back cover.

"There it is!" he exclaimed, throwing the almanac aside without a second thought.

"Careful, Holmes."

"Oh, don't worry about that old thing. Dreadful book, barely worth the pulp it's printed on. No, this is what I was looking for."

He snatched up the scrap of paper, poring over its text.

"Yes, this is more like it."

"And do you intend to share exactly what *it* is?"

"It's yours," he replied. "Or at least it was, until I liberated it from one of your medical journals."

"You did what?" I exclaimed, outraged.

"Come now, Watson. The crime took place some twenty years ago. Far too long to bear a grudge."

"I've only just found out about it!"

"Are you going to sit there and split hairs all night, or shall I tell you what it says?"

"Perhaps I should have asked you to pack yourself off to the Goring when I had the chance. Go on then. Astound me."

Holmes held the paper up so I could see a small illustration on the other side. Trying hard to ignore the jagged line where it had been ripped from one of my precious journals, I focused on the picture.

"Do you recognise anything?" Holmes asked.

"A scapula, but it has—"

"The same growth as our misplaced clavicle."

"Not so much misplaced as misappropriated."

"Whether it is in our possession or not, we now know what caused its mutation."

He passed the paper over.

"*Myositis ossificans progressiva*," I read.

"Quite literally 'muscle turns progressively to bone'. If you read on you will discover that it is one of the rarest diseases in the world, afflicting just one in every two million, thank heavens."

Read on I did, the horror of the condition becoming clear. According to the author, sufferers from the malady would in effect grow a second skeleton over the course of their life, extra bone sprouting from limbs, fusing them in place. Over time their joints would seize up, transforming them into living statues. The passage was short but chilling. I looked up at Holmes, barely able to imagine the torment the condition would bring.

"So the bone—" I began.

"Came from a victim of that dreadful condition," concluded Holmes, "although how it ended up in that operating theatre I have no idea. But perhaps tomorrow, after a good night's rest, we can throw ourselves on the mercy of your Harley Street colleagues. Surely someone in London must know more about the disease?"

CHAPTER NINETEEN

A MOST SINGULAR SKELETON

Rested, if not completely refreshed, we could be found the next morning up with the lark. My wife was courteous towards Holmes, although I received a reception so frosty that even an Eskimo would feel the chill.

It was a relief to make our exit into a thankfully dry morning. My head clearer than it had been for days, I decided to drive, pleased to take the wheel once again. As soon as we were entrenched in Queen Anne Street, I started consulting my books, looking for an expert in the rare condition Holmes had uncovered. We were in luck, and before the hour was out, were sitting in the consulting room of Dr Gapton of Harley Place, the country's leading authority on *Myositis ossificans progressiva*. He was a thin fellow, dressed smartly in a stiff collar and tie, with the look of a man who spends too long in the library and not enough in the sun. I must admit that seeing him did bring a shudder, as his pallid complexion awoke memories of the encounter with our unnatural assailant at Abberton Hospital.

I described the bone that had been taken, and Gapton

nodded, inviting us into an adjacent room. It contained a library of medical tomes and, most strikingly, a full human skeleton, but one unlike any I had ever seen.

"This fellow suffered from M.O.P.," Gapton said, stepping aside to let us take a closer look. "I treated him myself and when he died he left his body to medical science."

The specimen was ghoulishly fascinating, and I had to remind myself to treat these human remains, like others, with the respect they deserved. The skeleton, hung in the traditional way, was twisted, its bone structure smothered in the same growths as we had seen on the clavicle. However, the mutation itself was more advanced. Where there should have been ribs, a gnarled armour plate was grafted to the contorted frame, while the jaw of the skull was similarly fused together. He must only have been able to take soup through a straw. Chewing would have been impossible.

"This is appalling," I said. "His life must have been unbearable."

"The condition is debilitating, yes, although, as I'm sure you must have discovered over the years, Dr Watson, the human spirit is more resilient than the flesh it inhabits. The men and women I treat, why, they are some of the bravest souls you could ever meet."

"Is there a cure?" Holmes asked, his voice impassive as always.

Gapton showed us back into his main consulting room. "I'm afraid not, which is the tragedy, especially as, in most cases, the condition first manifests in infancy."

"At what age?" I asked, taking my seat.

"I've seen children as young as five years old. Symptoms often appear following a trauma, a fall or some such." Gapton fetched a book from a shelf and joined us, sitting behind his desk. "There have been mentions of the disease since the late 1600s, although the first clear description was made by John Freke of the Royal Society nearly two hundred years ago." The doctor found the appropriate passage in his book and offered it to me. I skimmed the page, finding a passage dated the fourteenth of April 1740. I read it aloud to Holmes.

"*There came a boy of healthy look and fourteen years of age, to ask of us at The Hospital, what should be done to cure him of many large swellings on his back which began about three years since, and have continued to grow as large on many parts as a penny-loaf* – Good Lord – *particularly on the left side. They arise from all the vertebrae of the neck, and reach down to the os sacrum.*" I looked up from the book to offer Holmes an explanation. "That's a triangular bone at the base of the spine, part of the—"

"Pelvis, yes, I know," Holmes interrupted.

"Very well. *They likewise arise from every rib of his body, and joining together in all parts of his back, as the ramifications of coral do, they make, as it were, a fixed bony pair of bodice.*"

"It's as good a description as any that has been offered since," Gapton commented.

I nodded, recalling the misshapen skeleton in the other room.

"Two hundred years and we are no nearer a cure," I commented.

"Not for want of trying, I assure you."

I raised an appeasing hand. "It was no criticism, Doctor. I often feel that while we have achieved so much in the last century, performing medical feats that would once have had us either praised as miracle-workers or condemned as witches—"

"There is still much that we do not know, or seem able to combat. I agree, which is why I have dedicated my life to this particular curse." He gave Sherlock Holmes a good-natured smile. "You have your mysteries to solve, this is mine."

"An admirable attitude, Doctor," said Holmes. "So, these swellings; they are the first symptom?"

"Usually, although there are other indicators that a child may suffer from M.O.P."

"Such as?"

I jumped in, still consulting Gapton's book. "There's mention in this report of an abnormality in the toes."

"The toes?" echoed Holmes.

"Yes," replied Gapton. "Sufferers are often born with malformation of the great toe."

"It is stunted?" Holmes asked.

"Why, yes," Gapton responded. "With a valgus deformity."

"Meaning that the bone is twisted away from the body slightly."

"Quite so. The greater the deformity—"

"The greater the severity of the condition."

"I see you've been doing research of your own."

"So, every time that the child is injured…" Holmes prompted, ignoring the suggestion.

"The condition goes to work," Gapton replied. "Normally, the immune system rids us of infection, while broken bones knit back together, but with M.O.P., the body's response is amplified. The muscle itself ossifies, encasing the original skeleton at the point of injury."

"And the extraneous bone cannot be removed?" I asked.

Gapton shook his head. "Not without more growth. It's a vicious circle. Before long the patient's joints seize up, leaving him with restricted movement at best."

"And at worst?"

"Complete immobility."

Holmes leant back in his chair, considering his next question. "How many patients are you currently treating, Doctor?"

"Well, as you know, the condition is thankfully extremely rare, although I do have one on-going case, here in London."

"Would we be able to interview your patient?"

Gapton looked uncomfortable at the suggestion. "That might

not be possible, Mr Holmes. The family in question values their privacy, and are wary of their son becoming a curiosity."

"It is a boy then?"

The doctor's expression darkened. "Why do I have the impression that I'm being interrogated? I welcomed you into my surgery as I believed you were interested in my work, not my patients."

"We are interested in both," I cut in. "The case we are investigating is of national importance." For all I knew, my claim was not a complete lie. The fact that everyone had turned us away, from the Metropolitan Police to Holmes's own brother, suggested that we had stumbled upon something of political import. "If we can understand this terrible condition, then we may be able to find a connection."

"Between your case and the bone you discovered."

"Exactly. Dr Gapton, as one doctor to another..."

The doctor examined my face before coming to a conclusion. "Very well. I shall contact the family and see if they will meet with you, but if they want to keep out of whatever this is – and I warn you, I suspect they will – then I shall have to respect their wishes. As a doctor, I am sure you understand the importance of the Hippocratic Oath."

"*Whatever I may happen to obtain knowledge of, if it be not proper to repeat it—*"

"*—I will keep sacred and secret within my own breast,*" Gapton finished.

Handing back his book, I assured the doctor that we quite understood. Holmes himself apologised for any offence and thanked Dr Gapton from the bottom of his heart.

After a congenial farewell, we retired to my practice to await Dr Gapton's verdict. As Holmes perused my library for mentions of the abominable disease, I had a question of my own.

"Holmes, how did you know about the toes?"

"What's that, Watson?"

"When Gapton was describing the symptoms you knew about the irregularity of the toes before he mentioned it. What was it? Something you noticed on the skeleton?"

Holmes smiled, returning his attention to the book in his lap. "Not at all, Watson. I was merely thinking back to the footprint we found in the operating theatre."

"The one in the blood? The woman's?"

Holmes nodded. "Quite so. I am surprised you failed to notice yourself, Watson. Her toe was stunted."

CHAPTER TWENTY

ON THE TRAIL

I was curious when Holmes suggested that we lunch at Bourne & Hollingsworth on Oxford Street, rather than in any of the numerous eateries near Queen Anne Street. He claimed that the short walk would help clear his mind, and yet, as we made our way along Wigmore and then Wells Street, he talked non-stop, pointing out every scrap of trivia that seemed to be flowing through that incredible head of his. This was not his way. When in contemplation, Holmes would usually fall silent, discarding useless facts and obsessing over observations that lesser men would have dismissed as irrelevances. Yet today it was as if Holmes were incapable of stopping the words, as he babbled about everything and nothing. What was more, the man was positively dawdling. Again, I was used to having to stride after Holmes; today, he seemed content to dilly-dally, much to the annoyance of anyone trying to walk behind us.

Even when eating, Holmes took his time, picking over his lunch while regaling me with more stories about life on the South Coast than I had ever heard before, or indeed wanted to know. I was subjected to village tittle-tattle and gossip; the ins and outs of local quarrels; and even a full review of the ales on offer in every hostelry within a five-mile radius of Holmes's house.

As we meandered back along Oxford Street, turning up Holles Street to amble through Cavendish Street Gardens, I began to think that the great man was suffering a relapse. Sudden changes in personality often followed head injuries. Maybe Holmes's recovery was less complete than I had hoped.

However, as soon as we were back within the confines of my practice, Holmes thanked me.

"For what?" I asked.

"For letting me ramble on for the last hour."

"More like two," I remarked. "I've never known you walk so slowly. Are you feeling quite yourself?"

"Never more so, Watson. And I apologise. I would have told you that we were being observed, but I knew that you would have unwittingly given the game away."

"Observed? Over lunch?"

"From the moment we left this building, dear boy. And by professionals, too. I counted not one tail but four, working together. They were subtle, switching positions at regular intervals."

"So that's why you were all but crawling along the pavement."

Holmes laughed. "Perhaps I should have literally crawled to see what they would do, but yes. When being followed, one's natural response is to quicken one's pace, to see if one's pursuers do the same. However, I always find it is better to meander, stopping as often as possible. It is very hard to follow someone who insists on walking slowly, not without being noticed."

"And were they in the restaurant too?"

"The woman in the brown dress, with the silver brooch. Did you notice her?"

"I can't say I did."

"Because your eye was taken by the lady in the red hat, as it was supposed to be. When our woman in brown picked us up on the corner of Great Titchfield Street, her outfit was hidden beneath a long black coat, which she had swapped for a navy-blue tunic by the time she entered the restaurant. Another sign that we are dealing with professionals: the changing of outer garments to confuse their quarry. Hats and coats are easily substituted; shoes, on the other hand, are not."

"And she wore the same shoes?"

"She did. Patent leather with a velvet top and a military heel. A style neither in vogue nor noticeably unfashionable. The perfect camouflage. Indeed, when she passed us in Cavendish Street Gardens, she had changed into a moss-green coat and matching hat—"

"And yet was wearing the same shoes."

"You're learning."

"So who were they?"

"Government I would say, rather than gangland, by the sophistication of the surveillance. No doubt the work of brother Mycroft, keeping tabs on his errant sibling."

"Then they would have seen us visit Dr Gapton this morning?"

"More than likely. I wonder if he is suddenly going to take a well-earned holiday?"

An appalling thought struck me. "You don't suppose they'll do anything to him, do you?"

Holmes dismissed my fear with a shake of his head. "Other than apply a little pressure, I doubt it. Or, at least, so I hope."

It was with a certain amount of relief that I received a telephone call from the doctor himself within the hour. He had contacted the family of his patient – the Sellmans of Hampstead – who had, to Gapton's surprise, agreed to see us. He passed on their address and telephone number, and impressed upon me that he did not wish to see the Sellmans inconvenienced in any way.

I assured him that we would treat them with the utmost respect, which he said that he believed in *my* case, and thanked him once again before returning the receiver to the cradle.

"So, I shall be driving to Hampstead this afternoon?" I enquired.

"Tomorrow, Watson. Let the hounds' trails grow cold, for tonight at least. We shall telephone the Sellmans from your house, as if we have nothing to hide."

"Which we don't!" I insisted.

"No, but others obviously do."

CHAPTER TWENTY-ONE

A HOUSE CALL

The following morning Holmes suggested that we take the tube to Hampstead, saying that public transport would offer a better chance to spot anyone on our tail. Now I realised why he had omitted to share his suspicions with me the day before. It was all I could do not to glance furtively over my shoulder at every turn.

As it was, I was convinced that I spotted the same car pass us on three occasions.

"Head forward," Holmes instructed as we descended to the platform. "Eyes ahead. You let me worry about our friends on the streets."

"So we're being followed again?"

"A bearded gentleman with a bowler and umbrella, a woman walking her dog and a fellow with a cloth cap."

"A cloth cap?" My mind immediately threw up an image of the sadistic visitors to my surgery two days previously.

"Do not concern yourself, Watson. There wasn't a bushy moustache in sight, and neither did he match the description of your bowtie-wearing assailant, Mr Burns."

"Are any on the station now?"

Holmes made a show of consulting the train timetable.

"On the platform opposite. The lady's canine companion seems to have slipped its leash. I do hope she is not too upset, although the way she is reading the latest edition of *The Gentlewoman* would indicate that she has not even noticed."

Knowing full well that I shouldn't, I turned to examine the opposite platform as nonchalantly as I could. There was the woman Holmes described, studying her periodical on a bench with an intensity I am sure I would have failed to notice had not my senses been heightened.

"I'm assuming she's not alone," I asked, careful not to turn as soon as I spotted her.

"No. Our friend in the bowler hat is at the end of the platform, although this time I suggest you trust me in the matter and avoid looking yourself."

Casually swinging his umbrella, Holmes led me down the platform towards the exit, and I thought we were going to leave when a sudden rush of air from the tunnel's entrance told me that a train was approaching. The train came to a halt and we stepped on board, Holmes whispering to me not to make myself comfortable. I knew immediately what he had planned. Checking that the individual wearing the bowler hat had also boarded a carriage, Holmes waited for the last moment before he grabbed the door and jumped from the already moving train. I followed suit, nearly losing my footing before chasing after him as he charged back up the stairs to the station entrance. I dared not glance back to see if bowler hat had followed us back out onto the platform, but spotted the woman who had been reading the magazine already outside the station. Holmes did not hesitate, even as a taxi rolled up beside us without being hailed and my friend opened the door.

"Holmes, this could be—"

"Get in, Watson."

I did as he insisted and soon we were being whisked away down the street.

"Good morning, Doctor," said the driver, touching a finger to his cap.

"Good Lord. Geller, is that you?"

The former Irregular, with the same squirrel-like cheeks and flattened nose I remembered from when he was a child, smiled back at me in the rear-view mirror.

"The very same. Good to see that you two are in as much strife as ever."

"I hope you don't mind, Watson, but I made use of your telephone before you awoke this morning to contact Geller."

"It was you who shadowed us on the way to the station?"

"Just following Mr Holmes's instructions, same as always."

"So you planned the whole thing?"

Holmes allowed himself a smile. "I have no doubt that agents will be awaiting us at our destination, just as they already know where we are going."

"Then why all that tomfoolery at the station? We could have broken our necks jumping off that train."

"He wanted to send a message, didn't you, Mr Holmes?"

"Quite right, Geller. If my brother knows that I am on to his cloak and dagger antics, it may force his hand. If he wants to stop us in our enquiries, then let him arrest us."

"I would rather he didn't," I insisted.

"And I would like to know what crime we would be charged with. Fleeing a hospital bed? Visiting an innocent family in their home?"

"If they're still there," I suggested, thinking of everyone else who had already disappeared.

However, as we drove up to the Sellmans' impressive house on East Heath Road, there was a light on in an upstairs bedroom.

"At least someone is at home," Holmes commented, thrusting some coins into Geller's hand.

"Shall I wait for you, Mr Holmes?" the cabbie said.

"If it's no trouble."

"None at all. I'll park on Well Walk. Just whistle and I'll come running. Well, driving anyway."

With a friendly wave, Geller drove off, leaving us alone. At least I thought we were alone. The street was deserted in both directions.

"Mycroft must be slipping," Holmes said, starting up the path to the Sellmans' front door.

"Or he has agents waiting for us inside," said I.

"You have a suspicious mind, Watson."

"Can you blame me?"

The Sellmans' house dated from the 1700s if my layman's eye could be trusted. Ivy clung around the bay windows, a small balcony having been added above the front door in recent years. While their home was less grand than either of its redbrick neighbours, the Sellmans must have been no strangers to money to reside in the village, especially these days. Since the turn of the century, the Heath had been highly favoured as a place to live. Even my wife, before settling on Chelsea, had toyed with the idea of relocating to these leafy avenues.

Reaching the threshold, Holmes rang the bell. Before long the door was opened by a woman with an austere expression and greying hair swept up in a monumental bun that was perched on her head as if gravity were a mere inconvenience. She wore a long black dress, buttoned to the neck; a pair of pince-nez gripped the bridge of her straight-edged nose, the safety chain attached to a discreet loop around her left ear.

"Can I help?" she asked, her Irish accent considerably softer than her countenance.

"Mr Holmes and Dr Watson to see Mr Sellman," my companion

announced, drawing a nod from the household's sentinel.

"Ah yes, the gentlemen who telephoned." The flare in her nostrils when she uttered that last word betrayed her evident belief that no man of honour would ever use such a device. "Please, come in."

She held the door open and we entered a bright, airy hallway, the walls positively plastered with watercolours.

"If you will wait in the drawing room," she said, showing us to another room filled with paintings, "I shall inform Mr Sellman that you have arrived."

"A housekeeper?" I asked as she left the room.

"Governess," Holmes replied, "if the smudges of chalk on her dress are anything to go by. And there was a book with similar marks on the hall table. *Ray's New Primary Arithmetic for Young Learners*. Obviously, the lady placed it there before opening the door to us. The housekeeper must be unwell. A governess does not expect her duties to include the answering of doors."

Whatever her station, the woman returned with a tall, handsome man in his mid-thirties. His hair was smartly parted and he wore a waxed moustache, every inch the modern man about town.

"These are the gentlemen," the governess said curtly. "Shall I have the maid bring tea?"

"Gentlemen?" our host enquired, turning the question to us.

"That would be perfect," replied Holmes. "Anything but lapsang souchong. I'm afraid I cannot abide the stuff."

The look on the woman's face told me that he would get what he was given.

"Mr Holmes and Dr Watson," the man said, crossing and shaking our hands when the governess had vacated the room. "It is good to meet you. We were so grateful to hear that you wanted to visit. Please, please take a seat."

"Mr Sellman?" I enquired.

"Yes, yes, of course. Forgive me. I'm afraid I have had quite a trying morning. My wife hoped to be here to greet you, but she has been staying with her mother for a few days. We are expecting her any minute, and so I stayed home from work in her absence and have been fielding phone calls for the last few hours."

"Trouble at the bank?" Holmes asked.

Sellman looked at him in astonishment. "Why, yes, but how on earth did you know that I am a banker? Does it show?"

"Only by the cut of your suit. I have read how the next generation of financiers have taken to wearing a narrow pinstripe, rather than the more traditional black attire of their forebears. Then there are your cufflinks, with their rather striking representation of a unicorn surrounded by coins. The symbol of the Gilmour and Buchanan Bank, is it not?"

Sellman chuckled, fingering his cufflinks. "A gift from my former manager when he retired."

"And you took his place, judging by their age. Passing the torch, as it were."

"Your reputation is well deserved, it seems," Sellman said, as a maid brought in a tea tray. Sellman thanked her and waited for our cups to be filled. "So, Dr Gapton said you are interested in our son, or at least in his condition."

Holmes nodded. "We are trying to understand the disease, in order to help us with a case."

A shadow passed over our host's pleasant features. "He has already suffered greatly, my poor child. Sometimes I wonder whether it would be better if we did not know what was to come, and yet the prognosis hangs over this house like a shroud."

A squeak in the hallway stopped Sellman before he could explain further. I looked up, to see a young boy of no more than eleven being pushed into the drawing room by the governess. The lad was confined to a wheelchair, his body twisted where he sat. His right shoulder jutted forward at an extreme angle, the left was permanently tucked behind his back. A lump the size of an apple projected from his thin neck, stretching against the skin, and his head was cocked to the side; he was presumably unable to move it. Despite the ravages visited upon his body, the boy gave us such a winning smile as he was trundled into the room that my heart broke in an instant. Gapton had talked of bravery, and here it was, personified in this unfortunate young fellow.

"Ah, that damned squeak," Sellman said, rising to greet his son. "It drives poor Frederick to distraction, doesn't it, no matter how much oil we apply."

"Yes, father," the lad replied, laughing. I saw something glint in his hand, something metal.

"That will be all, thank you, Miss Wilkins," Sellman said to the governess, who took her leave. Our host pushed Frederick nearer and introduced us.

"I have read your stories," the boy said. "I have some upstairs."

"Then we shall be sure to have Watson sign them for you," Holmes promised.

"And you too, sir?"

Holmes smiled warmly. "With pleasure." His eyes fell upon Frederick's hands. "What have you there?"

The boy beamed, revealing a small golden cube, no bigger than a matchbox. "It's clockwork," he said. "Shall I show you?"

"Please," Holmes urged.

Holding the cube in one hand, Frederick turned a tiny key with the other. It was impossible not to notice how gnarled his knuckles were, like those of an old man.

The key wound to its limit, Frederick worked a tiny lever and a sweet tune played out, a sea shanty that I half-remembered from my youth.

"It's a music box," I exclaimed, enchanted by the delicate melody.

"And that's not all," said the lad. "Look."

As we watched, a miniature sailing ship appeared through a slit in the top of the box, rolling and pitching in time with the music.

Mr Sellman smiled. "Clockwork automata are something of a passion of Freddie's," he explained. "You should see his room, full to the brim with drumming monkeys, flying angels and goodness knows what else."

"Aunt Elsbeth buys them for me," Frederick informed us. "Wherever she goes, she always brings one back for me. I got a unicorn last time. It gallops."

"I should like to see that," said Holmes.

"I can show you," said Frederick, eagerly.

"Perhaps later. First, I should like to ask you a few questions about your condition, if that is all right with you?"

The light went out of the boy's eyes, but he nodded politely, and Holmes began a gentle interrogation, discovering more about the onset of Frederick's disorder. It was a similar tale to that we had heard in Dr Gapton's consulting room. Frederick had fallen down the stairs as an infant, only to have his leg freeze as the damaged knee fused. Now, the boy's life was one of near constant pain, although one would never have known it from the young chap's demeanour. He was polite and courteous, which only made his plight all the more distressing.

However, I was unsure how the interview was going to help our investigation. Holmes questioned the father, asking him if anyone else had approached them, perhaps someone studying the condition.

Sellman shook his head. "Not that I am aware of, although I must say that unfortunately my work has kept me away from home. I'm trying to make amends for that, aren't I, Freddie?" He smiled sadly at his son, and I gained the impression that the man would have loved to reach out and ruffle the boy's hair, but was worried what the touch would do to the lad, how much pain it would bring. What a curse it must be to be afraid to embrace your own child. Even I, a childless man, could appreciate the torment that would bring.

All at once, there was a flurry of activity from the hallway. The front door had been flung open and a woman entered, wearing a navy-blue jacket and long gored skirt. She quickly removed a wide-brimmed hat, dropping a hairpin in her haste, and rushed into the drawing room, her face flushed. It was obvious that the lady had been running.

We all rose, Sellman smiling broadly at the new arrival. "Ah, you made it, my dear. Gentlemen, may I introduce my wife, Camille."

"Mr Holmes," Camille Sellman said, heading straight for my friend. "Thank you so much for coming. The good Lord has answered my prayers. I knew he would."

Even Holmes looked taken aback. "Madam, I thank you for making every effort to return from Reading this morning, but I am uncertain why you would think I am an answer to prayer."

"An answer to prayer or serendipity, I do not care which, as long as you say you will help us."

"In what way?" I asked. Surely this eager creature didn't believe that Holmes could unlock the mystery of young Frederick's condition, no matter how remarkable my friend's abilities were. With all due respect to Holmes, this was work for a doctor, not a detective.

"My sister, Elsbeth."

"Frederick's aunt?"

"Yes. She went missing, a year ago. Completely vanished, without a word."

Holmes urged Mrs Sellman to take a seat, his interest immediately aroused. "And you have informed the police?"

"Of course we have." The lady caught herself. "I do not mean to be rude, Mr Holmes, but I have been beside myself these last twelve months. To be honest, I had given up all hope. The police were next to useless."

"Camille," her husband warned.

"Oh, they were sympathetic, of course, and tried their best, I'm sure."

"But they found nothing," Holmes remarked. It was not a question.

"I was told that Elsbeth might never be found, that I should prepare myself for the worst."

Holmes looked grave. "My dear Mrs Sellman, while I sympathise, I'm afraid I am not taking on any new cases at present. My current investigation—"

She interrupted, talking over him in her agitated state. "No, no, you don't understand. I saw her, Mr Holmes. Just last week, in town. I was out shopping, and there she was, walking down Oxford Street."

"If that is the case," said I, "why would you need our help?"

"She is in trouble, Dr Watson. I know she is."

Her voice cracked, and Sellman took up his wife's story. "Camille confronted Elsbeth, on the street, asking her where she had been."

"And what was her response?" Holmes asked, unable to resist.

"She would tell me nothing," Mrs Sellman said. "I have never seen her like it, so drawn and distant. I took her for tea, tried to persuade her to speak openly, but still she remained unforthcoming. Then, just as I thought we were making some progress, when Elsbeth seemed to have relaxed a little, she shot up, staring out of the window of the tea room in horror. Before I could stop her, she ran out into the street, knocking the crockery from the table in her flight. There was a terrible fuss and when I myself got outside she was gone."

"Whatever had she seen?" I asked, captivated by the tale.

"A giant of man," came the reply. "Standing on the pavement outside, positively glaring through the window."

"A giant?" repeated Holmes. "Can you describe him?"

"Mr Holmes, I shall remember that face for as long as I live. Long, dark hair covered most of his aspect, and yet the scars were clear."

"Scars?"

"They crossed his face like roads on a map; deep, deep scars, and his skin, so pale. Like a corpse."

"My dear," Sellman said, leaning across to touch his wife's hand. "Please, think of Freddie."

Mrs Sellman ignored her husband, pulling her hand away. I gained the impression that this was a conversation that had played out many times in the last week. "I can only explain what I saw, George."

"And tell me, Mrs Sellman," Holmes said, his voice level, although I would wager that his heart was racing within his chest. "Tell me of this giant's eyes."

The lady looked at my friend with fresh intensity. "They weren't human, Mr Holmes. They burned yellow, like the sun."

CHAPTER TWENTY-TWO

ALL IN A NAME

"You know him, don't you, Mr Holmes?" Sellman asked. "You recognise the giant that Camille saw."

I looked to Holmes, my blood chilled. His eyes were still on our hostess, and he chose to ignore Sellman's question in favour of one of his own.

"What happened to the man? Did he follow your sister?"

Mrs Sellman's face was full of renewed hope. "I do not know. As I said, there was confusion in the tea room. The waitress was bustling about, trying to clear up the mess Elsbeth had made; the manager was asking what had happened, whether anything was wrong. He blocked my view of the window and I am ashamed to say I rather pushed the poor man aside. I doubt I will be welcome there again. Either way, the giant was gone."

"And your sister?"

"Likewise. There was no sign of either of them in the street outside."

"Do you have a picture of Elsbeth?" I asked.

"Of course." Mrs Sellman rose and crossed to the mantelpiece to fetch a photograph in an ornate silver frame. She passed it to me. The picture was of a striking woman, a few years older than our hostess, with dark hair in the popular pompadour style, swept up into a tight bun on her crown. There was a pretty lace collar at her throat, fastened with a brooch, a detail which Holmes immediately seized upon.

"A fascinating design," he said, taking the photograph from me.

"She was wearing it when we met last week," Mrs Sellman interjected. "I believe it was a present from our grandmother, Heilwig."

"A German name," Holmes commented.

"Swiss. My family were originally from Geneva."

"On your mother's side or your father's?"

"My father's. Klaus Honegger."

Holmes showed me the photograph once again. "On the brooch, Watson, at its centre. Some kind of bird, do you think?"

"A crow," Mrs Sellman confirmed. "Is it important?"

"Everything is important, if the right questions are asked."

"And what are the right questions, Mr Holmes?"

"Was your sister married?"

"No, never. There was a man when we were younger, a scientist like herself."

"She has always been a bit of a loner, from what I could tell," Sellman added.

"But she loved her family," his wife countered, a little defensively. "Yes, she may never have settled down or had children of her own, but she is devoted to Frederick, and used to spend as much time here as possible, when her work allowed."

"Her work? You say she is a scientist?"

"A biologist. She went to Newnham College at Cambridge." Mrs Sellman's pride in her sister was obvious. "Caused quite a stir in the family, a young woman striking out in a man's world. Mother was nervous about the entire venture, but Father encouraged her. We thought at one point that she would become a medical doctor, but she became fascinated with…" She sighed, struggling to find the word.

"Genetics," her husband supplied.

"That's right. Genetics and heredity. It was all she could speak about."

"Heredity," Holmes confirmed. "The passing of traits from one generation to the next."

"It was a particular hobby-horse of her tutor," Sellman said. "William something or other, and she converted to his cause."

"William Bateson?" Holmes enquired.

"That's it, yes," Mrs Sellman replied. "Elsbeth was devoted to him and his teaching. One could almost say besotted."

"Romantically? You mentioned that she once had a suitor."

"Oh no, Mr Bateson is much older, and happily married. His wife, Beatrice, took Elsbeth under her wing. I met them both once or twice. A charming couple."

Holmes turned to me. "William Bateson, a proponent of the ideas of Gregor Mendel. I read a paper of his a few years back: 'Genetic Inheritance and the Saltationary Nature of Evolution'. Quite fascinating. In fact, I have carried out a number of experiments based on his findings." He turned back to our hosts. "I keep bees," he added, answering their unasked question.

It was typical of Holmes to assume that I was ignorant of the man's identity. On the contrary I was familiar with Bateson, whose theories had caused a stir throughout the scientific and medical community. He had challenged Darwin's belief that evolution took place through tiny, advantageous variations, insisting that species developed in great leaps and bounds, changes which could be affected by specific breeding choices. It was obvious why Elsbeth Honegger had been drawn to them, a supposition that

Mrs Sellman confirmed in her next sentence.

"Elsbeth became convinced that Mr Bateson's theories offered hope for Frederick and those like him." She offered her son an encouraging, if sad, smile. "I found it hard to keep up with her. On leaving Cambridge, she travelled Europe, researching his condition."

"So when you said that she had been missing for a year..." Holmes pointed out.

"She always told us where she was going. Always wrote when she arrived. Most of her letters I could barely follow, let alone understand. I am afraid I share little of my sister's interest in academia."

"And this time, there was no warning that she was off on her travels?" I asked.

"None whatsoever. She had just come home from a visit to France and we were planning a holiday together, George, myself, Frederick and Elsbeth. It was late May, and we were due to meet to discuss the final details, but she never came. I tried to contact her, and there was nothing. No one knew where she was, or what she was doing."

"And she had seemed well on her return from France?"

"She was drained, utterly exhausted, which is why I had suggested the holiday in the first place. I hadn't wanted her to go to France, what with the war, but she insisted. 'Cammy,' she said, 'science doesn't stop because men decide to blow chunks out of each other.'"

"And she is correct. If anything, war stimulates scientific discovery, for good or ill. Do you have Elsbeth's letters?"

"Of course. I would be happy for you to see them, along with anything else you may need."

"Do you have any of her research papers?"

"I'm afraid not. When in England she kept lodgings on Chalton Street, near the British Library. It was the first place I looked, but she had paid her rent until the end of the month and moved out."

"And that was not her way?"

"No. She kept her rooms whenever she travelled. She'd been there since Cambridge. In fact, I think it was Mrs Bateson who informed Elsbeth of their availability. A friend of the family."

"What of her belongings?"

"Cleared out. Her clothes, her books, even her scientific equipment."

"Except for the painting," Mr Sellman added.

"The painting?"

"Another of Elsbeth's prized possessions," Mrs Sellman replied. "A family heirloom. It was still hanging on the wall after she left. I can't believe she would not have taken it with her."

"Indicating that even though she had settled her rent, she was in something of a hurry. Do you have the painting?"

Mrs Sellman rose from her seat. "I've had it hanging in our bedroom. Poor George is not fond of it—"

"But it helped Camille feel close to Elsbeth," the husband said kindly.

Our hostess left the room, and when she returned she had in her hands not only a packet of her sister's letters – which she placed in Holmes's keeping – but also the painting.

It was of medium size, roughly sixteen inches by twenty, and framed in a simple wood surround; Elsbeth Honegger was not one for 'frills', it seemed. The article itself was a pleasant, if unexceptional, oil painting of a large house, dated, Holmes estimated, around the mid to late eighteenth century. It was of little merit, and I could see why Mr Sellman would struggle to come to love it, divorced as he was from the sentimental value his wife placed upon the picture.

"A Swiss country estate," Holmes concluded. "Your family's ancestral seat?"

"Nothing so grand, I'm afraid," Mrs Sellman said, with the slightest of laughs, the first mirth we had witnessed in the woman since her arrival.

"Well, it certainly cannot be described as a shack. Twelve windows at the front and surrounded by substantial gardens. There was money in this house."

"Holmes," I said. "There's no need to be vulgar."

"No, Mr Holmes is correct. We do not know for sure, but Elsbeth always believed it was situated near Geneva. It's hard to tell. We know so little about our ancestors."

"Even as recently as the 1700s, relatively speaking."

"Our only link was Grandmamma, and she never spoke much of life before she came to England. I think there was a family rift, some kind of feud. She had very little to connect her to the past."

"Save for a brooch and this painting, both of which ended up the property of your sister."

"She always wanted to know where we came from."

"As a student of heredity, I am not surprised. Tell me, did your grandmother ever discuss your family's medical history?"

"As I said, she regarded our past as a closed book."

"But with young Frederick in mind, you must have been at least curious. Have there been any other cases of his condition in your family?"

"My great-uncle, Grandmamma's brother. He was said to have suffered from a severe rheumatism, even at a young age."

"Symptoms that could have been those of *Myositis ossificans progressiva*?"

Mrs Sellman glanced at her son. "That's what Elsbeth always believed."

Holmes afforded the young boy a smile. "You're being very patient, Master Sellman, having the adults talk about you as if you are not here."

"I'm used to it, sir," came the reply, with a touch more melancholy than an eleven-year-old boy should ever portray.

"He's a good boy," said his father.

Holmes returned his attention to the painting, commented on the brushwork, even sniffing it as if he might learn something about the paint from smell alone. Then he focused on the bottom right hand corner of the canvas, turning the frame towards the light of the bay windows.

"The artist's name," said he. "It has been purposely obscured. Here, Watson, you can see the ghost of the signature."

I took a closer look. "Yes. Painted over."

"Do you know which of your ancestors painted it?" Holmes asked Mrs Sellman.

"I'm afraid not. If Grandmamma knew, she never told us, although I do remember the name Joshua being mentioned, so that could have been the artist's name."

"Hebrew rather than Norse in origin. I suppose that is a possibility. May I borrow this, Mrs Sellman?"

Our hostess frowned. "The painting?"

"I realise its value to you, and will guard it as if it were by Michelangelo or Da Vinci."

"To Elsbeth, it is worth more than all their works combined."

"Which is exactly why it may yet unlock both our mystery and your own."

"You think the two cases are linked?" asked Mr Sellman.

"There is no doubt about it. The man you described. Frederick's condition. Our paths are intertwined."

"And you can find her?" Mrs Sellman asked, her expression achingly hopeful.

"I can and I will," my friend promised, and was rewarded by such a smile from our hostess that I half fancied she was going to throw her arms around him. She controlled the impulse, much to his relief I am sure. While Holmes could be as gallant as any soul I knew, and possessed as great a heart as he did a brain, his interactions with the fairer sex often resembled an anthropologist studying a distant and unfathomable tribe.

Holmes had one last question before we made our goodbyes. "Mrs Sellman," he said, "without prying too closely, did your sister suffer from a malformation of the great toe, one in keeping with Frederick's condition?"

Mrs Sellman flushed, but nodded her head. "We both do, Mr Holmes, as do all on our side of the family. It was one of the reasons that Elsbeth gave herself to her particular branch of science. She always believed that the key to Frederick's fate was to be found in our blood."

CHAPTER TWENTY-THREE

TWO OLD FOOLS

Found in the blood.

The phrase haunted me, even as Geller drove us back to Chelsea. A footprint, with a deformed toe, in dried blood.

A word also kept coming back from the conversation of the previous hour. Serendipity. I mentioned it to Holmes, commenting how peculiar it was to have been led from one investigation to another.

"Not so, Watson," came his reply. "Mysteries beget mysteries. And besides, you read it yourself: *Myositis ossificans progressiva* affects just one in every two million. A blighted bone discovered in an operating theatre, and only one family in London suffering from the same malady? If there had been no connection, I would have been amazed."

"And so, this missing woman—"

"Elsbeth Honegger. Precision is the life-blood of deduction, Watson."

"This missing Elsbeth, then. She was the woman in the hospital?"

"Yes, there can be little doubt that Miss Honegger was present when the operation, whatever it was, took place."

"Attempting to find a cure for her nephew's plight?"

"A distinct possibility, although why would she feel compelled to do so in such squalor and secrecy? She is a graduate of Cambridge, with an influential mentor. That's what makes no sense, Watson, that's the gap in her story that needs plugging."

"Just the one, eh?"

"The first of many, if you insist on splitting hairs, Doctor."

"Precision is the life-blood of deduction, Holmes."

"Touché."

"And then there's the giant."

"Most probably the man who nearly sent us both to early graves."

"Could he have been the other occupant of Abberton Hospital?"

"I think not. A man that size would require larger feet than even the mismatched footprints at the hospital suggest, but they obviously knew each other, the fiend and Miss Honegger."

"So what now?"

"Now, Geller takes you home, where I leave you with Miss Honegger's letters to study."

"And what about you? You're not still thinking about checking into some damned hotel?"

"Perish the thought. First things first. Geller is going to attempt to lose the Morris Bullnose that picked us up on Christchurch Hill."

"The what?" I went to turn in my seat, but was stopped by a restraining hand on my arm.

"Please, do not look, Watson. Give our shadows the professional courtesy of allowing them to believe that we are unaware of their presence."

"You think you can lose them?" I asked our driver.

"'Course I can," Geller replied with a grin. "I know roads that haven't even made it onto the maps, don't I? Piece of the proverbial."

"If you say so, but if you're not heading for the Goring, where will you go, Holmes?"

"The National Gallery. Do you remember Albus Woodbead?"

"The art historian who helped us with the case of the banshee's portrait."

"The very same. I helped retrieve a pair of Hungarian miniatures a couple of years ago. Quite extraordinary likenesses. He owes me a favour—"

"Which you hope to cash in with that painting."

Holmes patted the wooden frame. "I shall return this afternoon, and you can enlighten me as to the contents of the letters." He pushed the bundle of envelopes into my hand. "And here we are, Cheyne Walk."

The drive had taken nearly forty minutes, although I was pleased to see that, when I alighted onto the pavement, no Morris was parked on the other side of the road. Of course, if the car had been following us, and I had no reason to doubt Holmes, it could simply have been waiting on the corner of Lawrence Street, ready for Geller to drive on to the Embankment.

Still, I kept up appearances and strolled across the road as Geller drove away, fishing out my keys to open the door.

To my shame, I had given barely a thought to my wife all morning, but as I stepped into the hall, I wondered if she had already left for her sister's. The sound of her singing in the kitchen told me otherwise.

"My love?" I said, depositing my hat on its hook and the stack of letters on the hall stand. I found Mrs Watson pounding dough on the kitchen table, an act that I knew she only performed when she was nervous. After all, we had a cook for such business.

She was kneading with such fury, despite her cheery song, that I couldn't help but wonder who the dough represented in her mind.

"Hello John," she said, her nose smudged with flour. "I thought you and Sherlock would like some fresh bread for breakfast tomorrow."

Stepping into the kitchen, I took off my coat and draped it over the back of one of the chairs. "That would be lovely, but I thought—"

"That you would be rid of me?" she asked.

"Not at all, but you said—"

"That I was going to visit my sister." I would have given the world for her to stop ending my sentences for me. "Yes, that's exactly what I said, but I was angry with you. Furious."

"So I noticed."

Testing the elasticity of the dough, she transferred it into a large bowl and covered it with a cloth. "I don't understand this life of yours, John," she said with her back to me. "I never will. I'm not like Mary."

The mention of my first wife stung in a way I hoped was not deliberate.

"But like her, I knew what I was getting when I walked up that aisle. Sherlock Holmes is more a part of your life than I'll ever be."

"That's not true."

She turned and faced me with eyes that were neither sad nor accusatory. "He is you, John, and you are he. Two sides of the same coin. I used to think that he needed you, to centre him, to make him human, but it works both ways. You need him to make you feel alive, whether it's through reliving past glories, or creating new ones in burning houses."

I considered pointing out that the site of the conflagration had been a hospital, but was all too aware of the rolling pin that lay within her reach.

"But you need me as well, so you don't lose yourself completely."

"Lose myself?"

"The side of you that sits by the fire reading your books; listening to Gilbert and Sullivan on the phonograph. The side of you that comes home when the adventuring is done. That is, if you don't want to lose yourself, if none of that matters?"

At that moment, it felt that my heart was fit to burst.

"I'm sorry," I said. "I realise that all this has been difficult. When I invited Holmes to stay, I never dreamt that we would find ourselves so entrenched in a mystery again, save for which opera to see next."

"Then you are a fool, John Watson, and it's a good job that I love you."

I felt my cheeks burn. There was enough of the Victorian left in me to shy away from such declarations of affection. Fortunately, my wife saved me from further embarrassment.

"Now, while I clear up, why don't you solve the mystery of how to boil a kettle, and then you can tell me what's been happening over a cup of tea. No doubt you've already given this one a title. The Adventure of the Two Old Fools?"

I smiled, wishing that the facts of the case were half as light-hearted as my wife's gentle teasing.

CHAPTER TWENTY-FOUR

INTO THE DEN

Before I knew it, the afternoon had given way to evening and then to night. I sat in my study reading the neat handwriting of Elsbeth Honegger, trying not to think about the fact that Holmes had not yet returned. Eleven o'clock had come and gone. Where was the man?

The grandfather clock in the hallway, a relic of our time in Baker Street, chimed the half hour and, almost as if the person responsible had been waiting for such a cue, there came a rap at the door. Pulling my gown tight around me, I made my way to the door to find on my doorstep a London cabbie. I didn't know the man, who was dressed in a rather threadbare three-piece suit and was in dire need of a shave, but he knew me.

"Dr Watson," he croaked, his voice a hoarse whisper. "You need to come with me."

"I beg your pardon?"

"Geller sent me, sir. It's your friend."

"Holmes? What's happened?"

"I don't know. I'm only doing Geller a favour. Driving his cab, aren't I?"

Sure enough, Geller's automobile was parked in front of my house.

I hesitated, just for a moment. Could I trust this fellow? Days of being threatened, snubbed and followed had already shredded my nerves – but if Holmes was hurt? It might be a trap, but I had no choice but to take the bait.

Swearing softly beneath my breath, I told the driver to wait in the cab and rushed back into the house. Grabbing my doctor's bag, cane and coat, I hurried outside again. In a few short moments we were on our way.

"Where are we going?"

"Holborn."

"What's Holmes doing there?"

"'Fraid I can't tell you, sir. I really don't know anything about it. Geller just said to get you."

"What's your name? Do you know Holmes?"

"Harkness, sir. And no, I've never had the pleasure."

We fell into an uncomfortable silence, and sitting in the back of Geller's cab I gripped my cane as if my life depended on it. Perhaps it would at any minute. I kept imagining this Harkness screeching to a halt, the door opening and hands reaching in to pull me from the vehicle. The journey seemed to stretch on for ever, even though the streets were empty. Still, we had arrived at our destination by ten to midnight, turning off Eagle Street into a narrow lane. The driver stopped the car outside a bookbinding establishment that appeared to have seen better days, and stepped out, opening my door.

Cautiously, I climbed out of the car, regarding him with suspicion. My distrust must have been obvious.

"Don't worry, sir. You're quite safe. Well, as much as you can be after everything that's happened."

"I thought you knew nothing."

At least the fellow had the decency to blush slightly. "Sorry, sir. I'm just doing what Geller said. You'll understand."

Now I was convinced that I was walking into a trap. I considered bashing the damned fellow around the head with my cane and making a run for it, but the nagging doubt that Holmes might really be near kept me from fleeing. I looked around. A solitary gas lamp illuminated a pavement strewn with rubbish, discarded newspapers blowing over broken crates. No wonder the bookbinders looked to be on its uppers. Who in his right mind would venture down here?

Who indeed.

"So, where do I go?" I asked.

"This way," said the cabbie, leading me towards a narrow alleyway alongside the bookbinders.

Into the lion's den, John, I thought to myself and, steeling myself for attack, followed, my grip on my bag tightening. It was hefty enough that if I took a swing at a chap's head I could probably do some damage. There was in addition the ace up my sleeve, or more accurately in my coat pocket; my service revolver, recovered quickly from my study desk before I left the house.

I stepped into the shadows, following Harkness to a side door. He knocked once, and then twice more. There was another pause, and then four sharp raps. A code. A minute later came the sound of footsteps and a bolt was thrown. The door opened, not exactly flooding the alleyway in light, but chasing at least some shadows away with the flickering glow of a gas lamp.

Harkness stepped back, indicating that I should enter. Holding my breath, I stepped forward. A large figure was waiting to greet me.

"Oh, thank the Lord," I exclaimed, finally allowing myself to breathe. It was Geller, standing in the hallway. Harkness had been telling the truth.

"Quick, Doctor, he's upstairs."

"Holmes?"

"He's been asking for you."

I didn't wait for Geller to show me the way. I ascended the creaking stairs. The walls were bare and the entire place reeked of damp. My chest tightened. Why would Holmes come here? What had happened?

On the landing were two doors.

"The one to the right, Doctor," instructed Geller, coming up behind me. Harkness stayed at the bottom of the stairs, lighting a cigarette.

I gripped the door handle and, finding it unlocked, pushed my way into the room.

"Ah, there you are."

The room was bare, save for a poor excuse of a table, on which sat a bowl of water and a pile of bloodstained rags. Sitting on an equally unsteady chair was Sherlock Holmes. His jacket was gone and his shirt collar was undone; there was a dark red stain on his chest from the blood that had dripped from a laceration on his cheek.

"Good Lord, man, what has happened?" I said, rushing over to examine the wound. There were no other chairs, so I was forced to stand over him, gently taking his chin in my thumb and forefinger to angle it away from me. Close up, his injury was less severe than it had first appeared; nothing more than a deep graze across those sharp cheekbones, although it needed to be thoroughly cleaned before it turned septic.

"A minor inconvenience," Holmes said, swatting my hand away. "Nothing more."

I rested my medical bag on the table, which wobbled precariously, slopping dirty water over the side of the bowl.

"Minor? You left for the gallery hours ago, and that's not to mention all this." I indicated Geller, who was standing by the still open door, maintaining a respectful silence. "What is this place? One of your boltholes?"

"It is, although I am aware it hardly reaches the standards to which a Harley Street doctor is accustomed."

I poured disinfectant onto a ball of cotton wool. "I'm a Queen Anne Street doctor," I reminded him. "And we can discuss the conditions of your hovel after you tell me what really happened."

Before he could respond, I pressed the cotton wool onto the graze, perhaps with a little more force than was strictly necessary.

"Watson, have a care!"

"Says the man who obviously took none himself."

"If I explain all, will you desist from torturing me?"

"No, but do it anyway."

He sighed, wincing as I attacked a further portion of the wound.

"Very well. As I told you, I went to see Woodbead, who was delighted to see me. To be fair, I think he would have been delighted to see anyone, surrounded as he was by nothing but paintings all day."

"Get to the point, Holmes. You showed him the painting."

"Yes, and he thought it pretty unremarkable, although he said he would investigate."

"You left it with him?"

"I did."

"Mrs Sellman won't like it being out of your sight."

"She will if he helps me find her sister."

The application of further disinfectant brought another sharp intake of breath. "What's in that bottle, sulphuric acid?"

"So, Woodbead took the painting…" I prompted, preparing a dressing.

"And invited me for lunch. I agreed, assuming that you would be able to occupy yourself for a few hours."

"How kind of you to think of me." I applied the dressing to the now clean graze. "Where did you go, or shouldn't I ask?"

"The Ritz of all places. It appears art historians are paid well."

"As are *retired* consulting detectives."

Holmes ignored the jibe. "We ate a pleasant lunch – I can recommend the halibut – and Woodbead imbibed more than a little wine."

"While you abstained?"

"I may have enjoyed one or two glasses. The food was good, as, I admit, was the company."

"And then?"

"And then we said our farewells. Woodbead headed rather unsteadily back towards the gallery, while I decided to walk off my meal before calling a cab."

"What happened to Geller?" I asked, shooting an accusatory glance at the former Irregular.

"I needed to clear my head," Holmes cut in, saving the cabbie from embarrassment. "The afternoon had stretched on and I admit that I have less tolerance for alcohol than I possessed in my youth."

"You make it sound as though you were a drunk," I said, applying the dressing to his cheek. "If I remember rightly, drinking was one of the few vices you omitted to embrace with vigour."

"Still, a walk was required."

"Even after you had been followed for the last few days."

"A man is allowed to make a mistake."

"Not you."

I stepped back, admiring the dressing. Yes, it would do for now.

"None of this explains how *that* happened," I said, pointing to his cheek.

"I walked along Piccadilly, enjoying being back in the city, when it veered across the road, dazzling me with its headlights."

"It? A motorcar?"

"*The* motorcar, Watson. The Morris Bullnose that trailed us earlier. Now it was doing more than trailing; now it was trying to sandwich me between its grille and the wall."

"It tried to run you down? What did you do?"

"There was no time to think, let alone react. Fortunately, a passer-by had faster reflexes than I did. He pushed me aside before I ended up beneath the Bullnose's wheels. I hit the wall, giving me this." He gave the dressing a tap, flinching slightly. "Safe to say, if it had not been for my guardian angel, a scraped cheek would have been the least of my worries."

"And the car?"

"Ploughed into Swan & Edgar's latest window display. The dresser will have a nasty surprise waiting for him when he arrives for work tomorrow."

"You could have been killed."

"Maybe."

"Maybe? From what you have described—"

"Watson, Watson, Watson. Once again, you fail to ask the pertinent question, focusing instead on the trivial."

"And your well-being is trivial now, I suppose?"

"You stated earlier that *it* had tried to run me down, as if the automobile itself was in control of its own destiny."

"Well, the driver then," I snapped. "You know what I mean."

"I do indeed. Would you like to know who she was?"

"*She?*"

"None other than Elsie Kadwell."

"The singer from the Mallard?"

"*Formerly* of the Mallard. It appears that she and Albert's nephew have parted company."

"I'm not surprised after what she tried to do to the poor

fellow, but shouldn't she be behind lock and key for her part in Pritchard's scheme?"

"It appears that she was released; that she made a deal."

"With whom?"

"That is the question. I'm afraid I couldn't get much sense out of her. Not only was her leg quite broken, there was no mistaking the gin on her breath as she was pulled from the wreckage."

"So she followed us from Hampstead."

"I doubt it, from the state she was in. She had obviously been drinking for many hours."

"Dutch courage, to take her revenge for her ruination."

"Most likely. She wasn't driving the Morris earlier today, as she would have had at least two opportunities to finish me off. I spotted the car on my arrival at the gallery and on our walk to the restaurant."

"A different driver then," I suggested, "with orders to observe rather than intervene?"

"Which raises the question of how and when my would-be assassin clambered behind the wheel of the car."

"You said she struck a deal to escape prosecution."

"If I can believe her drunken rambling. 'He told me to do it,' she said over and over again. 'He wanted to scare you, to warn you off.'"

"The intention was not to kill you then?"

"If Mycroft is behind our surveillance I would certainly hope not. Perhaps this was a warning, like that given by Burns and Hartley."

"Surely they weren't sent by Mycroft?"

"At present, we have no evidence to the contrary. At least they were professionals, rather than a frightened girl manipulated by those who should know better. First Pritchard and now the mastermind of tonight's entertainment. Unfortunately, Miss

Kadwell will pay the price for their machinations."

"So, what happened? The police arrived, I take it."

"In large numbers. Thankfully, I lost myself in the confusion, slipping away."

"And the man who saved you?"

"He vanished."

I attempted to perch on the edge of the table, before thinking better of it. Holmes immediately sprang to his feet, offering his chair.

"Sit down. Your need is greater than mine. Besides, I have been patched up by the greatest doctor in London."

I didn't contradict him. "But how did you end up here? Piccadilly is two miles away."

"That'll be me," Geller piped up. "I didn't like leaving Mr Holmes alone, not after all that's happened, whether he'd dismissed me or not."

"Quite right. Good man."

"I heard what happened, and went looking for him."

"I admit that I was a little confused. I may have had the wits to avoid the police, but the events of the last forty-eight hours were starting to catch up with me."

"I am not surprised."

"And that's not all," Geller added.

"What do you mean?" I asked.

"Tell him," Geller said, drawing a withering look from Holmes.

"I remember when I was the one in charge."

"Long time ago, Mr Holmes. Long time."

Holmes relented. "As I blundered into Soho, I once again picked up a shadow, one of the individuals who have dogged our footsteps these last few days. And then he made his move."

"He attacked you?"

"An old man, befuddled by too much wine and a near-fatal accident? Of course he did. There would never be a better time."

"And what happened?"

"For that we need to go into the next room."

"What do you mean?"

Holmes walked towards the door and Geller, limping slightly. "You have the key?"

Geller pulled a chain from his pocket. "He's not going to like it," he told Holmes.

"Who isn't?" I asked, before realising the former Irregular was talking about me. "What am I not going to like?"

Holmes simply stared at me. "I trust you brought your revolver?"

"Shall I need it?"

"There's every chance. If you wouldn't mind?"

Shaking my head at his theatrics, I fished the gun from my coat pocket and released the safety catch. "Now, are you going to tell me what's going on, or should I use this on you?"

Geller unlocked the other door. "I told him this wasn't a good idea, Doctor, I promise I did." Without another word, he pushed it open.

The room was as bare as the first, this time boasting no table, decrepit or otherwise. It did, however, contain a chair, on which sat a man in his late twenties, glaring at us with murderous eyes.

CHAPTER TWENTY-FIVE

QUIS CUSTODIET IPSOS CUSTODES?

Instinctively, I raised my gun, but thankfully the fellow stayed where he was.

"Who the devil is this, Holmes?" I asked, not sure that I wanted to know.

"My attacker," came the reply. There was a creak on the stairs, and I realised Harkness had joined us. "There may have been gaps in my story, Watson, which is why you will always be the better author."

"You need to let me go," said the man, a Scottish burr to his voice. As he spoke he ran his fingers nervously against his chin, revealing a nasty graze on the side of his large hand. "You can't hold me here against my will."

I had to agree. "He's right, Holmes. Whatever he's done, taking a man prisoner—"

Holmes cut me off. "I didn't dismiss Geller, not really. I had already told him what I had planned; to persuade Woodbead to go to lunch, to over-indulge, or at least to give the impression that I had done so. Granted I never expected the car, but that only added to my performance. I knew that if I wandered into the side streets, I would be too great a target to resist. They would finally make their move, and so would I.

"I stumbled, and so did our man here. He grabbed me from behind, his arm going around my neck." Holmes turned to the prisoner. "'Just drop it,' that is what you said, is it not? 'Drop all of it, if you know what's good for you.' Dialogue worthy of one of your stories, Watson. He must be another fan."

I winced at the dreadful Americanism. "And you fought back?"

"Simplicity itself, even in my weakened condition. I arched forward, dragging him with me while delivering what I imagine was a painful kick to the shin. Not expecting an old man to retaliate, he was thrown off balance, long enough for Geller to rush to my aid."

Holmes regarded his prisoner with such pride that my blood boiled. This was too much, even for him.

"What now, then?" I asked. "You torture him? Make him tell you everything?"

Holmes looked appalled. "Torture? Please, you insult me, Watson."

"Says the man who kidnaps innocent folk in the street."

"Hardly innocent."

All this time, the fellow was watching us argue, no doubt waiting to see if he could make a break for it. I fancied that Geller and Harkness, Holmes's accessories, would be enough of a deterrent, even if he could get past my gun. Like it or not, I was a part of this now.

"What of the police?" I asked.

"What of them? They have turned their back on us, Watson, after years of service. Besides," he continued, "why would I need to torture someone to uncover the truth about him? Until yesterday this gentleman had a beard, for example."

"He did?"

Holmes sighed. "Use your eyes, Watson. The skin above his cheekbones is lightly tanned, whereas his chin is pale. There is also a tan mark on the little finger of his left hand, suggesting he usually wears a signet ring, but that he removed it in order to remain as anonymous as possible. That he wears it on his left indicates that he is right handed, knowledge that helped me remove his wallet from his left breast pocket during our scuffle."

"His wallet?"

With a flourish, Holmes produced the item concerned, a smart leather receptacle.

"Barely used, and without any marks of identification. Another attempt to remain incognito, although to that end he has failed. This, Watson, is our bearded friend from the Underground. The bowler hat and black suit may have gone, but his cravat is fastened with the same gold pin. I would also suggest that if we had addressed him on the platform yesterday, he would not have used that awful Scottish brogue. The fellow has never been north of the border. If I am doing him a disservice and he has, then he failed to notice the subtle differences between Dundee and Glasgow, as he mashes both accents together with gay abandon."

Holmes turned to the man in question. "Am I correct?"

The prisoner simply glowered at us.

"I could go on, explaining how he recently bought his sweetheart a posy of forget-me-nots, but I think my point has been made."

"But, if he won't speak—"

"He can remain as silent as the grave for all I care. That is not his function here."

"Then what is?"

There came a knock on the door in the hallway below. I started, and our captive used the momentary distraction to rise from his chair, ready to make good his escape. Even after all these years, my military training came to the fore, my gun arm stiffening. The fellow hesitated.

"If you'll excuse us," said Holmes, letting Geller step in and pull the door shut, locking it tight.

I lowered my revolver. "Now what?"

"Now we retire to what we can laughingly call the drawing room. Harkness, will you get the door?"

Harkness grunted in response and headed downstairs. Holmes ushered me back into the first room, shutting Geller out on the landing.

"You've gone mad, haven't you?" I exclaimed, shaking my head, as Holmes rushed to his former chair to reclaim the jacket that was draped over its back.

"I sympathise that it appears that way…" he replied.

"Sympathise? Holmes, since when have you employed louts to do your dirty work? Or is this an aspect of your operations that I have hitherto been unaware of?"

"Careful, Watson," Holmes said, buttoning his jacket. "Geller will hear you. He's a lot of things, but a lout he is not, as well you know."

"But what of that Harkness fellow? He lied to me, you know? Told me he hadn't a clue what you'd been up to—"

"Of course he did. We could ill afford the risk that someone was listening. I was unprepared to show our hand just yet."

"To whom?" I demanded, although Holmes gave no answer. Instead, he beckoned me to listen to the creak of the stairs. Someone was pulling heavily on the banister, puffing and wheezing all the way. I slipped my revolver back into my coat pocket, but kept my hand firmly around the grip as I moved to stand beside Holmes, who had his hands clasped behind his back, looking for all the world as if we were back in 221B Baker Street, ready for Mrs

Hudson to bundle in a prospective client.

Even Geller seemed to keep the pretence going. Through the warped wood we heard him say, "He's through here, sir," before opening the door. I tensed, and then my mouth dropped open.

An elephantine figure was squeezing his way through the doorframe.

"Sherlock," he growled.

"Mycroft," Holmes responded. "How good to see you."

CHAPTER TWENTY-SIX

HOLMES V. HOLMES

The two brothers stood there, Mycroft scowling and Holmes returning the gaze with such indifference that one would think they had never met, let alone been raised in the same nursery.

Mycroft's plump face was flushed, but I found it impossible to tell whether it was the result of his laboured ascent or the anger that burned in his eyes. Bizarrely he carried beneath his arm a copy of *The Times*.

I wondered which brother would break the impasse, but dared not do so myself. Neither would thank me for it, although Geller was obviously not a man to stand on ceremony.

"I'll just shut this then," he said, pulling the door closed. Mycroft glanced behind him to make sure that we were alone, as if the feeble door would offer much in the way of privacy, before returning his furious gaze to his sibling.

Holmes smiled thinly, stepping aside to show Mycroft a chair that was in no way capable of taking his weight. "Brother, would you care to sit?"

"What I'd care for, *brother*," replied Mycroft, pouring into the word as much scorn as he could muster, "is for you to tell me what the blazes you think you're playing at. He is in the other room, I take it?"

"He is indeed," said Holmes, not attempting to deny anything to a man whose powers of observation were nearly as well honed as his own.

"Have you injured him?"

Holmes snorted with derision. "Do you really have to ask?"

"Obviously I do. Sixty-five years and you still amaze me, Sherlock. Congratulations."

"Sixty-five years and still you do not trust me."

"Is it any wonder? I could believe a lot of things of you, but never this. Now, hand my man over before this damnable affair becomes worse than it already is."

"You admit he is yours then?"

"Why admit something you already know?"

"And I assume that you have not come alone?"

Mycroft pulled a mocking face. "You, Sherlock, assume? Perhaps you really *are* suffering from concussion."

"From the way your hand is bunched you either wish to punch me or call for assistance using the whistle hidden in your fist. As you cannot abide physical exertion of any kind, I would suggest it is the latter."

Mycroft's eyes flicked in my direction. "As for you, John, I am shocked that you would be party to such folly."

I bristled at the reproach. "Says the man who has had us followed these last few days. A man I thought was a friend."

"I tried to warn you—"

"You tried to bribe me!"

"To reward you for your service to your country, nothing more. Unfortunately, the only reward left for you is the dock."

"And now you resort to threats. What the devil is this about, Mycroft? Tell us."

Holmes was watching his brother, clearly enjoying every bluster. "Yes, tell us, brother. Why do we need your protection?"

That blindsided me. "His what?"

Holmes smiled at me. "It appears that we are ruffling feathers in Whitehall, Watson."

Mycroft sighed and walked forward, not to take the chair but to throw his hat and newspaper onto the table. "The worst kind."

"But why?" I asked. "The business with the hand?"

"And Abberton Hospital. Your involvement has been… unfortunate. Had I known that Inspector Tovey would come to you…"

"So you are responsible for his… redistribution," Holmes concluded.

Mycroft's monumental jowls wobbled as he nodded. "Tovey has achieved too much in his career to have it end over this. I needed to get him away, before he found himself in real trouble."

"And you are not at liberty to tell us what the trouble is?"

A shake of the head. "The Official Secrets Act," he said, as if that explained everything.

"Which Watson and I have both signed," Holmes pointed out.

"You have signed *an* official secrets act."

"And that means what?" said I.

"That some questions should never be asked."

"And some answers will never be given," Holmes added.

"But, *protection*?" I repeated. "You've had us put under observation. I was threatened in my own surgery."

"Which is precisely the reason I have had agents on your heels. Not to watch you, Doctor—"

"But to ensure our safety," Holmes interjected. "The man my colleagues and I waylaid – an act about which, incidentally, Watson had no idea until we brought him here – has an injury on his right hand, a scrape that he suffered when pushing me out of the path of the Morris Bullnose."

My mind raced to keep up. "He was the man who saved your life?"

"As he was employed to do. I was not so addled that I failed to recognise him before he slipped away into the crowd. I just pray he can forgive my repaying him with incarceration."

"I'm sure it is an indignity he will learn to live with," replied Mycroft icily.

Holmes turned to me. "You are the reason we have been followed, Watson."

"I am?"

"Or rather your unexpected visitors the other morning."

"As Sherlock mentioned," Mycroft said, "feathers have been well and truly ruffled. I tried to intervene as soon as I heard, but action had already been taken, those ruffians Burns and Hartley having been sent by worried parties in Whitehall."

"They weren't yours then?" I asked, a question that seemingly wounded my friend's brother.

"It saddens me that His Majesty's representatives would seek to employ such blunt weapons. For that, I can only apologise."

"Indeed," Holmes said. "Whatever you have thought of my brother of late, I doubt even he would sanction arson."

"The hospital?" I asked. "Burns and Hartley were behind that too?"

"Mycroft's agency had already done its work," Holmes replied, "scrubbing the place clean."

"Except for the lobby," Mycroft pointed out.

"Of course. How else would I spot your surprisingly prominent footprint?"

Mycroft bowed his head slightly in acknowledgement, prompting a smile from Holmes who continued: "Remember what I said about the signet ring, Watson. Our man upstairs removed it to go about his business. And no one in my brother's employ would wear something so conspicuous as a carnation, such as you described Burns wearing – especially when the self-same flower would wilt in the heat, dropping incriminating petals in the presence of a large fire."

"You noticed that too?" asked Mycroft.

"In the mud outside the burning building? As if I could miss such glaring evidence—"

"That you left *in situ* to be found by my people."

"Naturally. I thank you for watching over us, Mycroft, and indeed for venturing out into the capital for this meeting. I wish only that you had come to me directly without my having to reel you in by taking your man."

"We live in remarkable times, Sherlock."

"We do indeed. Talking of which, Miss Kadwell..."

"The singer."

"Indeed. While I would never condone her past crimes—"

"No charges will be pressed concerning her redecoration of Swan & Edgar. I've had her placed in protective custody."

"Another trip to the countryside?"

"She will have an opportunity to make amends for any transgression she has committed in the past."

I didn't care for the insinuation. "So, you're going to manipulate the poor girl after all she's gone through?"

"A poor girl is she now?" Holmes commented. "Amazing how one's view shifts over time, eh, Watson?"

The accusation rankled, but I let it go.

"She's a bright lass, if misguided," Mycroft said. "We can give her a new start in life—"

"None of which is our concern," added Holmes.

Mycroft sized up his brother. "So, we are done, Sherlock?"

"I would say not," I interjected, only to be silenced by a wave of Holmes's hand.

"Everything is in order, brother." Holmes walked across the room and opened the door to find Geller and Harkness standing guard on the landing. "Will you show my brother to our guest? They are both free to leave whenever they want."

"Right you are, Mr Holmes," nodded Geller. Mycroft picked up his hat and made his farewells.

"Until next time, John."

I refused to dignify the sentiment with a response, merely turning my back as Mycroft approached his brother.

"I am sorry not to have trusted you, Sherlock."

"As am I."

"But thank you for trusting me."

Holmes led Mycroft to the door. "To official secrets, brother."

Mycroft nodded. "To official secrets. Thank you, Sherlock. I suggest you and Watson leave the city for a while."

Holmes shut the door, and, before I could argue, placed a long finger across his thin lips. We waited in silence until Mycroft had been shown into the other room and he and his agent had been escorted downstairs. To his credit, the newly freed man uttered barely a word, but followed his master out of the building in silence.

"And that's it?" I exploded. "After everything has happened, Mycroft comes to us and you let him leave without a word of explanation?"

"You know why we have been followed, and on whose authority you were threatened."

"Hardly. We've ruffled 'the worst kind' of feathers in Whitehall? That's no explanation. I'm grateful that Mycroft's man saved your life, although I doubt you would have allowed yourself to be mown down in the street, but we are nowhere nearer knowing what this is all about."

Holmes smiled. "Is that so?"

"'I suggest that you leave the city', that's what he said."

"He did indeed."

"You know what he's going to do, don't you? Cover all this up. Make the problem go away."

"That is one of my brother's particular talents."

"And you are happy with that, are you? To give up after we have already gone through so much?"

"Look to the table, Watson."

"Look to the what?"

"The table," Holmes repeated. I turned to see that while Mycroft had recovered his hat, the folded newspaper was still lying beside the bowl.

I sighed in frustration. "He's left his *Times*. I hope you're not expecting me to go running after him like a delivery boy."

"I would never presume such a thing, Watson, just as you shouldn't presume that it is *The Times*."

"But your brother always takes *The Times*."

My curiosity piqued, I picked up the paper. As soon as I saw the masthead, I realised my mistake. It was a *Times*, but not the London *Times*.

"The *Manchester Weekly Times and Examiner*," I read in amazement. "But why is Mycroft reading a regional paper?"

"He wasn't reading it at all," Holmes pointed out, joining me at the table. "He was carrying it, before leaving it here."

"On purpose?"

"Look at the date, Watson."

I did as he requested. "Thursday, the third of July 1919. What of it?"

"Observe the three pin-pricks above the last digit in the year."

I peered closer to spy three tiny holes above the nine.

"A code with which Mycroft and I used to amuse ourselves as boys," Holmes explained, flicking through the pages of the newspaper. "Page nine, column three." He reached the page and jabbed his finger at the central column. "There it is!"

Leaning over the paper, Holmes read aloud.

"*Hulme Giant Committed. Following the attack on one Ellie Grimshaw in Hulme last Wednesday, Judge Mark Roberts of Manchester County Court committed the young lady's assailant to Prestwich Lunatic Asylum.*"

"Very sad, I'm sure, but what has it got to do with any of this?" I asked.

"If you will permit me to continue, that will become clear," Holmes replied curtly. "*The inmate is believed to have returned from the front line two years, although he has failed to be identified. Campaigner Mrs Cleone Stevens of local charity, Dignity for Ex-Servicemen, has appealed for information regarding the mystery man, in the hope that she can uncover more about his past. Mrs Stevens (34) said today: 'It is a tragedy that so many of our brave servicemen have returned from defending our country to be cast out on the street or locked away in the hope that they will be forgotten.' The man known as the Hulme Giant is described as being six foot nine inches tall, of a pale complexion, with peculiar yellow-coloured eyes and multiple scars across the face, arms and chest.*" Holmes looked up from the paper. "Yellow eyes and extensive scarring?"

"The man in the hospital? Could there really be a link?"

"Mycroft obviously thinks so, or he would not have brought the story to my attention. Perhaps we should leave, after all. Do you think your wife would forgive me if I spirited you away to Lancashire?"

CHAPTER TWENTY-SEVEN

SECRETS

I cannot say that my wife was happy to wave us goodbye late the following morning, but at least she had not complained when I informed her of our plans. Thankfully, she had not seen Holmes when we returned from his bolthole, dropped off by Geller who remained as cheerful in those early hours as he had throughout the entire sorry affair. By the time we had rested, Holmes was resplendent in a fresh suit and, save for the graze on his cheek, seemingly none the worse for the previous evening's perils. My wife had simply taken one look at the damage to his face and said that she didn't want to know, although she embraced me when Geller reappeared to take us to Euston Station.

"Come back safe," she breathed in my ear, before releasing me and reclaiming her composure. My heart was heavy and for a second I doubted my actions, hesitating at my gate, wondering if I should tell Holmes to leave without me. However, as Geller took our luggage and Holmes clambered into the back seat of the taxi, I knew that there really was no choice.

Indeed, by the time we arrived at Euston, all my thoughts

about remaining behind were gone. The intoxicating bustle of the station set adrenalin pumping through my veins. I had always embraced travel and the freedom it brought to body and mind. As I sat in our carriage, I felt the same thrill as I had experienced when I had first set out for Afghanistan all those years ago. My sole wish was that this journey would end less badly. I doubted a sniper would be standing ready to take me out with another Jezail bullet as soon as we arrived in Lancashire.

At least, I hoped not.

As we pulled away from the station, the pressure of the last few days fell way, the streets of London soon replaced with open fields and tall trees. Even the weather seemed better in the countryside, the storm clouds finally giving way to blue skies and summer sunshine.

"How many did you spot?" Holmes said, after twenty minutes or so.

"How many what?"

"Mycroft's guardian angels. I counted five, although it would appear that my saviour-turned-detainee has been given some much deserved time off."

"You almost sound proud of what you did to that poor fellow."

"You were the one pointing a gun at him."

"I suggest we let the matter rest," said I, gruffly. "And turn our attention to the envelope you received this morning."

"Envelope?" Holmes parroted with feigned bemusement.

"You aren't the only one with eyes and ears."

Holmes nodded in appreciation. "I am impressed, Watson."

I smiled. "My wife told me that you received a messenger while I shaved this morning."

Holmes threw back his head and laughed, before rising from his seat to reach up to the luggage rack. "Perhaps I should have employed Mrs Watson as my assistant all those years ago."

"Employed, was I? I must have missed the cheques."

Chuckling, Holmes retrieved a briefcase from the rack and placed it beside him. Looking back at my work now, I feel I have done Holmes something of a disservice. It appears that many of my readers consider Holmes a mirthless soul, devoid of emotion and humour. Nothing could be further from the truth. He had the most remarkable of laughs, infectious in the extreme and capable of lifting even the darkest of moods. I miss it to this day.

Still amused, he flicked open the case and pulled out the envelope in question. "This is from our friend, Mr Woodbead," he said, extracting the papers within, "who has been as good as his word and has duly investigated the Sellmans' family picture."

I sat forward in my seat, eager to hear what the art historian had to say. "And what has he found?"

"More than I expected. Do you recall the name of Mrs Sellman's ancestor, the one who she believed painted that scene?"

"Something biblical, wasn't it?" I replied. "Joseph or some such."

"Joshua," Holmes reminded me, "although I'd wager that she misheard the name as a child. Woodbead showed the picture around and one of his colleagues recognised it. As luck would have it, he had bought a picture of a similar scene many years ago."

"I thought you didn't believe in luck."

"I don't, and it also appears that I know little about art. What I had dismissed as a fairly average daubing turns out to be the work of a young artist who showed great promise, only to vanish a decade or so after he sprang onto the art scene. According to these notes, his name was Jostli."

"A Swiss name?"

"It is, from the Latin *jocus*, meaning gladness."

"Mrs Sellman did say her family was from Geneva." I sat back in my seat and rolled the peculiar name around my tongue. "Jostli Honegger. Quite a mouthful."

"Indeed it would be, if that were his surname. Jostli was born around 1805, the son of Ernest and Adelais Balmer, but he could find no other record of the Balmer family in Geneva at the time."

"They moved away then?"

"Well, they did, but that isn't the reason that no records exist. Ernest Alphonse Balmer was a Swiss diplomat of note, who would end up as ambassador to Germany. However, no birth certificate bearing his name exists. Now, Woodbead's colleague, quite the amateur genealogist, started to dig, and found this…"

Holmes handed over an official-looking document, a birth certificate no less, in German and dated the seventeenth of March 1777.

"Read the names, Watson."

"Ernest Alphonse, born of Alphonse and Caroline Frankenstein."

"Intriguing, isn't it? For some reason the Frankensteins of Geneva changed their name to Balmer."

"When?"

"Sometime before Ernest became a diplomat."

"Do we know why?"

"Unfortunately not. All we know is that Ernest had two brothers, Victor and William. Other than that, the Frankensteins are shrouded in mystery. If our celebrated diplomat did change his family name, there must have been some kind of scandal."

"But one that surely has no bearing on our case?"

"No, but it is fascinating all the same." The envelope resting on his lap, Holmes sat back and tapped his index finger against his lips. "And there's something about the name Frankenstein that strikes me as familiar, although I cannot recall in what regard, and could find no mention in my index."

"You went up into the attic?"

"You really do take an inordinate amount of time to shave, Watson."

I handed Holmes the birth certificate and watched him stuff it and the envelope back into the case.

"Either way, I don't see how it helps us," I said, letting my gaze wander out across the landscape that whistled past.

"Neither do I, unless our artist, who by all accounts was destined for great things, had his career cut short by a debilitating disease."

"The curse of the Frankensteins?" I suggested.

Holmes smiled. "Already conjuring up a name for the short story? Or is this little distraction worthy of a novel?"

I chuckled. "Little distraction? Besides, do you really think Mycroft would let me publish it?"

Now it was Holmes's turn to regard the passing countryside. "Secrets everywhere, Watson. Official or otherwise. Just waiting to be uncovered."

CHAPTER TWENTY-EIGHT

MRS STEVENS

The rest of the journey passed without incident. Our distance from London seemed also to have a restorative effect on Holmes. It was only as I saw him relax, passing the time with anecdotes and reminiscences, that I realised precisely how much recent events had affected him. Before long, he was sitting a little straighter, becoming more effusive with his gestures and letting his laughter last longer, until both of us, on numerous occasions, were wiping tears from our eyes.

Finally we arrived at the ever-busy London Road Station, and stepped out into the throng of Mancunians. The sound was incredible, louder than even the great stations of the capital. Holmes and I made our way through the crowd, looking for the exit, only to be greeted by a serious-looking girl in a modest hat and coat. In her hands she held a card, with a single name written in clear block letters.

MR SHERLOCK HOLMES

"So much for anonymity," I grumbled beneath my breath.

Holmes ignored the comment, breaking into a smile as he approached the lady. "Mrs Stevens?"

"Mr Holmes," she replied, her warm northern vowels instantly making me feel at home. I had never lived in this part of the country, but there was something about the accent that exuded welcome. Some southerners dismissed the people of the north as downcast and gruff. I had always believed that it was the other way round. Anyone south of the Peak District could learn much about hospitality from our northern cousins.

"I am so glad that you got in touch," Mrs Stevens said, leading us to the taxi rank. "I couldn't believe it when I received your telegram. Sherlock Holmes coming here, to help us! Everyone at the campaign is so excited."

"Yours is a worthy cause," Holmes said, opening a cab door for the lady. She climbed inside and we followed suit. Holmes took the seat alongside Mrs Stevens and I sat with my back to the driver, enabling me to observe them both. She was a handsome woman, although her hair had turned prematurely grey. Her green eyes were bright with excitement and yet had the tell-tale signs of care, lines creasing the skin that she kept free of make-up. There was sadness to this woman, and I could scarcely help but notice that she wore black from head to foot. A widow then? There were a lot of widows these days.

"As soon as I read of this Hulme Giant I have to admit that my interest was piqued," Holmes continued. "While I have long since retired from practice, I wonder if my meagre talents might help identify the poor fellow."

Holmes's false modesty made me smile. Meagre talents indeed.

"We came as soon as we could," I added. "Any excuse to visit Manchester on my part. I find it such an exhilarating city, all this industry and commerce. A place where the future is forged."

She smiled, but there was little joy in the expression.

"It was exhilarating, once. No offence to the south, but we pride ourselves on being strong up here, ready to roll up our sleeves and get the job done. But with so many of the men gone…" Her voice faltered and, for a moment, she looked straight through me, as if searching the horizon. Then she was back, focusing on my face. "It's been hard," she concluded, "but we struggle on."

"*Concilio et labore*," said Holmes, smiling fondly at the young lady, who was obviously still grieving. He glanced over to me to explain: "The city's motto."

"By wisdom and effort," I translated.

Holmes nodded. "A fine maxim no matter where one lives. How did you become involved with Dignity for Ex-Servicemen, Mrs Stevens?"

Another kindness from Holmes. No doubt he could have dazzled the young woman with his detective prowess, gleaning everything he needed to know from her appearance, but this was no time for showmanship.

Mrs Stevens paused, as if summoning the courage to tell her story. "My Alfred never came home from the war. No one knows what happened to him. There are those who think he was taken prisoner, but they can't be sure. When the boys started coming back, I volunteered at the shelters."

"A noble calling," Holmes commented.

"No, a selfish one, Mr Holmes. Every night I worked there, I searched for him. So many faces, haunted the lot of them. The things some of them talked about, what they saw, what they had to do. Living nightmares. And then there were those who just sat there, staring at the walls, seeing God knows what staring right back at them. They say that war's hell, Mr Holmes, but for those men, peace is worse."

"Surely not," I said.

"At the front, they had a purpose in life. A regimented existence, in every sense of the word. Not now. Now they've come back, wounded and scarred, what reward do they receive? We turn our backs on them, Dr Watson. They fought for us, and now they're an embarrassment, an inconvenience." She gestured out of the taxi window with a gloved hand. "Look around you. You say this is where the future is forged. What about those men on the street corners, do you see them?"

How could I not? They were everywhere, leaning against walls or huddled in groups.

"There's more down by the canal. Hundreds. No one gives them the time of day. You see, they're not fit to work, that's what they're told. Men who dug trenches and buried their friends day after day. It makes me sick. What future have they got, Dr Watson? What hope?"

Her tone had gained a harder, accusatory edge. There was steel beneath this woman's sorrow.

"And it only gets worse for them," she continued, as the cab sped away from the city centre. "No jobs. No homes. Is it any wonder so many turn to crime, just to survive? We do what we can. We have a hostel, although there's only so many we can take in. For the rest, we become a voice when no else will speak up. The authorities would rather people forgot about them, but we won't let that happen. We owe these men far too much to let them fade away."

"Men like the Giant," Holmes prompted, bringing the conversation back to the reason we had travelled to Manchester.

"We don't call him that," Mrs Stevens said, although there was no condemnation in her voice. It was a statement of fact, nothing more. "John's no monster."

"John?" I asked.

For the first time since she started her polemic, Mrs Stevens smiled. "He needed a name. John seemed as good as any."

"It's a fine choice," Holmes said, catching my eye before turning back to the lady. "You have met him?"

"They allow me to visit him in the asylum."

"A progressive institution, from what I've read," I said.

"They like to think they are," came Mrs Stevens' reply. "Oh, I've seen worse, Dr Watson, trust me. Prestwich prides itself on seldom using restraints or even sedatives unless it's really necessary, but at the end of the day, it's not a hospital. Not really. It's a prison. Yes, there are exercise yards and activities, but most have no hope of being released, especially folk like John."

"What can you tell us about him?" Holmes asked.

"The papers have got one thing right about him, Mr Holmes. He is a mystery man. He has no memory, you see, other than flashes of who he used to be."

"Amnesia?" I enquired.

"Possibly. Although Dr Dougherty thinks it is shell shock."

"John has a doctor at the asylum?"

"Much good it's doing him. John has this tic, you see, in his cheeks, his muscles sort of twitch when he speaks. Dr Dougherty thinks that John was forced to run his bayonet through the face of a German. His body's reacting to the trauma—"

"His guilt made manifest," I interrupted. "I've read about this in the *Lancet*. The terrors of the battlefield haunt those who come home. Men who were trained as snipers lose their sight, for no apparent reason."

"Other than they don't want to see what they've done," Mrs Stevens cut in.

I nodded. "Other men report that one minute they are having normal conversations with their family and then suddenly they see the faces of those they killed, or hear their screams. Conflict demands behaviour that would usually be condemned. When violence becomes the norm, it's hard to go back."

"You sound like a man who understands, Doctor," Mrs Stevens observed.

"I served in Afghanistan, although my experiences were nothing compared to those of the men you care for."

"And this is Dr Dougherty's diagnosis?" Holmes asked. "That John is suffering from a wartime neurosis?"

"Something terrible must have happened to him," Mrs Stevens replied. "You read the descriptions of his face, all the scarring. We see a lot of deformity in the hostel, limbs lost, faces twisted beyond recognition, but this… this is different. It is as if John was pieced back together, but with such skill. His scars are extensive, but so neat. I wish I could sew with such a steady hand. Whatever happened out there, it's little wonder it unsettled his mind."

"And what of the woman he attacked?" I asked.

"Ellie Grimshaw," Mrs Stevens replied. "But he never attacked her. I know that's what the paper said, but it weren't the case. She was scared, of course she was. Why wouldn't you be? It was late, she was on her way home from the pub, and he comes at her, out of the shadows. While I don't approve of what the papers call him, he really is a giant of a man. Huge, and clumsy, like he can't always control himself. Another symptom, according to Dr Dougherty, the lack of co-ordination, as if his body doesn't want to work any more."

"But you say it was no assault?" prompted Holmes.

"He knew her name, even though she said she'd never seen him before, and trust me you'd remember if you had. He called out to her, wailing her name over and over. She tried to get away, but he wouldn't let go, holding onto her arms. He's strong. You can see that just looking at him. And his touch, it's cold, no warmth at all. Anyway, she screamed and men came running from the pub to pull him off her. There was a fight and one of them got his skull cracked open. Still in the Royal Infirmary he is, but John was scared, Mr Holmes. He didn't know what was happening. He's like a child."

"The only trouble," said Holmes, "is that according to the newspaper report, he is a child who needs six men to subdue."

"I understand why they put him away, Mr Holmes, really I do. But I can't leave him in there, not knowing who he really is. I keep thinking, well, what if it were my Alf? What if Alf is out there, not right in the head, not knowing how to come home? He's a big man, too, not as big as John, but..."

"There by the grace of God..." I said, hoping to be a comfort. It appeared I was anything but. Mrs Stevens' expression hardened once more.

"God has nothing to do with it, Dr Watson. It was us that sent people like John out there; us that put them through hell. And all the time God sat watching His creations rip each other apart. I've had people bless me for the work I do, saying it's the Lord's work. It's not. I don't want it to be. I'm not interested in saving anyone for the hereafter. I want them to find peace now, on earth, where it matters. People like John."

"If I can help John find peace I shall," Holmes said softly.

She smiled again, reaching out and grasping Holmes's hand. To his credit, Holmes didn't flinch. "Thank you, Mr Holmes."

She broke away, turning quickly so we were unable to see the tears in her eyes as she looked out of the window. "We're nearly there. This is Bury Old Road."

I twisted in my seat and saw an imposing redbrick building ahead of us. We had arrived at Prestwich Asylum.

CHAPTER TWENTY-NINE

JOHN

Like most institutions founded during the reign of Victoria, the asylum was a large gothic building, intended to inspire rather than intimidate. The terracotta-coloured walls were replete with elegant carvings, angelic faces peering out of swirling leaves and bountiful vines. The extensive grounds were equally beautiful, patients strolling between long avenues of trees, or working on flowerbeds and vegetable plots. Perhaps it was the warmth of the sun after days of rain, or the smell of freshly cut grass, but I felt my spirits lift, especially after the forlorn conversation in the taxi ride from London Road. I had begun to doubt whether enough was being done to care for the poor wretches who returned from the front, but here, in these verdant gardens, I greeted Dr Dougherty with renewed optimism.

The doctor himself was a genial enough fellow, approaching retirement if his crop of near-white hair was any indication. He was obviously proud of his institution, giving us chapter and verse as he led us through the doors and into the maze of corridors within.

"Prestwich opened in 1851," he said as we passed workshops

and wards, "a direct result of the Country Asylum Act." His impromptu lecture was directed at me, a fellow medical man, rather than Holmes who walked a few steps behind, those keen eyes sweeping the corridors. "Before that the afflicted would have been sent either to the workhouse or to prison, neither option what one would call conducive to rehabilitation. The original building was constructed to accommodate a mere three hundred and fifty patients, although now, I am pleased to say, we are the largest institution of our type in Europe."

"How many inmates do you have?" I asked.

"We prefer to think of them as patients, Doctor," came the reply.

I apologised, suitably chastised.

"We have the capacity for two thousand, three hundred," he continued, "both here and in the Annexe, which is situated three-quarters of a mile away."

"Good heavens."

"The estate covers over one hundred acres, with a road linking the two main buildings. It's a village in its own right. We have a church, St Mary's, and a fire station, bookbinders and printing shops. There is even a brewery."

"Most industrious," Holmes commented from behind.

"I wish we could do more, to be honest. Our numbers may sound grand, but in a county of two million, our work is a mere drop in the ocean, I'm afraid."

"What treatments do you employ?" I asked.

"Everything from hard work to good old-fashioned Bible lessons." I could almost feel the glower from Mrs Stevens at the mere mention of religious education. "We have a strict routine. Our female patients make clothes, run the laundry, do the cleaning and so on."

"And the men?"

"They work the garden, growing food for the kitchens as well as taking part in vocational training. Many a man comes through those doors an unskilled wastrel, but leaves a carpenter or farmer."

"And what of John?" asked Holmes.

Dr Dougherty's smile faded. "I am afraid he is not quite ready to be put to work just yet."

By now, we were in the heart of the main building. Dr Dougherty led us through a set of double doors and I noticed immediately that the decor had changed. The brightly coloured walls of the outer rooms had been bedecked with paintings, cheerful flower arrangements set upon regular tables, no doubt utilising blooms from the grounds. Here there were no such fripperies. We had stepped out of a home and into a hospital. The smell of disinfectant hung in the air, as did the disturbed cries of the folk Dr Dougherty preferred not to call inmates.

I had the feeling that this was where the real work of the institution took place. I glanced at Mrs Stevens and saw that she was noticeably holding her tongue. There was nothing unsavoury as such; everything seemed hygienic enough, if not as clean as before. Even the clothes of the patients in the open wards seemed shabbier than those at the front of the house. There was none of the chatter that we had previously heard, no one toiling away in workshops or playing musical instruments. Here, the patients lay pathetically in bed, or shuffled about the wards like somnambulists.

"You said that John was making progress," challenged Mrs Stevens. Dr Dougherty nodded in response, walking all the faster down the corridor.

"And he was, but unfortunately we had an incident overnight. I almost denied your request to visit today, such was its severity."

"What kind of incident?" I asked.

Dr Dougherty halted, turning to us. "John became agitated after lights out. Getting out of bed, roaming the corridors. He was shown back to his ward, and yet it happened over and over again, each time causing more distress for the other patients. Eventually, he refused to co-operate and we were forced to sedate him."

"You said you weren't going to use drugs."

"I said that was my aim, Mrs Stevens, but when necessary such measures must be taken. John was becoming violent. One of the orderlies was injured, struck around the head. We couldn't allow it to continue."

Mrs Stevens made no attempt to argue the point, but it was clear from her face that she was seething beneath the surface.

"But we can see him now?"

"He's awake, and mostly lucid. As I said, I very nearly told you not to come, but when you telephoned and informed me that Mr Holmes and Dr Watson were on their way..." Dougherty turned to us. "I really hope that you are able to help him, gentlemen, in whatever way you can. He really is a gentle soul, but so disturbed. He weeps in his sleep every night. And then there's the strangest thing..."

"Go on."

"He suffers nightmares most nights, but cries out in fluent German."

"You think he picked it up on the front line?" Holmes asked.

"If that is where he was. There are certainly no records of any military service, and when he wakes, his mastery of German is gone, leaving him barely able to understand a single word. Indeed, most days he struggles to string together a sentence in English, let alone any other language."

"Another symptom of his neurosis?"

"Quite possibly. There's no way of telling. It's getting to the point where we are considering electric treatment."

"No," Mrs Stevens exclaimed. "You can't!"

"Please, keep your voice down," the doctor said. "I can't have the other patients disturbed." Dougherty returned his attention to me, looking for solidarity. "It's a last resort, Doctor, I am sure you understand. Maybe a shock to the brain would release the memories he has locked away. It could bring the real John back, whoever that may be."

Holmes spoke up. "And where is the patient now?"

"I've had him placed in a containment room." Dougherty raised a hand to stave off the rebuke that was sure to come from Mrs Stevens' direction. "He is still highly agitated. I'm afraid that for everyone's safety, we have had to place him in restraints."

"That is not acceptable," Mrs Stevens spat, her face flushed.

"But it is the only way for these gentlemen to conduct an interview. Do I make myself clear?"

Dougherty waited, like a schoolmaster laying down the law, and eventually Mrs Stevens conceded, nodding but not meeting his gaze.

"Excellent. If anything were to happen… well, the last thing we need is a public inquiry. We try our best here, but since the war…" Once again, the doctor turned to me. "We've worked hard to maintain standards, but it has been near impossible. Half the staff volunteered for service, our food has been rationed, and we have been forced to take more admissions than even our resources allow. Just keeping the therapeutic programme going has been a struggle. We haven't always time…" His voice trailed off. "Well, we haven't always the time to do everything we would like for these men and women."

Mrs Stevens spoke, but I was pleased to hear that it was not her intention to offer more recrimination. "What you have done for John so far has been nothing less than miraculous, Doctor. I'm sorry for my outburst. I just so want this to work."

I exchanged a look with Holmes, suddenly feeling guilty. Unaware of our ulterior motive, these people still believed that we were here for purely philanthropic reasons. That said, surely no one would complain if we could help this John in the process.

"Perhaps you can take us to him now?" Holmes said.

The doctor agreed, leading us to a door.

"I chose this room because it has a window," Dougherty explained. "John likes watching the birds. They calm him, and on days like today, every little helps."

He paused before the door. "Now, if I can ask you to be patient, and remain as passive as possible. No sudden movements or raised voices. If his condition worsens—"

"We understand," said Mrs Stevens. "Thank you."

The doctor smiled and fished a large ring of keys from his pocket. The door creaked slightly as it opened, revealing a featureless room with a solitary desk and chair at its centre, and three more chairs stacked against one wall, for us I presumed. John sat in the central chair with his profile towards us, gazing out of the small window.

What I was unprepared for was his size. The newspaper report said that he was tall, but the bulk of the man was immense. It looked like pure muscle too, albeit misshapen. He had a pronounced hunch on his back and his left shoulder was bunched up, as if it had been broken and not set properly. The arms beneath the flimsy asylum tunic were solid, and one could see at a glance the scarring Mrs Stevens had mentioned. It ran up and down those enormous arms, and across his thick neck.

And then there was his head, a grotesque mass of sutures knitting together anaemic skin. His dark hair was cropped short, ridged eyebrows jutting out beneath a monumental forehead.

We stood there for a full minute with no sign that the man was aware of our presence. Dr Dougherty gave a polite cough.

"John? It's Dr Dougherty. You have visitors. John, can you hear me?"

Perhaps it was the sedatives, still lulling the man into a stupor.

Mrs Stevens tried this time. "John, it's Cleone. I've come to see you."

At the sound of her voice, that great head swivelled towards us, revealing more of the man's ravaged face. The biggest scar of all ran from the top of his lumpy forehead, slashing across a flat nose to end on his right cheek, but it was the eyes that I could barely bring myself to look at. They were the same watery yellow as those that had glared at me in the corridor of Abberton Hospital.

Recognition flooded into the man's face, bringing life to those dead eyes, and tugging his scored lips into a hideous approximation of a smile. What few teeth he had were jagged and almost as yellow as his eyes.

"Cleone," he echoed, drool running down his square jaw. "Cleone here."

It was the voice of an imbecile, sluggish and raw.

Mrs Stevens looked to Dr Dougherty and, when he had nodded his approval, took a step forward. "That's right, John. I said I'd come back, didn't I?"

A flicker of confusion registered on his brutish features.

"John?" She took another step. "That's the name we chose together, do you remember? Until we find out who you really are. You said you liked it."

John nodded, like a puppy wanting to please his mistress. I glanced at the shackles that were attached around his ankles, the skin raw against the metal. How could a man such as this be a threat?

"Like it. Yes. John. Like it."

"I've brought someone to visit, John. Someone who might be able to help work out where you came from, who you are."

"Help?"

"Yes, John. Help." She indicated where we were standing. "These are my friends, Mr Holmes and Dr Watson."

"Friends, good," said John, still not taking his rheumy eyes from Mrs Stevens.

"Yes, they are. Very good. Would you like to meet them?"

John nodded so hard that, ridiculously, I feared that the stitches on his neck would split open. "Yes. Meet friends. Yes."

Dr Dougherty indicated for us to enter, warning us again not to excite his patient. John was already shaking his restraints in eagerness. We approached cautiously, and Holmes and I unstacked the three unoccupied chairs for ourselves and Mrs Stevens. John's eyes nervously flicked from Cleone Stevens to us, and he sank back into his chair.

Mrs Stevens took the chair furthest from the door and made soothing noises. "That's it, John. Nothing to worry about. Remember, these are friends. They've come to help."

"Yes. Friends, help. Friends, good."

"Friends are very good," said Holmes, never breaking eye contact with the terrified man. "My name is Holmes and this is Watson."

John shot a look in my direction. "Hair on face."

I laughed, and the man chuckled with me. "That's right. It's a moustache."

"Moustache. Funny."

"Do you like it?"

"Yes. Like moustache."

"Well, I'm glad to hear it. My wife isn't keen."

The laughter stopped and John frowned, his slab-like brow creasing. "Wife."

Mrs Stevens' head cocked to one side. "You've never used that word before, John. Did you have a wife?"

There was no response, the patient rocking slightly in his chair.

"John?" she tried again.

Suddenly the spell was broken and John laughed again,

pointing at me with his shackled hands. "Hair on face. Hair on face."

"Yes, yes," I said. "I suppose you are right. It does look rather funny."

There came another lightning-fast change of subject, as John showed his hands to Mrs Stevens, with a movement so abrupt his restraints clattered against the bolt on the table. Dr Dougherty made to jump forward, ready to intervene, but there was no need.

"Put John in chains," the patient explained. "Look."

"So I see," said Mrs Stevens. "Is it very sore?"

"Sore, yes. John, bad."

"No, no you're not."

He nodded again, this time solemnly. "John hurt man. Man trying to help. John sorry." He looked piteously at Dr Dougherty. "John want to come out now."

"You will," replied the doctor. "After your friends have gone."

That seemed to please John. He turned back to us and smiled that strange gappy grin. "Yes, friends. John friends."

"Can your friend ask you some questions, John?" Holmes enquired.

Another nod. "John like questions. Fun."

"Yes, they are, aren't they? Do you like it here, John?"

The man glanced at the window. "John can see birds."

"No, I don't mean in this room. In this building, where you live?"

"John live here now."

"Yes."

"John like it. Men kind." Another shadow passed over his face. "John hurt man. John, bad."

Mrs Stevens went to interject, but Holmes continued. "Where did you live before, John?"

The patient stared at Holmes as if he were incapable of understanding the question.

"John live here."

"Yes, but before. Before you came here. Where did you live?"

John shook his head. "Nowhere. John nowhere to go. No one to go to."

"Were you in France, John? Before you came here. Before you saw Ellie."

A jolt went through the man, as if he had received the electric charges Dr Dougherty had already planned.

"Ellie. Saw Ellie."

"Careful," warned Dr Dougherty, looking decidedly uncomfortable.

"Yes, you saw her, didn't you? Saw Ellie, your wife."

This time Mrs Stevens did cut in. "No, Mr Holmes. You'll confuse him. Ellie Grimshaw was definitely not his wife. She never married."

"Not wife," the man confirmed. "Not Ellie."

"I think we should try another line of questioning," Mrs Stevens suggested.

"I agree," the doctor concurred.

"Fiancée," said John.

Mrs Stevens blinked. "What did you say, John? She's your fiancée?"

"Yes," he replied. "Ellie. Come back to me. Come back to me."

"Is that what she said to you, John?" Holmes asked, looking the man straight in the eye. "Before you went away?"

"Not John. Didn't say to John."

"Then who did she say it to?"

"Come back to me. Ellie. Come back."

Dr Dougherty was watching his patient, studying every twitch of the man's face. "This is fascinating. We've never seen him react like this. Please, Mr Holmes, carry on."

At the sound of his voice, John looked at the doctor, distracted.

"No, John," Holmes commanded, his voice sterner. "Look at me. I'm talking about Ellie."

"Fiancée."

"Your fiancée?"

"Not John."

"No, because you're not John, are you? That's not your real name."

"Come back to me."

"Before you went away. Before you went to France."

Again, Mrs Stevens interrupted. "He says he's never been to France."

"But you have, haven't you?" Holmes said, not breaking the man's gaze. "Is that where you got that tattoo on your chest?" I looked at the man's neck and saw that, yes, there were three lines on his chest, poking out of the tunic.

"Is it a lion, John?" asked Holmes.

John looked down as if he had never seen the ink before. He went to pull his shirt over the markings, but the restraints stopped his hands. He tried again, more forcibly.

"Calm down, John," warned Dr Dougherty.

"But you want to see it, John, don't you? The tattoo you got on your chest in France. Because you were in France, weren't you?" Holmes's voice was becoming harder by the second, and the patient was looking more and more confused. Beside us, Mrs Stevens was quite literally on the edge of her seat.

"Mr Holmes, I think that perhaps this wasn't such a good idea. I thought you would just want to see him, to—"

Holmes raised a hand to silence her. "But John wants to talk to us, don't you, John? You want to tell us about Ellie, your fiancée, about getting your tattoo. In France."

"No," he moaned.

The doctor stepped forward, saying that the session was at an end.

"Not France," John continued. "Not been. Mother cared for me. Mother knows best."

"Your mother?" Holmes asked.

"He talks of his mother a lot, and yet can't tell us her name," Dougherty said.

"Mother looks after. Mother cares."

"We think that he's reverted back to childhood memories," continued Dougherty. "Yet even those evade him."

Holmes had never taken his eyes off the patient. "Can you remember your mother's face, John?"

John looked uncertain, cocking his great head as if the movement would dislodge his trapped memories.

"Caw, caw," he cried out, mimicking a bird. "Caw, caw."

He looked at the window, searching for his feathered friends.

"Caw, caw."

"No, John, tell us about your mother. Tell us what she looks like."

John gave a sharp shake of the head, still not looking at Holmes. "No. Can't say."

"Can't, or won't, John? Like you won't tell us about France."

John shifted in his chair. "Not been. Not been."

"Yes, you have," insisted Holmes. "You left Ellie to go to France; so smart in your uniform, ready to serve, to fight. For King and Country, John, do you remember? For Ellie."

John shook his head violently now. "No. No France."

"Yes, France. Wanting to go back to Ellie. She wanted you too, but when she saw you, she didn't recognise you, did she? Didn't know your name? What is your name?"

"Mr Holmes. I must insist—"

"John. Name John."

"No. Your real name. The one that Ellie knew. The one she said when she told you to come home. Tell me that name."

"No name."

"Mr Holmes."

"Tell me that name, soldier!"

"Mr Holmes, you should leave."

"Danny."

Everyone froze and looked at the man, who was staring at Holmes with a terrifying intensity. "Danny. Danny. Danny."

"And that is your name. The name you had when you went to war? When you left Ellie? The name your mother gave you?"

The giant was rocking now, back and forth, still staring at Holmes, his chain creaking against the metal hook.

"Come back to me," he muttered, over and over again. "Come back to me, Danny. Caw, caw, caw."

Holmes wouldn't let it go, despite the man's obvious distress. "But you did come back."

"Yes."

"And she didn't recognise you?"

"No."

"Because of the way you look, because of your injuries."

"No Danny."

"Is that what she said? That you weren't Danny? Is that what Ellie said to you?"

Holmes had pushed the man too far. Screaming Ellie's name, John rose, sending his chair tumbling across the room. The restraints snapped as if they were paper and the giant grabbed the edge of the table, spinning it over so we were forced to jump out of the way.

"Orderlies!" Dougherty called out, but John had already lunged across at Holmes, his still manacled hands wrapped around the detective's throat. I tried to grab the man's arm, but it was like trying to wrestle a statue to the ground. He lashed out, throwing me aside. I landed heavily on my bruised shoulder, crying out in pain.

The room was in chaos, Mrs Stevens shrieking at John to stop, the giant shaking Holmes's head back and forth. Asylum staff poured in, trying to pull the madman from my friend, looping their arms around his monstrous chest, yanking at that immovable grip. And all the time he yelled: "Danny! No Danny! No Danny!"

Finally, when I feared that Holmes's neck would break, Dr Dougherty himself stepped into the fray, thrusting a needle into the man's own bulging neck. John screamed in fury, releasing Holmes to crack his elbow into the side of the doctor's face. Dougherty went down, blood spurting from his nose, but the orderlies had hold of the patient now, stopping those murderous hands from returning to Holmes's throat. I scrambled up, pulling Holmes free as they manhandled their patient to the ground, whatever drug Dougherty had pumped into his system finally taking effect. As he settled, the yellow eyes rolling up into their sockets, the last word he slurred was the name Holmes had plucked from his head.

"Danny. Danny. Dan…"

And all was quiet, save for our ragged breath.

Leaning back against the wall, Holmes rubbed his bruised throat. "Well, that went better than expected," he rasped.

CHAPTER THIRTY

PROGRESS

"An eventful trip," said Holmes, as we headed back towards London on the 8.15 to Euston the following morning.

"And there was I thinking you were a master of deduction," said I, "when your real talent lies with understatement."

Following John's outburst at the asylum, we had been directed to the front door by Dr Dougherty. The brouhaha had set off something of a chain reaction through the surrounding wards, the other patients driven wild by the commotion. Never had Bedlam been a more accurate description.

"You know the way," Dr Dougherty snapped at Mrs Stevens, before darting towards a neighbouring room where an inmate was jumping on his bed and howling at the ceiling. We passed similar scenes of pandemonium before we stepped into the outer, more civilised area of the building. Even then the atmosphere had become electrified, the behaviour of the gentler patients becoming agitated as if madness were sweeping out in waves from the hospital's secret heart. My relief was considerable as we followed Mrs Stevens' determined march towards the gates. She didn't look back, but I could tell from the line of her shoulders that we would feel her wrath the moment we stepped out of the grounds. I felt like a naughty child waiting to be scolded, and had to fight the urge when we were back out on the pavement to walk briskly in the opposite direction.

Mrs Stevens took a few angry steps away from the gate and then whirled around.

"That," she hissed at my colleague, "was not what we agreed."

"I beg to differ," Holmes replied. "You asked me to uncover something about the man's past, and I discovered his name."

"We don't know that, and I never asked you to drive him into a frenzy. If you've undone all the good work Dr Dougherty and I have done with John—"

"With Danny," Holmes pointed out.

"We are sorry if we caused distress," I interjected quickly.

"You didn't do anything," she all but spat. "In fact, from what I could see you just sat back to see what happened. Good show, was it? Material for another story?"

"Now, look here—"

"No, *you* look. You two have put me back months. Do you think Dr Dougherty will welcome me back to his hospital after that performance?"

"You wanted me merely to observe?" Holmes said. "To take a look at the man and work out his past from the way he combs his hair, or the food caught between his teeth?"

"That is what you do, isn't it?"

"Not this time." There was anger behind Holmes's words. No, that wasn't it. Frustration. "I was unable to tell a thing about him, nothing anyway that made sense. That person in there is impossible, and I do not believe in impossibilities. I do not deal in impossibilities."

"What is that supposed to mean?"

"That I cannot tell anything from his hair, because it is not his hair. At least it doesn't belong to his face. Often there are differences between a man's beard and the hair on his head; a fellow with jet-black locks discovers that he has a ginger beard when it grows out, for example. But nothing – *nothing* – matched about that man. His hair was chestnut and yet those striking brows were blond, as opposed to the stubble on his chin, which was dark. As for his teeth? Nothing on earth could persuade me that the maxilla matched the mandible, and before you suggest one or both sets were false, no dentist with any pride in his work would produce false teeth of that colour and condition.

"I could also mention the misshapen neck, the strangely bunched deltoids, or the fact that one of his hands was free of hair, while the other was so matted that it would have not looked out of place on the arm of a chimpanzee."

By now, Mrs Stevens' eyes were wide. She turned and walked away, shaking her head. "You're mad. I shouldn't have brought you here."

"If I am insane, then you brought me to exactly the right place," Holmes said, walking after her. "But you must see it, Mrs Stevens. You must see what we are dealing with here."

The lady stopped short, spinning around. "And what is that, Mr Holmes?"

"A person who should not exist. A person who, somehow, has been fabricated from multiple bodies. A homunculus. A golem."

This was too much, even for me. "Holmes, calm yourself. You're talking nonsense."

"Yes. Yes I am," my friend responded. "And you know me, Watson. You know how even uttering words such as these is anathema. However—"

"—When you have eliminated the impossible, whatever remains, however improbable, must be the truth?" Since we first met Holmes had repeated the phrase time and time again, but this was different. What Holmes was suggesting wasn't merely impossible, it was abhorrent. The thought of stitching together body parts to form a new soul? It was laughable. Worse than that, it was unholy.

Still Holmes refused to let it go, no matter how ridiculous he sounded. "The stitching, Watson, on his face and arms. Did you see it?"

"Of course I did."

"And it reminded you of something?"

I was reluctant to answer. Thankfully, he gave me no chance to do so. "The hand, on the banks of the Thames. It was the same suture work, the same precision that Mrs Stevens so admired. So clean. So tight."

I was all too aware that Mrs Stevens' mouth was hanging open with incredulity. "The hand? On the bank of the Thames?"

Holmes ignored her. "And his skin. That waxy complexion. No, that is not the right word. Marbled. That's it. The capillaries, beneath his cheeks and around his eyes, clear for all to see. What did they remind you of?"

"Holmes, that is enough."

"Tell me what they reminded you of!"

"Of a corpse!" I responded, louder than intended.

Without a word, Mrs Stevens turned and walked away, her heels clicking on the pavement. Ahead of her was the cab that had been waiting patiently to take us to our next location. I had a suspicion that the lady would now favour travelling alone.

"Mrs Stevens," Holmes called.

"Leave her, Holmes. You've done enough."

"Mrs Stevens!"

She reached the car, pulling open the door without looking back. Holmes caught up as she climbed inside, addressing the lady through the open window.

"Go and see Ellie Grimshaw," he instructed. "Ask if the name Danny means anything to her. If it does, we will be staying at the Palace Hotel on Oxford Street."

At her command, the taxi drove off, leaving Holmes on the pavement.

After that, for the rest of the day, Holmes had festered; there was no other word for it. We had hailed another cab, making our way to the hotel, where our overnight luggage had already been delivered. We checked in, but while I freshened up in my room, and later availed myself of the restaurant for afternoon tea, Holmes sat in the lobby, glaring at the revolving doors. After fetching a book from my room, I waited with him. I had seen him in such a state before and, even though his earlier behaviour had been unfathomable, nothing good would come of pressing the point, for the time being at least.

Even as I tried to concentrate on the novel, reading the same passages over and over again, I was unable to shake my own unease. The reason I had reacted so badly to his outburst was that I recognised some truth in his words, truth that I had been unwilling to accept sitting opposite John. The man's body was simply wrong, mismatched even. The length of the arms compared to his torso, the width of his shoulders to the waist. At first, I had put such idiosyncrasies down to an unknown trauma on the battlefield. The scarring. The hunch. The obvious damage to the brain.

Mrs Stevens had chided me for sitting in silence during the interview, but in all honesty, I had been fighting the urge to run. I was incapable of articulating it at first. There was, however, a sense that we were in the presence of someone – of some*thing* – unnatural. As I sat there, rooted to my seat, I had told myself not to be so stupid. I had merely been disturbed by those long sterile corridors, and the tension of being in a room with a man in shackles, a man who was obviously not in his right mind. I had been in similar places before, had even sat in front of similar men, but my skin crawled as if infested with lice and I could feel a scream building in my chest. I was fascinated and frustrated in equal measure by my reaction, not understanding where it came from – until Holmes had ranted on that thankfully empty street, appalling and no doubt scaring Mrs Stevens; until he had forced me to utter those dreadful words:

Of a corpse.

And that had been the truth of it. The skin. The eyes. The broken veins. If I had seen them on the mortuary slab, I would have flinched not at all, but to see them animated, the black lips smiling and snarling, spittle running down John's chin…

In that moment, on that street, I knew that, implausibly, unimaginably, we had been in the presence of a living cadaver. Worse than that. An amalgam of cadavers. A patchwork devil.

Everything I thought I knew about medicine, about science, had been turned on its head with that single admission. And it terrified me.

So, sitting in the lobby, silently accompanying Holmes in his vigil, I put it out of my mind, denying that the thought had even occurred. It had been a momentary lapse of reason, a fevered fancy. Whether or not Holmes was willing to admit it, we were no longer the men we had been when we first met all those years ago, in the prime of our lives. My wife had been right to pour scorn on this silly adventure.

All I wanted was to go home.

The revolving doors at the entrance turned, as they had turned all morning. Beside me, Holmes remained still. Yet, when Mrs Stevens stepped into the lobby, he sat forward in his seat, silent but alert.

Unlike my friend, I stood as she approached, her face a tight mask. She took a seat across from mine. I sat down again, even as Holmes held her in his level but expectant gaze.

To her credit, she stared straight back, like a cobra staring into the eyes of its charmer. Only once did her eyes shoot across to me before looking almost instantaneously back at Holmes, her tight lips twitching before she spoke a single sentence: "Ellie Grimshaw was engaged to be married."

"To a man called Danny," Holmes said softly. It was not a question.

Mrs Stevens gave the curtest of nods. "Daniel Blake. He worked on the canal, before volunteering for service."

"But Daniel is not the man who accosted her in Hulme."

"So she insists."

Holmes sat back, falling silent again.

"So how did he know the name?" Mrs Stevens asked, her expression troubled. "Why say it?"

"A coincidence?" I suggested, knowing that Holmes would tell me that there was no such thing. He made no response. "Or perhaps Danny was his friend on the Western Front. In his confused state—"

"He returned to find Mr Blake's intended?" Holmes intoned, finishing my sentence.

"It's as good a theory as any."

"Other than that there are no records of 'John' ever serving in the war."

"There was his tattoo," I pointed out. "You said so yourself. Men had them done in the trenches."

"As they do in every town in England," Holmes said. "Did Miss Grimshaw have a photograph of Daniel?"

Mrs Stevens looked shocked. "How did you know—"

"That you would ask? You are an intelligent woman, Mrs Stevens. You will not rest until you understand all of this."

She looked at Holmes for a second, before reaching into her bag to retrieve a dog-eared photograph. She handed it to Holmes, who gave it a cursory examination before passing it in turn to me. A handsome young man, standing self-consciously in front of the camera, peered back at me. If this had been the same man we'd met today, and who had loomed out of the shadows at Miss Grimshaw, then his mutilation on the fields of France must have been more terrible than any of us previously thought. There was not the slightest resemblance. This was not the Hulme Giant.

I returned the picture to Mrs Stevens, who stowed it safely in her bag.

"All that nonsense, on the street," she said, looking from one of us to the other. "About cadavers. Corpses. What was it?"

"Thinking aloud," was Holmes's only response.

"But you don't believe it. You can't. It's—"

"Horrible?"

"Ludicrous."

He took a deep breath. "The last week has seen me making one promise after another. Yesterday I promised a woman I would find her sister."

Mrs Stevens' eyes narrowed. "Sister? What has that got to do with all this?"

Holmes ignored the question. "Today, I promise you that I shall discover what links the man in that photograph with our friend in the asylum. Whether any of us believe the answer when it is found remains to be seen. In the meantime, I shall write to Dr Dougherty and apologise for my behaviour, imploring that you be allowed to continue working with and for John. I applaud you for your endeavours, Mrs Stevens, and sincerely hope that through them you find peace."

The lady had left our company less than satisfied, but Holmes had been as good as his word and before running for the train this morning, had written a letter on crisp Palace Hotel notepaper which was duly posted to Prestwich Asylum.

"What now?" I asked as the carriage swayed and rattled on our way back to London.

Holmes considered my question, before letting out a tired breath. From the rings beneath his eyes, I could see that sleep had not come easily to my friend last night, whereas I had fallen into a deep slumber, albeit one plagued by dreams of corpses writhing on mortuary slabs, each cadaver sharing John's ruined face and calling like birds.

Caw, caw, caw.

"Now, we try to piece together what we have learnt," Holmes said, "which is still precious little, save for the fact that our assailant at Abberton Hospital is not alone in this world."

"So you think that he too is, like John, a..." The words trailed off, as I struggled to bring myself to describe the man using the terms Holmes had employed.

"A composite," the detective said. "Disparate body parts moulded together to form a whole." He gave a wry chuckle. "Even now, it seems a ridiculous thing to say, but at least it is a theory that finally explains Samuel Pike's severed hand. We know that Pike met his end two years ago."

Our conversation in Scotland Yard came flooding back.

"Replantation," said I. "You believed that the hand had been reattached to Pike's body."

"But what if it were not Pike's body? What if, instead of replantation, it were transplanted onto another arm?"

"One of these patchwork devils."

"A devil with one foot significantly larger than the other?"

"The footsteps in the dust."

Holmes sighed and rubbed the bridge of his nose.

"The theory matches the facts, and yet is too outlandish for words. Have you any idea of the torment this brings, Watson? All my life I have prided myself on possessing a rational mind, and yet now rational thoughts lead to conclusions which can only be fantasy."

"Unless..." I began, hardly knowing how I should continue the sentence.

"Unless we have stumbled upon a monumental leap in medical science, whereby suddenly, despite everything we know, such procedures are now a possibility. In which case, our world view is about to be shaken beyond recognition."

"But for it to happen in a disused hospital?"

"No, that is stretching credulity to its limit. No one could achieve such things in those conditions. If it happened at all, then it happened elsewhere."

"On the battlefields of France, then? Is that any more plausible?"

"War and innovation go hand in hand. If it were not for trench warfare, would the tank ever have been invented? There was a problem, a stalemate, and science and technology provided the solution."

"And with aircraft, too," I pointed out. "Who would have thought we should see machine guns mounted on biplanes? But surely, Holmes, this is different. Vehicles and weapons are one thing, but the human body? To transplant organs, entire limbs? It's incredible, not to say terrifying. Holmes, at the beginning of all this, you castigated me for not moving with the times, but when the pace of change is so fast, so unbelievable, how can any of us keep up?"

Holmes did not answer, but instead retreated into a fretful silence. There he stayed, looking out of the window, watching the countryside hurtle past. In that instant, all I wanted to do was to stop, to take a breath, but that seemed as impossible as the thought of sewing together a man as if he were nothing more than a doll.

I just wanted to be at home, to see my wife.

However, hours later, as afternoon became evening, and a cab delivered us back to Cheyne Walk, any thoughts of comfort disappeared. The door to my house was open, a policeman standing guard outside.

While Holmes paid the fare, I flew up the front stairs, bursting through the door. The house was in chaos. The cupboards were open, their contents strewn across the floor next to overturned furniture, my beloved books yanked from their shelves.

I could hear Holmes talking to the policeman at the door, even as I found my wife sitting in the drawing room, in the presence of another officer.

Seeing me, she rose from her seat and flung herself into my arms.

"Whatever has happened?" I asked, addressing the policeman over her shoulder.

Holmes replied for him, appearing at the door. "You have been burgled. Mrs Watson interrupted the perpetrator in the midst of his crime."

I eased my wife from her embrace and, with what I hoped were comforting hands on her arms, asked her if she were hurt.

"I'm fine, John," came the shaky reply. "Oh, but you should have seen him."

"The thief?"

She nodded, tears flowing freely. "He was huge. A giant. Seven, maybe eight foot. And the scars..." She hesitated, and my blood turned to ice at the word. "He had scars all across his face, John. Deep, deep scars."

CHAPTER THIRTY-ONE

FACE TO FACE WITH A MONSTER

After some discussion, bordering on an argument, the policemen finally left. We assured them that we would look after my wife, and would report any further incident. Reluctantly they took their leave, and I had to wonder about their place in the conspiracy that had formed around our lives. To whom would they be making a report? Mycroft? The ruffled feathers of Whitehall? Chances were that they would merely be filling out a report for their sergeant, but it was so hard to know.

Ignoring the state of the kitchen, the drawers scattered on the floor and the crockery smashed, I made a pot of tea and took it through to the drawing room.

Holmes was there, questioning my wife, his voice calm and concerned, easing details from her. It took every ounce of self-control I possessed not to jump in, but such an interruption might result in my missing a vital detail that would help Holmes get to the bottom of all this. I had to be patient, and so I tried to distract myself by pouring the tea.

"So, you came in at a quarter past five?"

My wife nodded. "I knew something was wrong, straight away. He was in John's study, ripping the place apart."

It was true that my study was in chaos. Books had been thrown from the bookshelves, my desk ransacked. The thought of that brute rifling through my possessions was only erased by the tightening of my chest I felt every time I imagined him coming face to face with my wife.

I placed her cup on the table beside her chair. She thanked me, but left it where it was.

"I didn't know what to do," she admitted.

"You should have got out," I cut in, sitting in my usual chair.

"I know, but I was scared. For a moment, I thought it might even be you, that you had lost something."

"But the rest of the house?"

"I didn't notice the mess at first. It was all so confusing. I called your name and it went silent. I went to the study…"

"What did he do when he saw you?" Holmes enquired.

"He shouted. But his voice, it was strange."

"In what way?" I asked.

"It was cultured, that's the only way I can think to describe it. The voice of an educated man. Not what I expected at all, considering his appearance. 'Where are they?' he demanded. 'Your husband and his associate. Tell me!' I asked what he was doing in my house, what he wanted with us. He just repeated the same question. 'Where are they? What have they discovered?'"

"Much that we can't believe," I said, quietly.

"And then he came at me, crossing the hallway in one stride, or so it seemed. He had me pinned against the wall, his hands on my arms, holding me tight." She rubbed her right forearm, shuddering. "His hands were so cold."

"Did he hurt you?" I asked. "Show me."

She let me come across to her and rolled up her sleeve. There were four livid bruises left by gigantic fingers, the thumb mark a huge purple circle. "Oh my darling," I said, kneeling beside her.

"I screamed," she recalled, her hands in mine. "I'm not ashamed to admit it, and he shouted at me to be quiet, but it was too late. Someone had heard me on the street. He flung me aside, cracking my head on the wall. And then he was running through the kitchen, through the back door, out into the garden. I dragged myself to my feet and opened the front door, asking my saviour to fetch the police."

"And nothing of note has been taken?" Holmes asked.

"Not from what I can see," I said. "I'll need to make sure, but our valuables, such as they are, are safe. By the look of things, the villain raided both bedrooms upstairs, before searching the kitchen and my study. I've no way of knowing if he reached the attic, as it already looks as though a whirlwind has blown through it."

Holmes nodded. "If Mrs Watson had not come home when she did, no doubt the drawing room would have been next."

"But what was he hoping to find?"

"Notes on our case perhaps?" Holmes turned his attention back to my wife. "Now, I realise that this will be unpleasant, but can you describe him to me?"

"I shall remember that face until the day I die. He was disfigured, heavily scarred, his face like a jigsaw puzzle."

"And his eyes?"

"Yellow. Bright yellow. I didn't even think that was possible."

"It's not," I said, sadly.

"His hair was long and as black as night."

"What was he wearing?" Holmes asked.

She shrugged. "Nothing of note. A shirt, which once would have been white, and dark overalls, equally dirty."

"What colour?"

"Navy blue."

"But covered in earth, or only in general grime?"

She shook her head. "I can't remember."

"Please, Mrs Watson, do try. Even the smallest detail could be of vital importance."

She reached for the tea, her hand shaking as she raised the cup to her lips. Then she paused, as a thought occurred to her.

"There was something."

"Yes?"

"You'll think it foolish, but as he stepped over me, to run to the kitchen, I noticed white marks on his overalls, as if he had wiped his hands on his trousers."

"What kind of marks? Paint?"

She shook her head. "No, more like chalk."

"Could it have been plaster?"

"Possibly. It all happened so fast."

"And yet you have done remarkably well, Mrs Watson."

"Does any of it help?"

"More than you can imagine. Now..." he glanced at the clock on the mantel. "It is late, but there will still be trains."

Her brow furrowed. "Trains?"

I realised what Holmes was saying. "You talked of going to visit your sister," I explained.

"Yes," she replied, a little sharply. "But we agreed that I would stay."

"That was before all this happened," I said, taking the cup and saucer from her and replacing it on the table so that I could rest my hands on hers. "I need to make sure that you are safe."

She stiffened, pulling her hands free. "By sending me away?"

"Do you really want to stay?"

She gave no answer at first, thinking the question over, before countering with her own proposition. "Come with me."

"To Hastings? I can't."

"You want me to be safe? I shall be safer with you."

"I must stay here, to put this place right."

"No," she said, shaking her head. "You'll be going after him, but you mustn't. I have seen him, John. He is a monster."

"As have we," Holmes interjected, the revelation silencing my wife. "In the hospital by the river. The man who attacked both of us matched the description you gave, Mrs Watson. Scarred face, black hair, yellow eyes."

"He nearly killed you!"

"But he didn't," Holmes insisted. "And I wonder if that was his aim at all? He came here looking for something, as he did at Abberton Hospital."

"The bone?" I asked.

"Maybe. But he didn't hurt Mrs Watson."

"Have you not seen the bruises on her arm?"

"Not purposely, then. He could have silenced her, for good and all."

My wife tried to stifle a whimper at the thought.

"Forgive me," the detective said. "I do not wish to upset you any more than I already have, but the fact that he fled without inflicting serious injury suggests that he is not out to take lives. When we encountered him at the hospital, he was cornered, trying to escape. We were simply in the way, some of us more than others."

"He near as damn it put you in a coma."

"Because I attacked him to protect you. If I had been less hasty, he might very well have continued to run. He left us both alive, didn't he? In bad shape, yes, but still breathing."

"I can't believe you're defending him!"

"Like John in Manchester, he is a man of great strength."

"Even so—"

"Even so, Mrs Watson is correct."

My wife blinked. "I am?"

"John must go with you. I have placed you both in danger as it is."

"None of this is your fault."

"It isn't?"

"No!" I insisted. "I am a part of this, whether you like it or not, and I intend to see it through." I turned to my wife. "I know you're scared, and in all honesty, so am I, but you understand, don't you? We have a friend, a taxi driver. I'll pay him to take you straight to Sissy's. Door to door. No trains."

"But you won't come with me?" she asked.

"I can't, if only because I want to hold this rogue to account myself."

"You could leave it to the police."

"I could, but I won't. And I know how stubborn that makes me sound, how stupid maybe, but I need to see this through to the end, especially now. Especially as he has done this to you. Please tell me that you understand!"

She gave no answer, but instead turned to Holmes. "And you'll make sure that John is here, alive, when I return."

Holmes nodded solemnly. "You have my word."

"And I shall hold you to it," she warned, her fists clenched to stop her jabbing an accusatory finger in his face. "If anything happens—"

"Then a marauding giant will be the least of my worries," Holmes conceded.

"So, you'll go?" I asked.

She brushed down her skirt and stood. "I shall go and pack. Will you phone Sissy, and ask her if it is convenient?"

"Of course I will."

"But don't scare her," she added, quickly. "Tell her that I've been under the weather and need some sea air. It's not too far from the truth."

"Thank you for understanding."

"I never said I did," she replied, and climbed the stairs to face the devastation in our bedroom.

"Geller will take her?" I asked Holmes.

"I have no doubt, although I, not you, will be picking up the fare."

Leaning on my wife's chair, I stood. "That won't be necessary. She's my wife, and I'll look after her. Besides, you have more pressing matters to attend to."

"I do?" Holmes asked.

"Yes. You need to tell me where I can find the man who assaulted my wife."

Holmes gave a grim smile. "That should be no problem."

CHAPTER THIRTY-TWO

THE CENOTAPH

The following morning, I waved my wife goodbye, and Geller telephoned just a few hours later to say that they had arrived in Hastings and all was well. My wife had been safely delivered into her sister's care and he was to stay nearby to keep a watchful eye on both of them.

Holmes had helped return the house to some semblance of order. We soon discovered that my first instincts had been correct and that nothing had been taken, but that by no means assuaged my desire to get hold of the villain.

That evening, settling down for a nightcap, Holmes explained how he hoped to find the fiend.

"The white powder on his overalls," he said, taking a sip of my best brandy.

"Plaster, you suggested."

"I did."

"How can that help us? There must be hundreds of places in London where a chap could get himself covered in plaster. Thousands even."

"There are. However, there is also a major construction project running through this city."

He produced the newspaper that had been delivered that morning. Neither of us had given it more than a glance, but he threw it across the room, where it landed, still folded, on my lap.

"Examine the front page."

I unfurled the paper to reveal the picture of a tower being constructed on Whitehall.

"The victory monuments?"

"The victory monuments, constructed from wood and covered with plaster, although if you read the report you will see that there are already calls to make at least one a permanent structure."

"All very noble, but how does it help us?"

"The photograph, Watson. Look at the workers."

I did, and saw that they all wore dark overalls. Of course, there was no way of telling the shade of their garments in the black and white photograph, but it could have easily been navy blue.

"The interesting thing about the project," Holmes continued, "is that the government has purposely employed those poor souls who have returned from the front with disfigurements that may preclude them from securing work in so-called polite society."

"Men with scars."

"Now, look at this," Holmes said, fishing a folded handkerchief from his pocket. He leant forward and, placing it on my wife's prized coffee table, unfolded the cloth to reveal a splinter of wood in its centre. "I discovered this on the carpet in the hallway," he explained. "It's oak, and rough enough to come from timber. Now tell me, what are they using to construct the monuments?"

I glanced at the report, and looked up at him, a smile on my lips.

"Oak," I said.

* * *

As we walked through the streets the following morning, I tried not to let my hopes run away with themselves. This was a long shot, and without my wife being able to identify the overalls, we had no idea if we were on the right track, but it was as good a place to start as any.

The site of the first monument led nowhere, but at the second tower, Holmes called over the foreman. He repeated the patter we had tried at the first site, explained that we were looking for an old friend, describing the disfigured giant. Did he work on this site?

"And who's asking?" the fellow had replied, his eyes lighting up when I produced a banknote in the sum of ten shillings.

"Someone who wants to remain anonymous," I said.

"Don't we all," said he, pocketing the note. "Although, from your description, I reckon you're looking for Aggie. Can't imagine there's two of *him*. Least I hope there isn't."

"Aggie?"

"Giant of a man, that one. You should try the Cenotaph, do you know it? The one near Downing Street. If Aggie's anywhere, he's there."

However, on arriving at the site, it seemed that we would be disappointed once again. The centre of the street was a hive of activity, the wooden frame of the Cenotaph being plastered in readiness for the procession. One couldn't help but be impressed. No structure could adequately represent the sacrifice of the war dead, yet even in its unfinished state this was a sight to behold, tall and majestic. A week in advance of the parade, men were already doffing their hats, an act of respect that was more touching than a thousand marching troops would ever be.

Again we approached a workman, another banknote in my hand ready to help loosen his tongue, but this time no bribe was required.

"Aggie, aye. He's here all right. Don't know him too well myself. One of the quiet ones he is. Don't say much at all."

He looked around, scanning his fellow workers. We spotted the brute at the same moment, but before I could hush him, the workman called out.

"There he is. Oi, Aggie! Over here. Some fellows to see you!"

The giant turned, his yellow eyes widening as he became aware of our identity. Then he was off, throwing aside the pallets he had been hefting, to flee across the road.

"Watson!" Holmes called out as he sprinted after the rogue, but I needed no encouragement. Ignoring the beeping horn of the omnibus that nearly mowed me down, I took off in pursuit of him. Unsurprisingly, our quarry's long strides had covered the road in seconds, plunging him into the crowd in the direction of Richmond Terrace.

"Stop him!" I shouted out, not caring who heard. A few days ago, I would have dared not be so bold, especially with Mycroft's men on our tail. Now I hoped they were still there, hiding in the shadows. If they were there to protect us, then surely they could serve us as well.

Yet no one came to our aid. Aggie, if that was the man's name, pelted through the crowd, knocking pedestrians flying. At least he was easy enough to spot, rising head and shoulders above the other Londoners.

"He's turned off," I called to Holmes as he disappeared to the right. We were having to manhandle our way through the throng, folk shouting at us to mind our manners. At this rate, we were going to lose him again. The devil could run like the wind. By the time we reached the corner of Richmond Terrace he would have made it to the river. There was no way we could catch up.

Yet, as we puffed our way onto the terrace, we found our prey standing stock still, his enormous arms high in the air.

In front of him, a revolver in his hand, stood the portly figure of Inspector Tovey, a stern smile etched on his face.

"I'm assuming that you'd like a word with this individual, Mr Holmes," Tovey said, never taking his eyes from the giant. "I know I would."

"I thought you were in Cornwall, Inspector," Holmes panted.

"So did a lot of folk, but you know me. I'm a city boy, always have been, always will be. And as for you, Goram…"

With his gun hand steady, Tovey raised a whistle to his lips and blew hard.

CHAPTER THIRTY-THREE

ELIMINATE THE IMPOSSIBLE

"Are you sure this is safe?" I asked Inspector Tovey as we walked through long dark corridors.

"Nowhere's safer than Scotland Yard, Doctor, no matter what Mr Holmes's brother may say."

"I for one am pleased to see you," said Holmes, walking a few paces behind us, no doubt in order to observe the faces of the officers and administrative staff who passed by. "How was your case in the West Country?"

"Insulting, that's what it was. If the powers that be thought shipping me off to Fowey would get me out of the way, they could at least have found something to keep me busy." He adopted a suitably sepulchral tone, as beloved by hams in music halls the world over. "*Mysterious disappearances linked to a suspected witches' coven*. Load of stuff and nonsense. Ended up being a simple smugglers' ring, as I suspected from the moment I stepped off the train."

"And your superiors?"

"Thought I was still down there, until we wandered through

the front doors with old Goram."

"You called him that before," I said, puzzled by the name.

"My little joke, Doctor. Goram was one of the giants who created Bristol."

"I beg your pardon?"

"According to the stories my Grampy used to tell when I was a nipper, anyhow."

"His workmates claim our giant is called Aggie," Holmes pointed out.

Tovey pulled a face. "Reckon he suits Goram better."

"But what were you doing in Whitehall?" I asked.

Tovey turned a corner. "I wasn't ready to announce my return just yet, so I headed for your place, only to find the two of you roaring off in that car of yours."

"And so you followed us?" Holmes asked.

"For all I knew you were a part of all this, especially as I'd heard that a certain Mycroft Holmes had been behind shipping me off to Cornwall."

"Trust me," I muttered, "we were just as much in the dark as you."

"Speak for yourself," Holmes rumbled behind us.

"I decided to hold back, just to see what you were up to. Even if it was nothing dodgy, the last thing you needed was me sticking my beak in where it wasn't wanted, but when I saw tall, dark and gruesome starting to run…"

"Inspector, I have never been so grateful for police interference in my life," Holmes said, warmly.

"I wonder if our prisoner shares the same sentiment." The inspector stopped in front of a solid wooden door and rapped three times. A tiny window in the door slid open, a pair of eyes peering out. Seconds later, the door opened. We entered another corridor, once again lined with heavy doors. Tovey led us to the third door on the right, and opened it to reveal a room containing a large, barren cell.

At least, it would have looked large, had the prisoner behind the bars been less imposing. Even sitting on the hard wooden bench that ran along the far wall, the monster of a man was intimidating, his long hair hanging across his blanched face.

Inspector Tovey had arranged for three chairs to be placed on our side of the bars. We chose to stand instead, waiting for Tovey to begin the interrogation.

The giant neglected even to acknowledge our presence.

"Playing dumb, are we?" Tovey said, breaking the silence. "And there was I wondering if you had a brain as big as your body. The thing is, we already have you for assault, not to mention breaking and entering. Wanting to add obstruction to the list, are you, Aggie?"

"Agares," came the brute's reply.

The inspector's brow furrowed.

"Beg your pardon?"

"My name is Agares."

"Interesting," said Holmes, taking the middle seat so as to be positioned directly opposite the prisoner. "Agares was a demon as described in the *Ars Goetia*, was he not?"

The man finally looked up, fixing his yellow eyes on Holmes, although he remained tight-lipped.

"*Ars Goetia*?" I asked.

Tovey answered for Holmes. "A seventeenth-century grimoire, translated at the turn of the century by those swindlers Samuel Lidell MacGregor Mathers and Aleister Crowley."

"I am impressed, Inspector," Holmes commented.

"You wouldn't be if you read the translation. Bloody awful."

Holmes laughed, although the giant made no sign that he shared the joke.

Holmes narrowed his eyes and continued. "According to the original text, the spirits of the *Goetia* are seventy-one demons summoned by King Solomon to do his bidding. Of the seventy-one, Agares was the devil who delighted in destroying man's dignity."

The prisoner's eyes bore into Holmes and when he spoke it was but one word.

"Devil."

The room fell quiet, neither Holmes nor the inspector choosing to fill the silence. Finally, the giant did so for them.

"That was the first word I ever heard my father speak. The first name he bestowed upon me. Names are powerful, Mr Sherlock Holmes. Mine has stayed with me ever since. If I had been painted a devil, then a devil's title I would have. The destroyer of dignity?" Agares uttered a single mirthless laugh. "In all my long life, I have never been blessed with dignity. It seemed strangely appropriate, do you not agree?"

The man's voice was extraordinary. So rich and deep, the voice of a poet in the body of a monster. Fascinated, I took a seat beside Holmes. Agares's eyes now followed me.

"Dr Watson," he said. "I must apologise to you and your wife. I meant her no harm."

I bristled at the words. "Then why did you attack her?"

In response, the man rather piteously raised his hands. "Even after all this time, I find it hard to judge my own strength."

"Which is why, I suppose, you nearly killed Holmes?"

"You should not have tried to entrap me." He glanced up at the bars in front of him. "I do not appreciate being caged."

"What were you doing in the hospital?" Tovey asked. Now those dead eyes swivelled to find him.

"The same as you, Inspector. I was searching for the truth."

"Do you know what happened there?"

"In the operating theatre? I thought that would be clear." He paused, before delivering his verdict. "Murder."

"Perpetrated by you?"

The giant raised his hands so we could see them, the same perfect stitching around his wrists. "Do these look like the hands of a surgeon?"

"Then who was it?" asked Holmes. "Elsbeth Honegger?"

The man's black lips drew back into a sneer. "Another name. Another lie."

"And what name should she have?"

"The most accursed name on the face of all the earth," Agares spat. "Frankenstein."

"Ernest Balmer's original surname."

"Before shame overtook his family, yes. The shame my father bestowed upon them."

"Your father?" Tovey asked.

"The man who christened you devil?"

The prisoner nodded. "Victor Frankenstein."

I glanced at Holmes. "But that's impossible. Victor Frankenstein was alive over a hundred years ago."

"Unless another of the family took his name?" Holmes suggested.

Agares threw back his head and laughed. "They would rather die first."

"Why? What was Victor Frankenstein's crime?"

"Was he a murderer?" I asked.

"The opposite," Agares answered. "He was a creator."

"You're not making much sense," Tovey said, vocalising the confusion that he and I shared.

"You want me to tell my tale?"

"That is why we are here," Holmes replied.

Agares smiled at the detective. "So you can pick holes in my story. The great detective." Another laugh. "You have no idea what you ask."

He paused, but when no one responded, he sat back against the wall and began to speak.

"It was November 1792. Victor Frankenstein was but twenty-two years old. A genius, able to see beyond the limitations of his peers. While attending university at Ingolstadt, he attempted to do what no man had been able to achieve. To create new life without a woman."

"How?" I asked.

"Using human remains," he replied, looking straight into my eyes. "Regenerated. Renewed."

I squirmed in my seat. "Preposterous," was all I could manage to say.

"Yes, I am," came the reply.

"You are his creature," Holmes stated.

"I am, for my sins. Or rather for the sins of my father."

"But, as my friend pointed out, Victor Frankenstein lived over a century ago."

"Yes," the prisoner agreed. "And died on the eleventh of September 1799. The date is branded on my stolen heart. I saw his body with my own eyes, and wept."

Holmes shook his head. "That is impossible. Despite your injuries, it is clear to see that you are no more than thirty years old yourself."

The giant smiled once again. "Impossible. As impossible as building yourself a funeral pyre, setting it alight and finding that your flesh refuses to burn? As impossible as discovering that, as a final insult, your creator was able to pass into the beyond, but you could not follow?"

"You're telling us that you cannot die?" scoffed Tovey. "Perhaps I should have tested the theory on the streets of Whitehall."

"Perhaps you should still try."

An uncomfortable silence descended once again, until Holmes

spoke. "So, if we were to believe such an outrageous account—"

"Why am I searching for my kin?"

Holmes nodded.

"I have travelled the world for over a century, searching for an end to my torment."

"For a way to die?"

"And then I hear of Elsbeth Honegger, following in Victor's footsteps."

I shifted in my chair, unable to keep still. "You're saying that Elsbeth is conducting her own experiments on the dead?"

"You have seen the results with your own eyes. I assume you followed up the newspaper report I found in your study? The Hulme Giant."

"He is like you?"

Agares spread his arms. "Surely you see the family resemblance? Seven years ago, Elsbeth was arrested."

"For what crime?" asked Tovey.

Agares turned to face the policeman. "Grave robbing, to find fresh material for her immoral procedures."

"Immoral?" commented Holmes. "You say that such experiments gave you life. Surely you would think them good."

The yellow eyes swung back to Holmes. "Nothing about my existence is good, Mr Holmes. You have no idea of what it is like to know that you are an abomination, to know that you should not exist. Those men alongside whom I have toiled, building monuments to those fortunate enough to die, they have seen such terrors, witnessed atrocities that would have driven you or I mad, and yet they could hardly bring themselves to look at me on the worksite. They know, as much as I do, that I am… wrong. Unnatural. That is the gift my creator bestowed on me."

"There's a problem with your story," cut in Inspector Tovey.

The prisoner smiled. "Only one?"

"Elsbeth Honegger was never arrested. I ran a check when we brought you in. She has no criminal record that we can find."

Agares looked at the inspector in disgust. "And there I was wondering if you had a brain as big as your body."

Tovey wrung his hands behind his back, trying not to show his displeasure at having his own words thrown back at him.

"You can be arrested, but never charged," Agares said. "It did not reach that point before *they* found her. Now, which of you is going to ask me, who are *they*?"

We waited, reluctant to give the man any more ground.

His smile turned into a leer. "The powers and principalities. Tell me, Dr Watson, what would you do if you were sending men off to war, wave after wave, like cattle to the slaughterhouse?"

I shifted uncomfortably beneath that yellow gaze. "Work to bring the conflict to a close, I should think."

"Would you really? Think of them, Doctor, all those boys on the front line. Fresh-faced, barely ready to shave. Terrified. And on the other side, more boys, more faces, more fear. What happens next?"

We let the question remain rhetorical. The monster looked at us, waiting for the moment, and then shouted: "Rat-a-tat-a-tat-a-tat!"

I am ashamed to say I nearly jumped out of my skin.

"The bullets start firing," Agares said, "the tanks start rolling. Mines. Guns. Disease – all working to the same end. Do you know what remains, when the sounds of battle fade?"

"Bodies," said Holmes coldly.

Agares clapped slowly. "Well done, detective. Bodies. Thousands and thousands of bodies. The honoured war dead, cluttering up the trenches, spreading disease, doing the work of the enemy. What use are they?"

"Use?" Tovey spluttered. "They've given their lives, damn you."

"But what if they could give their deaths," Holmes said quietly.

I looked to my friend. "What do you mean?"

"Mr Agares," said Holmes, "you implied that Miss Honegger was searching for bodies to recreate your creator's experiments."

"I did."

"Where better to find bodies than a battlefield?"

"You cannot be serious!" I exclaimed.

"Raw materials," Agares said. "That's all they are to her."

"But it wouldn't be allowed."

"Would it not? An army in desperate need of troops, fresh or otherwise. A body gets lost, in all the chaos. The telegram is still sent, sympathy expressed, but no body in the grave. No waste."

"So she used the bodies to create new soldiers," Holmes said, studying Agares's face.

"Soldiers who cannot die," he replied.

Not for the first time, I could scarcely believe what I was hearing. "Holmes, you cannot be giving credence to this macabre fantasy. It's tommyrot, the lot of it."

Holmes kept his eyes fixed on the giant. "Mr Agares believes it, wholeheartedly. Either that, or he has elevated deceit to an art form. You scratch your nose whenever you tell a lie, did you know that, Watson? You always have."

"An increase of temperature in the face, brought on by stress," the prisoner interjected, drawing a smile from Holmes. "Blood flows to the extremities, causing them to itch—"

"Hence the involuntary response. I see you are a learned man."

"I like to read."

Holmes turned his attention to Tovey. "The inspector has a similar tic. He taps his foot with every untruth. I've written a monograph on the subject, suggesting that the body shows more signs of deceit beneath the waist than above. Hand and eye movements are under conscious control, but the further the body part from the brain—"

"—the less aware you are that it is moving, especially during periods of stress," Agares completed. "I should like to read it."

"I'll send you a copy. However, in this case, you have made not a single movement, Mr Agares. In all the time we have spoken, other than turning to look from one of us to the other, there have been no hidden signs. No twitches. No scratches. No gestures at all. Indeed, the fact that you have looked each of us in the eye tells us a great deal. Even the finest actor struggles to conceal deceit. You believe every word that you say."

"I do."

"Which proves nothing," I insisted, unable to bite my tongue any longer. "A madman may believe he's Henry the Eighth. It doesn't mean that he is."

"What if an inmate says that he has never been to France?" Agares said. "What of that, Doctor? What if I could prove that he had, that poor wretch in Manchester?"

Agares shifted on his bench, and Tovey took a step forward as if worried that the giant was about to throw himself against the bars. Instead the man reached into the pocket of his overalls and pulled out a folded paper. He reached across, his arm span easily reaching the front of his cage, and offered the paper through the bars. Cautiously, Tovey took it, stepping away before opening it and passing it to Holmes.

It was a photograph, showing three soldiers in their uniforms, heads held high. Two were unknown to me, but the third…

Holmes had the same thought. "What do you say, Watson? That face, if it were scarred almost beyond recognition?"

There was no doubt. "It's John. It has to be. So he was in France?"

"His name was Michael," Agares informed us. He had folded his great hands in front of him again. "Michael Connick, although I think you will find the identity of the man next to him of interest. The fellow with the moustache."

Holmes turned the photograph in the light, trying to make it out. "I don't recognise him."

"There is no reason you would, but you might know his name. Daniel Blake. Known to his friends as Danny."

I looked at Holmes. "Ellie Grimshaw's fiancé."

"They died on the same day, in the same battle. Their bodies were reported lost. Telegrams sent. Sympathies expressed."

"No bodies in the grave," Holmes said.

My head was spinning. I took the photograph and examined it further. The soldier's resemblance to John was extraordinary, even without the scarring. We had talked to the man, deranged though he was. He had been alive.

"She took those men," Agares said, "and carved them apart, discarded the pieces that were of no use. And then, limb by limb, joint by joint, she made them anew. Michael Connick, I discovered, was shot in the head. Right here." The prisoner tapped his left temple. "His brain would have been damaged beyond repair. Daniel, however, took a bullet to the face. His jaw was ripped clean off, but his brain, that was unharmed. Dead, yes, but intact, ready to be reanimated. Ready to be born again."

I could hear no more of this. I rose to my feet. "I need to get some air. I'm sorry."

Agares's eyes never left me. "Difficult to accept, is it not? But I trust the person who gathered the bodies. He was French, or at least he thought he was. He was unable to remember. None of us can remember, not really. There are moments, random images that flash across the mind's eye like pictures from a magic lantern, but you have no idea what they mean. And then there are the dreams." Agares laughed humourlessly. "Your mind trying to process memories that should have died with the brain.

"The man who took Michael and Daniel's remains to her,

he was her firstborn, her greatest success to date. She called him Adam. The curious thing is that even though he spoke English, after a fashion, he could read French. Preferred it, in fact. When I last saw him, I gave him a book. A bribe if you will. *Le Triangle d'or.* He was so grateful. He kept turning it over and over in his hands. Before she removed them of course, his own mother, before she dumped his body parts into the Thames. All but one that she missed in her hurry. A hand."

I felt the gorge rise in my throat.

"Is it all becoming clear to you, Doctor?" Agares sneered. "Are you beginning to understand?"

"I'm sorry," I said again, and rushed for the door. The man couldn't be telling the truth. None of it was possible.

But when you eliminate the impossible…

CHAPTER THIRTY-FOUR

HERE BE DRAGONS

Holmes found me standing outside Scotland Yard, gulping air like a fish out of water. He did me the courtesy of not enquiring about my health and instead called a cab. We sat in silence all the way back to Chelsea, and exchanged few words until we were safely installed in my drawing room, supping a restorative brandy.

"Mr Agares affected you deeply," Holmes said.

"Deduced that, did you?"

"Come now, this is no time for sarcasm."

"What time is it then, exactly? Time for throwing years of medical and rational belief out of the window? You have spent the best part of our lives astounding me, Holmes, but never like this. That you, of all people, should believe that... man's story."

"I never said *I* believed it, only that *he* does. Unfortunately, at present, I have no other theory to offer, not one that fits the facts anyway."

"There has to be something. I cannot believe—"

"That human life, no matter how grotesque, can be manufactured on an operating table?"

I let out a deep sigh. "Yes."

"Neither can I, Watson, but what if I am wrong? Our forebears believed that the world was flat, that the sun circled the earth. They were wrong. They believed that odours and not germs transmitted diseases; that blood could not be transplanted from one body to another. They were wrong. No, that is unfair. They were mistaken. They did not have all the facts at their disposal. Discoveries were yet to be made.

"Today we heard that new life has been born out of necrotic flesh. We have seen evidence with our own eyes that perhaps such beings exist. We don't know how. We do not have all the facts at our disposal. But, if that creature in the cell had told us that Elsbeth Honegger was conjuring spirits from hell, I would not have believed him. If he told us that London was crawling with the nosferatu, I would have laughed in his face. What he suggested was that through scientific endeavour, such a feat has been made possible. No magic. No superstition."

"But science?"

"But science... There is so much we don't yet understand, Watson. It could be that, no matter how ghoulish it may sound, such a miracle is possible. Perhaps scientists of the next century will look back at us and laugh; those primitives, who didn't believe that bodies could be recycled. How backward. How stunted. No different from those who thought you could fall off the edge of the world if you sailed far enough."

"Here be dragons?"

Holmes nodded. "None of this sits easy with you, does it, old boy?"

"Not one bit."

"Nor does it with me, to be truthful, but Mr Agares is safely under lock and key and Inspector Tovey will see that he remains that way. He will provide the answers I seek, one way or another. I shall understand, Watson. I shall get to the bottom of it."

I went to speak, but stopped myself.

"What is it?" Holmes asked.

"I keep thinking about John, or Daniel, or whatever we are meant to call him. Could he really have been created by Elsbeth Honegger?"

"Mother knows best?" Holmes asked.

My stomach clenched. "Oh good Lord. You don't mean—"

"Maybe he wasn't talking about his mother sending him off to war. Maybe he was talking of a woman on the battlefield, bringing him life. Do you remember Elsbeth's brooch, Watson, the one that belonged to the Frankensteins?"

My mouth was dry. "The crow."

"Caw, caw, caw," croaked Holmes.

I shivered, despite myself. Could it all be true? I had thought that John was calling for the birds outside the window, but if he was remembering the clasp on his mother's collar... No, it was madness, but I knew one thing. While I struggled to believe Agares's wild story, I believed in Sherlock Holmes. If any man alive could make sense of all this, it was my friend, and I would stand by his side every step of the way.

Little was I to know that in doing so, I would nearly lose Holmes in the process. But we had been set on a path, one that beckoned us further just a few minutes later when the telephone rang.

"Oh, thank God," said the voice on the other end of the line.

"Mrs Sellman?"

"I've been calling all afternoon, I didn't know what else to do."

"What's happened? Is it Frederick?"

"No, you don't understand. It's my sister."

"Elsbeth? What about her?"

"She wrote to us, Doctor. She's alive."

* * *

The following morning we were back in Hampstead, being welcomed by Mr and Mrs Sellman. Frederick was up in his room, but the item which had prompted our summons awaited us in the drawing room.

"It arrived yesterday morning," Mrs Sellman informed us, showing us to the drawing-room table. "We were both out, so Miss Wilkins took delivery. Here."

At the centre of the table was a toy lion, roughly fifteen inches from nose to tail and standing beside a deep emerald cardboard box. The creature was covered in flocked material, with a bushy mane made from what looked like real fur.

"Another automaton?" Holmes enquired.

Mr Sellman nodded. "It was all I could do to prise it out of Freddie's hands this morning. He thinks it's simply marvellous."

"And for good reason," said Holmes, bending to examine the toy. "Such craftsmanship. Look, Watson, those eyes are positively lifelike, and as for the teeth!" He reached out and touched one of the sharp incisors that lined the toy's jaws. "Made of ivory no less. May we see it in operation?"

Mr Sellman produced a small bronze key. "Of course."

Our host inserted the key into a hole in the beast's side and began to wind. When he removed his hand, the key started to turn of its own accord, driven by the clockwork mechanism inside. Springing to life, the miniature lion nodded its head, the jaws opening and closing. After repeating the motion four or five times, the automaton sat back on its haunches, emitting a throaty mechanical roar. I found myself chuckling, but then started as the clockwork beast leapt once more to its feet.

"Enchanting," cheered Holmes, applauding the device. "Most ingenious. I can see why your son is so enamoured."

"But how do you know it is from Miss Honegger," I asked, "other than by her fascination with automata?"

With a shaking hand, Mrs Sellman passed me an envelope. “This was in the box.”

The envelope was plain, but inside was a note written on light cream paper. In neat, crisp handwriting it read:

Darling Freddie,

Sorry that I had to go away so suddenly. Here is a friend to keep you company until I return.

Your loving aunt,
E.

Tears had formed in Camille Sellman’s eyes by the time I passed the note to Holmes. It was easy to see that many tears had been shed over the last twenty-four hours.

Holmes sniffed the paper before reading. “Your sister doesn’t care for perfume.”

“She never wears it,” Mrs Sellman confirmed.

“And is not fond of crowds either.”

Mr Sellman looked confused. “She is a solitary soul, but how can you tell?”

Holmes reviewed the handwriting again. “She leaves considerable room between words, a sure sign that the writer enjoys freedom and doesn’t like to be encroached, with a tendency to become overwhelmed at large gatherings.” He looked up from the paper and smiled. “Graphology is such an intriguing subject.”

“The analysis of a person’s handwriting,” I explained. “Holmes believes that an individual’s personality spills over into his – or her – script.”

“Each one of Elsbeth’s letters is tiny,” he continued, “indicating a meticulous, even obsessive person, while the slight slant to the right, no more than five degrees, indicates that Miss Honegger is ruled by her head, rather than her heart, repressing emotion wherever possible."

"Not when it comes to Frederick," bristled Mrs Sellman.

Holmes favoured the comment with a smile, before asking how the package was delivered.

"In the post."

"Excellent. May I see the postmark on the wrapping paper?"

Mr Sellman's face darkened. "I'm afraid not. Miss Wilkins, with her usual efficiency, threw it away before we returned home."

Holmes nodded twice. "I see, but all is not lost." He held the paper up to the light to inspect the watermark. "Your sister is in Germany, Mrs Sellman."

"Germany?"

"This is a product of the Gaertner-Melnhof Paper Mill, a stock sold only to their domestic market."

"Has she been to Germany before?" I asked.

"Not that I know of," admitted Mrs Sellman.

"You did say she has travelled a good deal?"

"For her research, but she is a very private person. She wouldn't always tell us where she had been."

"Thankfully, our friendly lion is less reticent," said Holmes, reaching for the clockwork toy. "May I?"

"Of course," Mrs Sellman replied.

With great care, Holmes turned the toy over in his hands, running his thumb against the seam of its belly and, placing the beast back on all four feet, removing the key from its side.

"Yes, I thought so. May I also see the box? Thank you."

Holmes removed the lid and turned it over to reveal a crest and a company name printed on the reverse.

"Foerstner Automaten GmbH," Holmes read. "The abbreviation stands for *Gesellschaft mit beschränkter Haftung*,

German for a limited company."

"Yes," said Mr Sellman, "I'm aware of what it means, but where are they based?"

"I'm afraid I do not recognise the crest above the name, although it is undoubtedly a coat of arms," Holmes admitted, turning the lid to face me. "Watson?"

I took a closer look, but was none the wiser. Beneath a typically Germanic cross lay a solitary key with a diamond-shaped head and square teeth. "I'm afraid I have no idea," I admitted, "although the presence of a key suggests a financial connection. A centre of commerce, or some such?"

Holmes nodded. "A fair assumption." He replaced the lid neatly on the box. "Either way, a visit to your attic will reveal its identity, I am sure."

"The doctor's attic?" Mrs Sellman said, looking from Holmes to me.

"It's a long story," I told her, not relishing the thought of facing Holmes's vast collections of books once more.

"And one that will soon be at a close," Holmes added. "Once we have identified the coat of arms, finding your sister will be simplicity itself."

"George will pay your travel expenses, of course," Mrs Sellman insisted.

I was unsure who looked more shocked, Mr Sellman or myself.

"We're going to Germany?" I asked.

Holmes gave me a knowing smile. "*Reisen bildet und erweitert den eigenen Horizont, Herr Doktor.*"

CHAPTER THIRTY-FIVE

ALL ABOARD

Whether or not travel expands one's horizons, the coat of arms had indeed borne fruit. Two days later, we were thundering through the countryside of north-western Germany, heading for Bremerhaven, a port at the mouth of the river Weser.

Holmes had found the crest within a minute of flicking through one of his gazetteers. That it took him the best part of the morning, crashing through the attic, to find the book itself need never be mentioned again.

Disembarking at Bremen railway station, we checked into our hotel and asked the concierge for help locating Foerstner Automaten. The shop, a charming establishment whose window display was packed with all manner of clockwork toys, was near the town hall, not a ten-minute walk from the hotel.

We entered, a tinkling bell alerting the proprietor of our arrival. He appeared from a door behind the counter, a man in his fifties with a neat grey beard and two pairs of half-moon reading glasses, one perched on his nose and the other resting on the top of a hairless head.

"Herr Foerstner?" Holmes enquired, in perfect German.

The proprietor smiled warmly. "The same. How may I be of assistance, gentlemen?"

Holmes held out his hand. "It is a pleasure to make your acquaintance. My colleague and I have travelled from London to meet you."

Foerstner took the proffered hand, but looked at us in concern. "London? Why would you come all this way for me?"

Holmes threw out his arms to take in the contents of the small shop. "For the sake of all this," he offered in explanation.

Surrounding us were dolls and animals and carousels and castles. It was a veritable Aladdin's cave that would send any child into rapture, although I found the experience of having hundreds of glass eyes staring in my direction somewhat unsettling. I was unable to shake the feeling that they would all come alive at any moment.

"We are reporters from *The Times*," Holmes continued, smiling broadly. I fought the urge to peer at my friend in order to discover *his* personal sign of deceit. "We are writing an article on automata, and recently had the pleasure of witnessing one of your exquisite creations. You, sir, are a true artisan."

The flattery worked. Foerstner positively preened, his eyes sparkling. "It is kind of you to say so, but if I may enquire, which piece did you see? I do not send many of my toys overseas."

"Which is why we had to visit," Holmes insisted. "Yours is a rare talent that our readers will want to experience for themselves. I dare say that you'll receive a good many orders from English enthusiasts, keen to add a Foerstner original to their collection."

"You are very kind, but the piece?"

"Ah, yes," said Holmes, feigning absent-mindedness. He pulled a notebook from his pocket and flicked through to a page covered in shorthand. "A lion that, once wound—"

"Sits back and jumps," Foerstner interrupted. "Yes, yes, I was particularly proud of that one. The growl was quite difficult to perfect."

"And yet perfect it you did. Can you talk me through the creation of the masterpiece?"

We listened as the craftsman explained his methods in minute detail, learning more about clockwork than I thought possible, or indeed wanted to know. All the time, Holmes nodded and jotted down notes. Finally, when I thought that I might be able to build one of the wretched contraptions myself, Holmes consulted another page of his notebook.

"The lion was purchased by a Miss Elsbeth Honegger." He leant in surreptitiously. "A present for her nephew, who simply adores the beast."

Again, Holmes's flummery did the trick.

"Ah, a delightful woman," Foerstner gushed. "So interested in the work. She was a pleasure to talk to."

"I'm glad to hear it, as we should very much like a word with the good lady ourselves. Could you pass us her telephone number, or perhaps an address?"

Foerstner's expression faltered. "I'm afraid that won't be possible."

"You don't have them?"

"No, it's not that. I would feel uncomfortable handing out a customer's private details. It just isn't done, you know?"

"I understand, but all we would require from her is a short statement about the quality of your work; what attracted her to your shop, how she was impressed by your service and so on. Everyone wants to read about a happy customer, don't they? Especially before making a purchase themselves. You know, I have even heard that His Majesty the King collects automata for his children. Just imagine if he read the article?"

Foerstner hesitated before relenting, reaching beneath his desk for a ledger. "I'm sure she won't mind," he said, "if you explain why you are calling."

His finger stopped on the relevant entry. "I'm afraid I don't have a telephone number, but I can give you gentlemen her address."

"That would be ideal," Holmes said with a smile.

According to Foerstner, Elsbeth Honegger had taken lodgings at 28 Löningstraße, near the port. We made our way to the address, but as we approached the three-storey building, we spotted the lady herself pulling the front door closed behind her. Holmes clasped my arm, guiding me behind a nearby market stall.

"What are we doing?"

"Observing," came the reply.

There was no mistaking Miss Honegger. She wore her hair in the pompadour style we had seen in the photograph owned by Mrs Sellman, and bore a startling resemblance to her sister in person, even down to her purposeful walk.

"Should we not simply approach her?" I asked.

"I would rather see where she's heading," said Holmes, "especially in such a hurry."

"You would think she'd take a cab in such weather," I said, turning up my collar. It had been raining steadily from the moment we arrived and looked to be getting worse, a storm brewing in the air. Holmes waited for the lady to continue halfway down Löningstraße before stepping out from our hiding place. We set off in gentle pursuit, Holmes refusing to open his umbrella in case it drew her attention. Pneumonia it was then!

What was that my wife had said about Holmes being the death of me?

Miss Honegger went straight to the port, breezing past the

dockworkers as if she owned the place. Finally, she approached a large steam ship that was moored alongside the dock. The port was a hive of activity, dockhands loading cargo from a nearby warehouse onto the ship. She stopped to talk to them. At first, I thought she was asking for directions, but it soon became clear that she was taking them to task over their heavy-handed treatment of the cargo. *Her* cargo.

Holmes read the name of the freighter. "*Das Rabe*. Notice something odd about it, Watson?"

"I'm hardly what you would call an expert," I admitted.

"Neither am I, but look at the main mast."

I did as he asked. There *was* something odd about it.

"Looks too tall," I said.

"As if it has been extended, and where are the sails? The secondary masts have them, but there's no rigging on the central pole."

"There's something on there. Rope, is it?"

"Possibly. It is peculiar, though."

We watched the men continue to haul crates onto the deck.

"Surely they're not thinking of taking her out in this?" I said.

The rain had increased, fierce winds rolling in from the sea. On the dockside, Miss Honegger was holding onto her hat, struggling to remain upright in the gale. The crates being winched onto the ship swayed alarmingly, and even behind the pile of containers that we were using to conceal ourselves, rain stung our faces.

The discussion had become an argument, although the voices dropped to silence as a stern man in a sharp suit descended the gangplank. He approached Miss Honegger, standing just a little too close for comfort, clearly trying to intimidate the woman, although she held her ground. We were too far away to hear what was being said, the heated conversation muffled by the rain, but both of us were shocked when the gentleman in question seized her arm and marched her up the ramp and into the ship, a burly sailor stepping out of the way to let them gain entrance.

"Holmes—" I started, but a hand on my shoulder stopped me from breaking cover.

"We'll be no good to her in there, especially as most of those men are armed."

He was right. Peering through the downpour, I could just make out a gun in its holster on every docker's belt.

"You would have us do nothing? If they are leaving..."

"I've not come all this way just to lose the lady again," Holmes said. "We're going aboard that ship."

"And how are we going to do that? Is *The Times* about to publish an award-winning piece on German maritime affairs?"

"Shipshape and Bremer fashion? I doubt those fellows are as gullible as Herr Foerstner."

"What then?"

He glanced at the open warehouse. I followed his gaze and saw more crates lined up, ready to be loaded. A couple were open, their lids loose across them.

"Those crates look big enough to hide a fellow or two, don't you think?"

"You can't be serious."

"I assure you I am."

"But how are we supposed to climb inside them without being noticed?"

Holmes nodded towards the ship. "An Englishman always keeps his eye upon the weather."

I followed his gaze, seeing the crate on the winch rock precariously in the wind. All at once, it slipped from its bonds and tumbled to the ground, splitting open. Men came running, the foreman shouting orders. This was our chance. Complaining under my breath, I followed Holmes into the now deserted warehouse. He pulled aside one of the lids to reveal coils of cables and wires.

"What is all this for?"

"Now is not the time to ask questions," said Holmes, glancing up at the chaos on the dockside. "Now is the time to get in the box. There should be just enough room for you."

"How small do you think I am, and what about you? There isn't room for both of us."

"There's more than one crate. Get in."

Still grumbling, I clambered in, lying on my bed of cables. "You saw that crate fall, didn't you?"

"I did, yes," Holmes hissed, grabbing the lid.

"And you're not worried that lightning will strike twice?"

"Worse things happen at sea. Besides, these crates are smaller. They will probably be carried up the ramp."

"And if they're not?"

"Bon voyage, Watson!"

He lowered the lid, closing me in. Panic hit me almost immediately. It was like being shut inside a coffin. Outside I could hear scuffling, and imagined Holmes entombing himself in one of the crates. Then all was silence, save for my own breathing, before voices approached. What if they lifted the lid? Worst of all, what if they hammered the crates shut for good and all? Then where would we be?

It was all I could do not to cry out as I felt the crate lift off the floor. The dockworkers swore, calling over to their mates for help.

"What has she got in here?" one of them asked, and I prayed they wouldn't check. Instead, I was carried forward, the patter of rain on the lid telling me we had left the warehouse. There was more grunting, more swearing, and then I slid on the cables as the box tipped to the left. I imagined myself sprawling across the dock as the crate overturned, guns pointing in my face – but instead we continued, the dockhands lugging my dead weight up the ramp. The drumming of the rain stopped. I was on the ship.

I closed my eyes, willing the indignity to be over. It seemed that I swayed back and forth for ever, before, with a thud that jarred my entire body, the crate dropped to the floor. Elsbeth Honegger wouldn't be happy about that. I can't say I was either.

There were more boots outside now, and another thud, this time on the lid of the crate. To my horror, I realised what had happened. The idiots had piled another container on top of mine. How would I get out?

I froze, waiting for the sound of the boots to fade. Then, when I was sure I was alone, I pushed against the lid. It wouldn't budge, the weight of the box on top too great. I was trapped. I banged my clenched fist against the side of the crate, not caring if the noise was heard. If I were discovered, I would be let out. I would also probably be shot, but that was a risk I was willing to take.

The side of the box refused to give way, and soon my hands were raw from pummelling the rough wood.

With a scrape and a clatter, something dropped to the floor outside. I froze again, my eyes searching the darkness. More boots scraped and then there was a crash, deafening within the confines of the crate.

I went to push up against the lid one last time, when it was raised, and the face of Sherlock Holmes looked down at me.

"Watson," he snarled, "get out of there and help me."

"What the devil happened?" I asked.

"Not now," he said, giving me his hand. "They're on their way back. Quickly."

I scrambled out of the crate and took in my surroundings; we were clearly in the hold of the ship. Holmes turned and threw cables back into the overturned crate that lay on its side next to my own. He eased it back onto its base and continued refilling it. I helped as well as I could, and when everything was back where it should be, he told me to replace the lid on my crate. I did so, and we piled the other box on top.

"Were you in that one?" I whispered.

He gave no answer, but yanked me to the back of the hold, into a small curtained vestibule. I fell quiet and we listened as the men returned, slapping more crates into place.

"That's the lot," one of them growled in German.

"And not before time. The captain's casting off. Come on."

Holmes waited for them to leave before peeking out from behind the curtain. The hold was empty, save for the crates – and a pair of stowaways.

"I can't believe you made me do that," I hissed.

"Neither can I. You must be going soft in your old age," replied Holmes. "You used to put up much more of a fight."

"Don't tempt me. So, now what?"

Holmes put his finger to his lips and slipped past the curtain, checking that the coast was clear. When he was sure, he beckoned me out.

"Now, we find Miss Honegger."

"Where?"

"If I knew that, we would have no need to search. The ship is not a large one."

"It's not a small one either. What if we are spotted?"

"You have your revolver?"

I nodded, patting my coat pocket.

"And I have mine. Let us pray we don't have cause to use them."

There was a low resounding clang deep beneath us, and the sudden roar of engines. The entire ship reverberated, the deck vibrating beneath our feet.

"We're on the move," Holmes commented, throwing out an arm to steady himself.

"And already being tossed from fore to stern."

"A storm is coming."

"And if we need to abandon ship?"

"I'm sure there are lifeboats, Watson."

CHAPTER THIRTY-SIX

THE EYE OF THE STORM

In only a short time the ship was rolling. Usually, I have my sea legs, but even I was struggling as we bounced down a corridor. Luckily, the poor conditions seemed to be keeping the crew busy, so there was little chance of our discovery. Only once did we almost come face to face with a couple of sailors, but I pulled Holmes back into an open doorway where we hid until the men staggered past.

"This is hopeless," I whispered. "We can't blunder around below deck, hoping to find her."

A voice sounded from up ahead, shouting to be heard over the groans of the ship's superstructure.

"Take these to the Fräulein. The storm is coming in faster than expected."

Again we sank into the shadows, waiting for the deckhand to pass. I saw that he was carrying a small crate, piled high with cables.

We waited a few moments and then slipped out into the corridor, following his footsteps. Pausing at a bulkhead, we heard him knock on a door, a faint female voice sounding in response. There was a creak and he entered.

"Place it over there," the female voice said in faultless German, while we scurried past the door and reached the next section. There we waited for the sailor to exit, hoping that he would return the way he had come. For a moment, it looked as though he was about to walk straight towards us, when shouts from above caused him to double back and head towards the foredeck.

Breathing a sigh of relief, I followed Holmes to the door and exchanged a look, before he turned the handle and stepped over the raised partition into the room beyond.

"What now?" said Elsbeth Honegger, her back towards us. "I've told you that I cannot do this unless—"

She turned and stopped, not expecting to see two grey-haired Englishmen staring back at her. I, for one, shared her amazement. The room was built into one of the holds of the ship, but thankfully it was enclosed against the elements. Instead, the rain hammered down on a glass ceiling that stretched the length of the compartment, save for multiple heavy industrial cables that snaked down through a hatch from the central mast. Those cables, not ropes, were what we had seen on the sail-less mast.

I followed the cables down from the hatch's rubber seal to the most bizarre of contraptions. There, on a raised dais, sat something that resembled a bronze beer kettle, the kind used to ferment ale in breweries the world over – but never had one such as this been constructed. Its lid was suspended on chains above the base, weighted down so it would not swing with the roll of the ship. However, every time the deck bucked beneath our feet, a strange yellow liquid slopped over the edge of the base to splatter on the floor. It was thick, and gave off such a chemical reek that it was all I could do not to gag.

"Who are you?" she said in German. "What are you doing here?"

Holmes took a step forward, replying in our native tongue. "My name is Sherlock Holmes."

Her eyes widened.

"This has to be some kind of joke."

"I'm afraid not. I am here on behalf of your sister."

"Cammy?"

"She is most concerned for your safety, and, after seeing the way you were treated on the harbourside, so were we."

The lady came towards us, unconsciously wiping her hands on her white medical coat, leaving behind stains from the viscous yellow liquid. "You cannot be here. How did you get on board?"

"That is unimportant," Holmes said, his eyes flickering over the equipment behind her. "Although I have some questions of my own."

She broke to the left, racing towards a communication tube. Holmes sprang after her, grabbing her arm before she could reach the voicepipe.

"Release me at once!"

"What are you doing here?"

"Holmes," I cautioned, worried that my friend would hurt her.

"Look in the kettle," he commanded, even as she squirmed in his grip.

"Let me go, I say!"

"Do it, Watson!"

I seesawed across the lurching room, grabbing hold of the handrail around the platform. Pulling myself up, I peered down into the glutinous pool within the kettle. There, submerged on a metal frame, lay a naked body, strapped by thick lengths of leather around its chest, waist and legs. Its head was held in place with a brace, its eyes closed. Even through the liquid I could make out the marbled effect on its skin and the tight stitching that had now become so familiar.

"Good Lord," I murmured. "It's all true. Every word of it."

"Don't touch him," Elsbeth Honegger shrieked, breaking free of Holmes's grip and racing towards me. The ship hit a wave and was tossed to port, sending her diving across the deck. I fell back against the copper, my hand splashing into the creature's – what, amniotic fluid?

Behind me, I heard Miss Honegger approach. Pulling out my revolver, I spun around, bringing the weapon up to bear.

She froze, staring down the barrel of my gun.

"My friend asked you a question," I said, the revulsion in my voice plain for all to hear. "What are you doing here?"

Now it was Holmes's turn to give counsel.

"Watson, steady."

"I dared not believe it was possible," said I, glowering at the woman. "But here it is."

"Please," she begged me. "Lower the weapon. It is almost time."

"Almost time for what?" Holmes asked.

"Her infernal experiment," I snapped, answering for her. "This abhorrence. Why a ship?"

"What?"

"Why not do this on land?"

"I would think it is the storm," Holmes said calmly. "Power for the… resurrection."

She glanced at him. "You seem to know a great deal of my business."

"Your business?" I spat. "Grave-robbing? Blasphemy?"

She pointed at me now, ignoring the gun. "He volunteered his body for the benefit of medical science, and that, not blasphemy, is exactly what is being carried out here."

"Body or bodies?" Holmes enquired. "We have seen your handiwork, Miss Honegger. Or at least what we have been told is your handiwork. On the Western Front, experimenting on the dead. On Daniel Blake?"

Her eyes narrowed. "Who?"

"You don't even know their names?" I asked, incredulous.

"I never ask," she said. "I do not concern myself about what they are, only what they will be."

"Your creatures," Holmes said.

"They don't belong to me."

"Really? What about the man you slaughtered? In Abberton Hospital? Did Adam deserve to die?"

She at least had the decency to look surprised. "You have indeed been following me. I took no pleasure in that, I can assure you."

"I should think not!" I exclaimed.

"I was offered a way out, but Adam declined to take it."

"A way out from what?"

She turned to face Holmes. "How much do you know?"

"That you sought to carry on Victor Frankenstein's work—"

"To play God," I interrupted.

Holmes ignored me. "But you were arrested, yes? For desecration. And yet, when the authorities discovered what you were attempting, what science you had at your fingertips…"

"Who told you all this?"

"I think you know."

"He lies, without hesitation."

"And yet the lies are compelling. Offered a chance to continue your experimentation, a supply of fresh meat, no questions asked – until the war ended, until they realised that if anyone found out what they had allowed you to do, what they had sanctioned – the British Empire, experimenting on its own dead… No wonder you ran."

"I had nowhere else to go."

"Nowhere except home. The lure was too great. A loving family, a favourite nephew; but official secrets rarely stay secret for long. Germany may have lost the war, but she still has spies. They discovered what you had achieved, and offered you a way out. Oh, this is a private vessel, but the markings on the cargo, they are military, as are most of the sailors on board, I would think. The money that all this would cost, you were unable to find it yourself, otherwise you would hardly have been operating out of a derelict hospital on the banks of the Thames. Although I must congratulate you on the generator. I always appreciate the ability to extemporise in the face of adversity."

"Do you expect me to thank you?"

"As you thanked Adam?"

"He refused to come. The thought of turning to the enemy he had been created to fight was a step too far."

"So you took what you had given, killing him in the hospital, dismembering him piece by piece so that his body would never be found. Well, not all of it, unfortunately."

When he paused, she asked but one simple question, her face without expression.

"So, it is I whom you consider the monster, not they."

"You're a scientist, a brilliant one if the stories are true, but you are also a murderer. We were brought in by Scotland Yard to find a killer, and we have found one."

"I thought you said you were sent by my sister?"

"The two cases have dovetailed."

Above us lightning flashed in the broiling clouds, thunder crashing through the heavens a second later. We were nearing the eye of the storm.

The ship pitched, buffeted by a wave, and I fell forward, stumbling from the dais. My gun skittered across the deck, but the lady had already made good her escape. Before Holmes could stop her, she had raced to the door, flinging it open and calling for help.

At least, that was what she tried to do. Her cry was cut off halfway through and she stopped short, before backing into the room again. Looking up from where I had fallen, I saw two men follow her in, guns raised. Two men I recognised all too well.

"Dr Watson," the first of them said. "I didn't think we'd be running into you again." The tweed suit and bow tie had gone, but it was the same sneer he had worn when he and his companion walked into my surgery. Burns and Hartley. "At least, I hoped we wouldn't."

Hartley, that damned moustache twitching, turned sharply to cover Holmes in his sights. "Everyone stay still."

"Who are these men?" Elsbeth Honegger snapped, not taking her eyes from the unwavering gun barrels.

"Old friends," said Burns.

"Hardly," I replied. "Believe it or not, these two louts work for the British government. How did you get on board?"

Holmes answered for them. "The shouts from above."

"I didn't think it would work, to be honest," said Hartley. "Jerry isn't known for compassion, and yet, would you believe it, they saw our little boat bobbing around out there, heard our cries for help—"

"And rescued you," said Holmes.

Burns grinned, showing tobacco-stained teeth. "Worst mistake they ever made. Still, they're not worrying about it any more."

"You followed us here," Holmes realised. "Straight to Miss Honegger."

"I was wrong about that too," said Hartley. "I thought we'd scare you off when we paid our little visit."

"Isn't that what you were supposed to do?" I asked, glancing around for my gun. It had slid beneath a bank of equipment. There was no way I could reach it before the thugs squeezed their triggers.

Hartley shrugged. "They said it would just make you dig your heels in, and try to find Madam here."

"They?"

"Our lords and masters. And the curious thing is, they were right. Stubborn pair of codgers, aren't you?"

"We try our best," drawled Holmes.

Elsbeth Honegger stood her ground. "So what now? You kill me too?"

"Nah, we're taking you back. There's still folk at home who have use for you." His eyes flicked to the copper device behind us. "And what you can do."

"But they shut my experiments down."

"That was before the Germans showed an interest," Holmes cut in, glancing over to the table where Honegger had been writing notes. "Headed notepaper, from at least two of the major German pharmaceutical companies. Germany is in crisis. A new crop of medical advances would be timely, especially if they could be patented and sold overseas. After all, that's why you are doing this, is it not? To find a cure for your nephew?"

"Enough chat," interrupted Burns, and fired at Holmes. I cried out as the bullet slammed into my friend's shoulder, sending him pirouetting to the floor. I scrambled over to him, not caring a jot if I was about to receive a bullet of my own. Burns fired again, but the pitch of the ship sent his aim wide, the bullet ricocheting off the copper with a loud clang.

"No!" shouted Miss Honegger, running back up to the dais.

"Stay back," Burns warned her, but she whirled around.

"Listen, I shall return with you. I don't care who foots the bill as long as I can continue my work, but would your masters not prefer that we take my crowning achievement back with us?"

"They just want you."

"Because they have not seen him yet. But when they do…"

Lightning flashed high above us, and the ship rolled again. Holmes cried out as he tumbled onto his injured arm. I rolled him onto his back and examined the wound. It was pumping out blood. Sitting him up, I glanced around. I searched for bandages or gauze, anything I could use to stem the flow.

Behind me, Honegger continued her plea. "Trust me, he is perfect. Better than any of them. I have no wish to flounder around in the mud any more. Say what you want about the Germans, but they've given me what I need."

Thunder crashed, and Elsbeth Honegger looked up into the dark sky. "It may happen at any moment. When lightning strikes that mast…"

Hartley glanced at Burns. "We don't have time for this."

"Are you seriously thinking of escaping from this ship in the middle of a storm?" she asked. "Let me complete my task, and then we shall go together. They will thank you for it."

I didn't have time to watch for the thugs' reaction. I had found a store of gauze and folded it into a pad. Now pressed over the wound in Holmes's shoulder, it was already drenched in blood.

"Hold it in place, old boy," I told him. His face was as white as a ghost. "I'll find bandages."

The last thing I expected was to hear Elsbeth Honegger calling for me.

"You. I need your help."

I looked round at her in puzzlement. "What?"

She was working a pulley, lowering the lid of the kettle into position. The louts had relented, but I had no intention of abandoning Holmes.

"You're a doctor, are you not?" she said, struggling with the apparatus. "Trust me, this will be the operation of your career."

"I'm busy," I snapped back. "Ask those two."

Burns's gun swivelled towards me. "I'm going nowhere near that thing. Do as she says."

"Go to hell."

"You will be there before us if you refuse. And then where will your friend be, bleeding to death all alone?"

"Do it, Watson," Holmes said weakly, his hand holding the now scarlet dressing. "I find myself unable to move."

I looked from my friend to the gun pointing in my direction, before struggling to my feet. "Very well," I said, as I tottered over to the platform. "What do you need me to do?"

CHAPTER THIRTY-SEVEN

NEW LIFE

"Steady," Elsbeth Honegger said as she guided down the lid. My shoulder burned as I lowered the pulley, but it was in no way as serious as Holmes's injury. I glanced across at my companion. He was sitting where I had left him, his hand pressed against his shoulder and his eyes closed. Was he even breathing?

"Concentrate!"

Miss Honegger's sharp command brought my attention back to the kettle. Glaring at her, I lowered the lid until the two metal components met with a clatter.

"That's it," she said, checking the seal. "Now, help with the bolts."

She moved to the far end of the kettle, fastening the first in a series of hinged latches that would clamp the two parts together. I did the same at the other end, moving in to meet her in the middle.

Through the windows in the copper I could see the ghastly thing on its cradle, oblivious in death. *Perfect.* That was what she had called it. Certainly, it was less misshapen than the poor soul in Prestwich Asylum, less hulking than Agares, but it was still unnatural, made out of who knew how many cadavers.

The final latch in place, Honegger stood with her back to Burns and Hartley.

"When the lightning strikes, there will be a flash, brighter than anything you have experienced before."

"What do you mean?"

"I mean that anyone not wearing goggles is going to be blinded."

"Goggles?"

She walked away from me, calling over to the men. "We are nearly ready."

Before they could answer, she plucked two pairs of welder's goggles from a hook and, turning, threw one at me. I caught them, marvelling at this remarkable woman. As she walked back to join me, our eyes locked and I knew what she expected me to do. When the light flashed, the men would be blinded, whereas I, thanks to the goggles' filter, would still be able to see. As I fixed the rubber band around my head, I glanced at Burns and Hartley, judging the distance between us. They were more than seven paces away. For just how long would they be dazzled? Could I move that fast?

The ship swayed and I caught hold of a handle on the lid of the kettle.

"I wouldn't touch that," Elsbeth said. "If it starts to conduct—"

Thunder sounded, but not from the sky above. It came from below, a tremulous rumble accompanied by a vibration that travelled from the floor up into our bodies. Immediately the ship listed to starboard, throwing us against the copper, but the movement felt different from the effects of the storm. There was another sound beneath our feet, the clamour of rushing water. The entire ship seemed to groan, as if its metal skin were tearing itself apart.

"We're taking in water," Burns shrieked.

"What?" Elsbeth Honegger shouted.

"The hull is breached," I shouted as the deck sloped. I hung onto the platform's rail, stopping myself from being thrown against the copper – and not a moment too soon.

Lightning forked across the sky, striking the main mast. The mass of cables absorbed the inconceivable energy in an instant, channelling it down towards the chamber, the glass ceiling shattering above us. I threw up my arms against the sudden shower of sparks and broken glass, the coruscating electricity flooding into the copper drum.

The moment the charge met the swirling chemicals within the kettle, a luminescent glare flared through the windows. Even behind my protective goggles, it felt as if my eyes had been boiled away. All around was chaos. Rain lashed down into the exposed compartment, the delicate equipment that lined the walls erupting into flames. There was a scream, shrill and panicked, and I looked up to see Burns where he lay in a growing puddle of blood, the side of his face having been sliced clean off by a shard of falling glass. Hartley was staggering, his gun lowered, desperately rubbing his eyes with the palm of his free hand. Even in my addled state, I remembered what I had to do. This was my chance, I could disable him; but even as I half-tumbled from the dais, a terror struck me, more deadly than any lightning. The door to the chamber was open, and silhouetted by the light from the corridor outside was a monstrous figure, eight feet tall.

Agares clambered into the room, snarling with fury, like a monster from hell.

Hartley turned, hearing the noise behind him, and blindly emptied three bullets into Agares's chest. The giant roared, but did not fall, swatting the thug aside with one swipe of his mighty arm. Hartley flew across the room, carried by the pitch of the ship, and cracked into the wall, his neck snapping like a twig. I fell to the floor as Agares loomed towards me, hair plastered against his bloodless skin and eyes burning with hatred. For a moment I thought that he was about to pluck me from the ground and send me sprawling like Hartley, but he stomped past, heading for the platform. I twisted, fragments of glass slicing into my hand, but I paid no heed.

There on the dais lay Elsbeth Honegger, her body limp.

"No," bellowed Agares, snatching her from the floor and pulling her upright. Her head lolled back and I could see the vivid burns across her face. She must have fallen against the copper as the lightning hit, the electricity ravaging her body. She hung in the giant's grip, like a marionette with its strings cut.

Agares shook her violently, her head flapping pathetically back and forth. "I was supposed to die, not you! You were supposed to show me how. You were supposed to end the curse!"

The deck reeled, the ship sinking deeper beneath the waves by the second, and even Agares teetered on his feet, Elsbeth's corpse falling from his hands. Seizing the rail, he threw back his head and howled at the heavens like a wild beast.

A hand grasped my shoulder. It was Holmes, leaning heavily upon me.

"Watson, we need to get out."

"You," snarled Agares, spotting us, the only people left alive on the doomed ship to behold his rage. "Did she tell you? Did she reveal the secret?"

"Now," shouted Holmes, throwing his good arm around my shoulders. I hoisted us up, almost immediately slipping on the water, and tottered forward. The ship creaked and tilted further, sending us crashing to the floor. Holmes cried out, and then the monster of a man was upon us. He flipped me over as if I weighed no more than an infant and yelled into my face.

"Tell me what she said!"

I tried to wrestle his hands from my lapels, but it was hopeless. He was too strong, and I had used up what remained of my already depleted resources.

"Tell me how to die!"

There was the crack of a gun, and my world was painted red. Agares slumped down upon me, crushing from my lungs what little air remained in them. I tasted copper in my mouth, my sight obscured by a crimson sheen.

I reached up, pulling the goggles from my head. Holmes appeared beside me, throwing Burns's discarded gun aside. He yanked at Agares's body with his good arm, screaming as his wounded shoulder took the strain. I pushed upwards, attempting to roll the dead weight off me. Agares had wanted to know how to die, and Holmes had showed him, delivering a shot to the man's head, but I was determined that we should not join the devil in hell just yet. I wriggled from beneath his body and grabbed Holmes. Fighting against the yawing deck, I pulled him up to the door, crying out with the effort.

As I thrust Holmes out into the corridor, I glanced back and froze. Now it was the detective's turn to urge me on, yelling at me that we had to reach the lifeboats before the ship went down.

His shout broke the spell, and I hauled myself through the door, flinging Holmes's arm around my shoulder. As I propelled us along the corridor, what I had seen in the chamber clawed at my mind.

It wasn't the sight of Agares's body rolling over on the deck, his yellow eyes meeting mine, that had chilled me more than the rain that fell from above.

No, it was the pale face in the window of the copper drum, pressed against the glass, screaming to be saved.

CHAPTER THIRTY-EIGHT

BRAVE NEW WORLD

"You imagined it, of course," Holmes said, when I finally told him what I had seen as we made our escape. Sitting in my drawing room, with the early August sun streaming through the window, it was hard to believe that our bizarre experience in the North Sea had happened at all.

We had made it to a lifeboat, the only living souls left on board, or so I kept telling myself. We crashed down onto the waves, moments before the sea finally claimed *Das Rabe* for its own. With Holmes lying at my feet, I had found a flare, firing it up into the stygian sky.

Thankfully, a courageous fisherman heard my cry for help and braved the storm to find us. Finally, I could let myself be a patient, safe in the knowledge that Holmes was being cared for. We were taken straight to hospital, where a member of the British consulate was waiting for us, armed with an official communiqué from Mycroft.

Holmes had fared worse, of course. His bullet wound was less serious than I had feared, although his body, finally giving in to the ravages of the last two weeks, succumbed to pneumonia.

Mycroft had us shipped back to England, Holmes being afforded the greatest possible care. For a time it looked as though we would lose him. For the second time in a month, I prepared to say goodbye to my greatest friend, but Holmes rallied and was soon attempting to discharge himself at the first opportunity.

We said nothing of the ship until we were alone, other than Holmes expressing a wish to inform Camille Sellman of her sister's demise. We owed her that much, although Mycroft was ahead of us once again. He surprised us both by revealing that he had visited the Sellmans personally, explaining that Elsbeth Honegger had been employed on official state business but had suffered an accident. There was truth in the lie, of course. Elsbeth had been conducting state business, although for a foreign power rather than our own. Now, the entire affair was in Mycroft's hands. Elsbeth Honegger's work had been lost with the ship, her lodgings in Bremerhaven having been searched and found empty. The senior Holmes brother had insisted that we never speak of the matter again, even going so far as to have us sign a written agreement, which he assured me would protect us from the employers of the late Messrs Burns and Hartley. I had no reason to disbelieve him, but spent the next few days looking over my shoulder all the same.

My wife returned to London and proceeded to wrap me in cotton wool, a task she likewise attempted to perform on Holmes when he too returned to Chelsea to convalesce. Needless to say, she was encouraged in no uncertain terms to leave him be. However, I could tell that Holmes was grateful to her, and she in turn treated him like one of the family, which was exactly how it should have been.

Finally, after days of studiously avoiding the subject, I broached what we had witnessed on the ship.

"How did he find us?" I asked, as we sat alone in the house, my wife having gone out earlier in the morning.

"Agares?"

"I thought Inspector Tovey was keeping him under lock and key."

Holmes's eyes sparkled. "As you were supposed to."

I sighed. "You knew he was free."

"Tovey was to release him the moment we left the country, letting slip where we were going first, of course."

"To what end?"

"To bring all the pieces together, what else? I must admit, the appearance of Burns and Hartley was something of a surprise. For once, I had no idea we were being followed."

"Used to sniff Elsbeth Honegger out, you mean."

"And there I was thinking that Inspector Tovey was the bloodhound."

"But how did you know Agares would find his way onto the ship?"

"I didn't, although I am glad he did. Mr Agares turned out to be more resourceful than even I predicted; following the ship out to sea, blowing his way through the hull."

"Using what? Dynamite?"

"What else could he use? His bare hands?"

I was beginning to wonder.

"But what did he want with Elsbeth Honegger?"

"What he said. He wanted to know how to die."

"You gave him that answer."

Holmes gave the ghost of a smile. "As we have already discussed, Agares believed his fantastical tale, believed that he was the creation of Victor Frankenstein."

"Cursed with immortality."

"And yet, he knew that Elsbeth Honegger had killed one of his own, butchered Adam at Abberton Hospital. That is what he was looking for in the hospital, not the bone, and that is why he followed us halfway across Europe. The man wanted to die, and thought she was the only one who knew how to achieve his goal. He wanted release, the mad fool."

"You believe he was insane, then?"

"The last few weeks have led me to question much about existence, Watson. I am uncertain what I believe at present, but I am grateful that even as my life reaches its end—"

"Come now."

"Its twilight years then. I am grateful that there are still lessons to learn, still mysteries waiting to be solved."

"Still miracles to be performed?"

My friend's smile grew. "You really believe what you saw as we fled, do you not?"

I sighed, shifting in my chair. My body ached even after all this time.

"I don't know what to believe, Holmes. Agares rolled over."

"The tilt of the ship, nothing more."

"He looked straight at me."

"A trick of the light."

"He's dead then?"

"How could it be otherwise? He went down with the ship."

"And what of the face in the window? He was calling for help, Holmes. He was alive."

"Did you want him to be?"

"I beg your pardon?"

"Did you want to believe that after everything that had happened, Miss Honegger's work would be a success?"

"You said yourself that it was the only plausible explanation for the body, for John."

"A *possible* explanation; I am not so sure that I would describe it as plausible."

"But all that business about science, the world being flat and so on."

"I stand by what I said, and I admit that I don't know for sure. As a young man, such an admission would have been unbearable, but now..."

"Don't tell me you're changing with the times, Holmes, no matter what they bring?"

My friend sat back in his chair and closed his eyes. "It's a brave new world, Watson, full of new thoughts and new men to think them. As for myself, though it pains me to say it, some things are best left unknown."

My friend, Sherlock Holmes, it seemed, was finally accepting that there were answers he would never find, mysteries he would never solve.

I didn't believe him for a moment.

ACKNOWLEDGEMENTS

Thanks first of all to my good chum Mr George Mann for introducing me to Titan Books' queen of Sherlockery and all-round brilliant editor, Miranda Jewess. Miranda, in turn, has been simply wonderful. Thanks for the support, the notes, the pots of tea and, most of all, a good helping of silliness en route.

Nearer to home, a big, big thank you to my darling wife Clare for reading the book chapter by chapter and persuading me that it was working at the moments I thought it wasn't. Oh, and all the cups of coffee. Definitely the coffee.

There are so many other people I should properly thank; the authors of the various books on Holmesian lore I kept by my side (particularly Leslie S. Klinger of the spectacular *New Annotated Sherlock Holmes*), Emily Cartwright of the London Transport Museum for her timely assistance regarding the London Underground in 1919 and Dr. Matthew Sweet for pointing me in the direction of *Dope Girls* by Marek Kohn.

Finally, thank you to Sir Arthur Conan Doyle and Mary Shelley for creating two of the biggest obsessions in my life. It's been an honour to bring them together in this book.

ABOUT THE AUTHOR

Cavan Scott is the author of over ninety books and audio dramas including the *Sunday Times* Top 10 Bestseller *Who-ology: The Official Doctor Who Miscellany*, co-written with Mark Wright. He has written for such popular series as *Doctor Who*, *Star Wars*, *Vikings*, *The Sarah Jane Adventures*, *Warhammer 40,000*, *Pathfinder*, *Blake's 7*, *Judge Dredd* and *Highlander*. Find out more by visiting www.cavanscott.com, or follow him on Twitter @cavanscott.

SHERLOCK HOLMES

THE THINKING ENGINE

James Lovegrove

It is 1895, and Sherlock Holmes and Watson learn of strange goings-on in Oxford. A Professor Quantock has built a wondrous computational device, which he claims is capable of analytical thought to rival the cleverest men alive. Holmes and Watson travel to Oxford, where a battle of wits ensues between the great detective and his mechanical counterpart as they compete to see which of them can be first to solve a series of crimes. But as man and machine vie for supremacy, it becomes clear that the Thinking Engine has its own agenda…

"The plot, like the device, is ingenious, with a chilling twist... an entertaining, intelligent and pacy read."
The Sherlock Holmes Journal

"Lovegrove knows his Holmes trivia and delivers a great mystery that fans will enjoy, with plenty of winks and nods to the canon." **Geek Dad**

"I think Conan Doyle would have enjoyed reading this story: the concept of an intelligent, self-aware Thinking Engine is brilliance itself." **The Book Bag**

SHERLOCK HOLMES

THE ARMY OF DR MOREAU

Guy Adams

Dead bodies are found on the streets of London with wounds that can only be explained as the work of ferocious creatures. Sherlock Holmes is visited by his brother, Mycroft, who is only too aware that the bodies are the calling card of Dr Moreau, a vivisectionist who was working for the British government, before his experiments attracted negative attention and the work was halted. Mycroft believes that Moreau's experiments continue and he charges his brother with tracking the rogue scientist down before matters escalate any further.

"Succeeds both as a literary jeu d'esprit and detective story, with a broad streak of irreverent humour." **Financial Times**

"Deftly handled… this is a must read for all fans of adventure and fantasy literature." **Fantasy Book Review**

"Well worth a read… Adams is a natural fit for the world of Sherlock Holmes." **Starburst**